'... one of the best young adult novels I have read in a long time.'
The Book Bundle

'A fabulous debut that had me looking over my shoulder while reading.'
Thoughts from the Hearthfire

'... a brilliant book that captures the true nature of secondary school so very well.'
Mostly Reading YA

'... clever, sophisticated storytelling and one of the best thrillers I've read in a long time.'
Cosy Books

'A tense and terrifying debut novel with some wonderful characters and a brilliant location. Highly recommended.'
The Book Bag

'The opening lines saw me hold my breath and I didn't breathe again until the end of the first chapter. I honestly thought I might need medical assistance. What an amazing opening to a book'
Serendipity Reviews

'This book blends important teen issues, teen angst, witch-craft and murder mystery, creating a delectable cocktail of a book. Best sipped slowly so you don't miss a single drop.'
Bookangel's Booktopia

'If you are craving a chilling tale, laced with suspense, *Hollow Pike* is the book for you.'
Realm of Fiction

'*Hollow Pike* is the perfect book for teens who love spooky stories or just great literature.'
Book Zone for Boys

Hollow Pike

Juno Dawson

Indigo

First published in Great Britain in 2012 by Indigo
This paperback edition first published in 2012 by Indigo
This edition published in 2017 by Hodder and Stoughton

7 9 10 8 6

A CIP catalogue record for this book
is available from the British Library.

ISBN 978 1 78062 128 9

Printed and bound in Great Britain
by Clays Ltd, St Ives plc

The paper and board used in this book are
made from wood from responsible sources.

Orion Children's Books
An imprint of
Hachette Children's Group
Part of Hodder and Stoughton
Carmelite House
50 Victoria Embankment
London EC4Y 0DZ

An Hachette UK Company
www.hachette.co.uk

www.hachettechildrens.co.uk

This book is dedicated to anyone
who has ever hated school.
Unlikely gang forever, x

Part One

*Alas! Experience tells us that there
is no number to girls, and consequently
the witches that spring from this class
are innumerable.*

THE MALLEUS MALEFICARUM, 1486

Owls

Lis knew she was dreaming, although this brought little comfort as the blood ran over her face. It rushed up her nostrils and caught in the back of her throat. The metallic taste choked her, panic creeping in.

This was not the first time she'd knelt in the red stream. She had encountered this nightmare many times in recent weeks and each time the vision became more realistic, more visceral.

Sometimes, the focus of the dream was her long, wet hair matted to her face. Sometimes it was the freezing rain and howling wind. Sometimes it was the frenzied screams far away in the distance. On this particular visit, Lis was very aware of the pebbles, so cold and round and perfect under her hands. They scraped her skin but somehow she knew that the blood rushing over her body was not hers.

In a twisted way, she was starting to enjoy these nightly terrors. Every dream brought a new piece of the jigsaw puzzle, although she remained far from seeing the picture on the box. In reality, she had never seen her dream brook or the forest it trickled through, or maybe she had ... a distant childhood memory, eroded by time.

The desperate screaming grew closer, coming in loud, distorted blasts as her head dipped in and out of the water.

She became aware of her own panting and groaning. How much farther could she crawl?

Every movement felt laboured and slow. Even adrenalin could not counter the exhaustion in her arms and the water may as well have been treacle. She fought to keep going regardless of the pain in her bleeding knees. Her sodden clothes clung to her body, pulling her back.

Far overhead, owls circled the charcoal trees. They were there for her, she knew that much, although she couldn't be certain why. She had no time to worry about that now; she had to get away.

But she knew what was coming. The dream always ended the same way. Sure enough, she recognised the icy hand now reaching into her hair. Such was the grip that it was impossible for Lis to turn and face her assailant. Not once had she set eyes upon her attacker. She let out a howl before her face was plunged into the inky water.

There was no moonlight to illuminate the stream and Lis was submerged in blackness. Air bubbles rippled against her cheek as the vice-like grip pushed her deeper; all the way to the bed of the stream.

Lis tried to relax. She knew she would wake up any second now. Her chest seemed to shrink inwards and she tried to inhale oxygen that wasn't there, her lips parting uselessly. This was the end.

Lis's eyes snapped open. She always felt she should spring upright and pull sweat-soaked sheets from her body, just like in the films. But she was safe, curled up under her duvet; cosy in her familiar old bedroom.

She reached for her mobile. No texts and the clock display

read 2.14 a.m. She rolled over to try to get back to sleep, knowing that it was utterly pointless.

For today was the day she moved to Hollow Pike.

The Copse

Opening her eyes, Lis immediately recognised the Yorkshire Dales. The twisting, turning country lanes had caused her sleeping head to bang against the window as her mother followed the snaking road to Hollow Pike.

'Wakey-wakey, love,' her mother said. 'We're almost there.'

Lis blinked and hoisted herself upright in the seat, her new outfit now more than a little crumpled. All her old hoodies and trainers had been left in Wales. She'd wanted new clothes for a new start. 'How much further?' she croaked.

'Oh, not far at all. You can see Pike Copse from here.'

Leaning forwards, Lis squinted towards the horizon and saw the furry blanket of trees covering the hills ahead. Her mum was taking the back way into town. 'How come we're going this way?'

'There are roadworks, love. I can't be bothered with temporary traffic lights; we'll be there all year. I've never been this way, but Sarah says it's a short cut.'

Lis bit her tongue to stop herself saying anything sarcastic about her mother's dubious history with short cuts, the incident in Tenerife where they'd nearly driven over the edge of a cliff being a particularly terrifying memory. Instead she rolled her eyes and turned back to the road. The tiny silver Corsa passed onto an ancient bridge that vanished into the looming trees ahead, and she wound down the window to get a better look.

Staring down at the rushing, chattering stream beneath, Lis felt a sudden shiver ripple down her spine as she recalled her dream. She quickly did what she always did with that unwelcome memory and pushed it to the back of her mind, focusing on thoughts of anything else: what it would be like living with Sarah, whether her mum was right and her new clothes did look 'a bit much' (Lis had aimed for 'pretty but chic' with some new skirts and cute tops), whether anyone at Gwynedd Community College would even notice that she'd gone.

Of course Bronwyn Evans would notice. *She* was the reason Lis was moving in the first place. Her old school had refused to acknowledge any 'real bullying' was taking place, so her mum had cooked up the plan to move her up north with Sarah. Lis had jumped at the chance. Her mum was so busy with her new fiancé (soon to be husband number three), that Lis sort-of wondered if she'd even be missed. Lis had dreamed of living with her big sister ever since Sarah had moved to Hollow Pike years ago to care for Gran. Really, in Lis's mind, this suited everyone.

Within moments it was as if the car had driven from day into night. Inside the copse, only long diagonal fingers of light pierced the leaves and Lis peered into the gloom to see where the road led. The wood closed up behind them, sealing them inside its damp foliage. It felt like being swallowed by some huge, green whale; Lis shuddered at the thought.

As she looked more closely at her surroundings, she realised that the copse was very much alive. Every surface was covered in moss or lichen, and the birds ... the birds were deafening. The density of the trees caused the radio to lose reception so only an eerie hiss filled the car, and for a moment Lis felt that it was the sound of the forest itself – growing, moving, breathing.

Her mum squeezed the brakes as the road became narrower. Broken branches hung perilously close to the car and it seemed as if the darkness itself were edging nearer, becoming more intense as they advanced through Pike Copse.

'Mum . . .' Lis didn't really have anything to say, but hoped that fishing for chitchat would lighten the suddenly sinister atmosphere.

'I know, love. Sarah and her short cuts, eh?' Deborah smiled a thin smile.

Instantly regretting giving her mother an opportunity to criticise her sister, Lis turned off the radio static and reached into her mum's box of cassettes. For once, the thought of Deborah attempting to sing along to hits of the seventies was a comforting one.

Without warning, her mum slammed on the brakes. Lis's forehead smacked into the dashboard. 'Ow!' she yelped. 'Mum, what are you d—'

'Bloody animal!' her mum exclaimed.

Lis sat up to look at whatever had caused her mum to brake so sharply. In the centre of the road stood a single, black and white magpie, playing chicken with their car. It simply waited, watching them with beady black eyes, alight with intelligence.

Deborah pressed on the horn, a short blast, but the bird didn't move a muscle, didn't even flinch. Instead it seemed to peer even more intently at Lis.

'What's it doing?' Lis murmured.

'Do I look like an animal psychologist?'

Her mum edged the car forward, but the magpie stood its ground, blocking entry to Hollow Pike. There was no way they could drive around it.

'Will you shoo it away please, Elisabeth? It'll be dark at this rate.'

Lis dutifully unclipped her seatbelt and opened the door. Swinging her legs out, she stepped into freezing water. She recoiled and looked down. The car had come to a halt in a shallow, trickling stream.

'Careful, love, don't ruin your shoes.'

As soon as she was out of the car, the magpie, bigger than she'd anticipated, took one final look at her and darted for the safety of the trees. But Lis barely noticed. She was struggling to breathe as she looked around, taking in the full scene for the first time. Everything seemed so familiar: the water, the thick, earthy air. *This was her dream – the stream, the blood, the darkness.*

Tears started to prick her eyes and Lis told herself to get a grip. This couldn't be the forest she so often saw in her dreams because she'd never been here before. And, when you got down to it, all forests and streams looked pretty much alike. She was just upset by the creepy, staring bird and the move and her mum and, oh, everything today – the sooner she got to Sarah's, the better. She drew a steadying breath.

'Elisabeth, are you going to get back in the car or not?'

Lis dragged herself out of her stupor, tiptoed through the glacier-cold brook and clambered into the passenger seat.

'Bad luck, that is,' her mother said as Lis slammed the passenger door.

'What is?'

'Seeing one magpie. What is it they say? *One for sorrow.*'

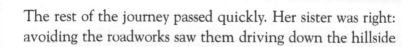

The rest of the journey passed quickly. Her sister was right: avoiding the roadworks saw them driving down the hillside that led directly to Sarah's new home in no time. And there it was – cut into the landscape like some sleek, modern sculpture – her sister's dream house. Max, Lis's brother-in-law, had recently completed work on the building, nicknamed 'The Cube' and Lis could see how it had earned that title. It was as if a giant had carelessly abandoned a block of glass and wood at the edge of the copse. Lis thought it was nothing short of stunning – and she got to live there.

As the car finally pulled into the driveway, Lis was sure that she could still hear the whispering of the branches in the wind and, if she really strained, the busy little stream making its way towards the river. She shook her head firmly; she had to get over herself, she wasn't a baby any more. Who makes such a drama out of a few bad dreams?

Sasha, the lumbering family setter galloped to meet the car. Lis flung herself out and allowed the shaggy russet beast to jump up at her chest.

'Sashey!' she cried in a munchkin voice. 'How's my doggy dog?'

'Elisabeth! Don't get all dirty!' her mother put in.

A new voice interrupted from above, warm and affectionate but with an air of exasperation. 'Leave her alone, Mother! You're always nagging!'

They both looked up to see a tall, striking blonde standing on a balcony that ran all the way around the first floor. Sarah, twelve years older than Lis, was her half-sister from their mum's first marriage, but Lis couldn't possibly have loved her more if they'd had the same dad.

'Leave all your stuff in the car,' Sarah instructed. 'Max is on his way down to lend a hand. Come on up, you two, the kettle's on!'

Lis ran up the wooden stairs to greet her sister. Sarah wrapped her up in a bear hug and the pair tossed greetings at each other – Sarah actually complimenting Lis on her chic new clothes – until Deborah arrived and received a similar embrace.

Sarah invited them inside and, looking around the huge kitchen, Lis could feel warmth and love radiating from every beam and tile Max had installed. Huge windows filled the whole house with heavenly light. Everything was clean and modern, but in no way cold or minimalist; if anything the space was cluttered, filled with the beautiful furniture that her sister had collected and restored, not to mention a scattered selection of baby toys.

'Lis? Do you want to come and see your new room?' Sarah asked. 'I hope you don't mind, I've put some pieces in there. If you don't like them, I can find somewhere else for them.'

Lis resisted the urge to bounce up and down. Her sister restored vintage furniture for a living, so this promised to be *good*. 'Yes please!'

Sarah grabbed Lis's hand and pulled her through the lounge and upstairs to the next level, where two of the bedrooms were. One was in use as a study and the other was evidently Lis's room.

Lis gasped. It was like walking into a magazine spread. Sarah had installed a massive white sleigh bed next to French windows leading onto the back terrace. Other exquisite choices included a mirror and chaise longue – no doubt lovingly crafted in the basement workshop.

'You like?'

'Sarah, I love, love, *love*!' Lis beamed and gave her sister a second massive hug. 'It's like a princess room or something!' It was as if her sister had read her mind across county borders, sensing her wish to move away from her childlike, poster-filled life in Bangor, and step into a glamorous, sophisticated new skin here in Yorkshire.

'I'm glad you like it. You have no idea how long it took us to get that bloody bed through the door. We'd need a chainsaw to get it out!'

Lis laughed and crossed to the glass doors. The terrace was beautiful: Parisian-style table and chairs and a little fish pond. She could already see herself reading a book with a huge cup of hot chocolate beside her, and chatting with Sarah in a way she could never chat with her mum. She felt a million miles and a hundred years away from the Elisabeth London who'd spent last summer caring about best friends, Bangor and ... Bronwyn. This was more than she could have ever hoped for. She'd miss Mum, sure, but this was worth it.

'Mum's making the tea; I'll go give her a hand. And then I want to know all the Bangor gossip!' Sarah said.

'I'll be down in a sec.' Lis sat on the chaise longue, tenderly stroking the gorgeous upholstery. Her shoulders relaxed and Lis realised how tense she'd been – whether it was the weird incident on the way, or the worry that somehow this new chapter of her life wouldn't be what she'd hoped, she didn't know. She breathed out, closed her eyes and counted to five. It was fine ... Bangor was all in the past and she was safe now. Safe from Bronwyn Evans. Free from the taunts, jibes and whispers. She stood, ready to go and join her family.

As she turned she saw another lone magpie hop across the terrace and come to a standstill before her bedroom windows. For a second she wondered if it was the one from the copse. *Oh, come on*, she told herself, *how many magpies must there be in this town?* It cocked its black head, staring straight at her with shiny onyx eyes – there *was* something awfully familiar about it ... Curious, she pressed a hand to the glass and it was enough to send the bird into retreat.

The magpie flew away, but she couldn't so easily forget what her mother had said: *One for sorrow.*

Fulton High

I should have rolled in the mud, thought Lis. Her pristine uniform stood out a mile; she may as well have carved 'new girl' into her forehead with a scalpel. Eyes burned into the back of her skull, and even though she knew this would pass in a matter of hours, she hadn't anticipated how wretched it would make her feel. Boarding the school bus, she'd felt as fresh and confident as a toothpaste commercial, yet just five minutes into the journey she felt anything but.

The weather had clearly understood that it was the first day of autumn term, providing students with an unrelenting spray of fine drizzle to accompany them on an already depressing day. The whole world was the colour of slate. Worse still, as the bus filled with soggy pupils, it became more and more like a sauna. Peering through the steamed-up window, a slender, isolated figure at the side of the road swam into focus. Lis rubbed a little porthole for herself, but the silhouette remained shrouded in the murk.

With a hiss, the bus scraped to a halt and the damp newcomer boarded. There was a pregnant silence before an electric ripple of hushed giggles, lowered voices and meaningful glances ran down the bus. The newcomer's presence was intense. Lis watched, fascinated, as the new arrival made her way down the aisle towards the back seats.

She was a fearsome Amazon of a girl, approaching six feet

tall and with a shock of spiky black and purple hair that only added further inches. Lis couldn't even think of a word to describe her futuristic style: her skirt was the shortest Lis had ever seen dared as part of a uniform, and massive black construction boots finished off endless legs. Oh, and safety pins were lined neatly up the side of each ear. But by far the most striking feature was her face. Lis kind of thought of herself as pretty, but this weird girl was *beautiful* – mixed race, with flawless brown skin and twinkling blue eyes.

Lis knew she should look away but she was mesmerised. Craning her neck around, she saw the girl join two other oddities already tucked away at the very back of the lower deck. How had she not noticed *them*? The second girl was much shorter than the first, although equally stunning – a living china doll. Lis had never seen such a mass of bright red curls. They tumbled down almost to her waist. Red had also managed to radically reinterpret the dress code, swapping the regulation skirt for a flowing floor-length one. She had tiny ballet flats on her feet and thick NHS glasses balanced on her petite nose.

Their male companion was a stark contrast. A pale young man, he huddled in the corner by the fire escape, his uniform almost as immaculate as Lis's own. His hands were thrust tightly into his duffel coat and his eyes were fixed on his lap. He was neither handsome nor *un*attractive, but next to his outlandish female companions, his neutrality was shocking in itself.

Lis tuned into the nearest whispers and, although much was lost in the roar of the bus pulling away, she was able to make out the occasional word such as *Freaks!* or *Gay!*.

Lis was suddenly haunted by a familiar dread. The same sensation she'd fought every morning on her old school bus when Bronwyn and her mates had been whispering about *her*. Oh God, what if Fulton was no different? The dread intensified and Lis gripped the edge of her seat. *One day*, she thought, *I'll be living in New York or Paris and none of this will matter. Just hang on in there*.

She stole another glance, and was surprised to see the 'freaks' staring at *her*. Apparently, no one was above glaring at the new girl. The shy young man gave her a half-hearted smile that said *I know*. Red grinned and whispered something in his ear, giving Lis a coy wave. Lis returned the smile. In Hollow Pike, she was determined to rise above the ridiculous social pecking order that had blighted her time at her previous school. That school had had its own group of freaky outsider kids. They had been mocked and harassed, a shared punch-bag for the whole school. Once upon a time she had figured they'd brought it on themselves by dressing so crazy. She knew better now.

Turning to the front, Lis found herself looking straight into the face of a delicate blonde girl with slightly pointed features.

'You don't wanna go talking to them,' she said in a low, genuinely concerned voice.

'No?'

'No. That tall girl is like a proper lesbian. She'll totally try to rape you. It happened to our friend, Laura.'

'Oh, right. Thanks for the advice,' commented Lis with mock gratitude. The first blonde girl ('Platinum Blonde') and her equally blonde companion ('Honey Blonde') nodded earnestly, flicking poker-straight hair out of their eyes. 'You are *so* welcome. We were all new once.'

OK, so the blonde girls seemed vacant, but at least they'd deigned to speak to her. Lis knew she probably shouldn't shun prospective friends at such an early stage. Anyway, for all she knew the tall girl *could* have attacked someone. She was certainly intimidating enough.

'I'm Fiona and this is Harry,' said Platinum Blonde.

'Not like Harriet, like Debbie Harry,' explained Honey Blonde.

'Wow, cool name,' smiled Lis. 'I'm Lis. Lis London. And today is my first day.'

Fiona and Harry grinned broadly at each other, wordlessly communicating.

'You are going to like Fulton so much. Are you Year Eleven?' gushed Harry in her broad Yorkshire accent. She was wearing so much foundation, her skin was matt.

'Yeah, I am.' An imitation accent slipped out before Lis could stop it.

'Excellent,' nodded Fiona who hadn't seemed to notice. 'We will totally show you round and stuff. Our friends are, like, really nice. You'll so fit in.'

'Thank you! I'd love that.' Lis felt her mind-set quickly adapting to fit in with her new guides. 'I'm totally freaking out about starting a new school!'

'Don't worry.' Harry reached forward and squeezed her arm. 'We'll *totally* look after you!'

Thank God for Harry and Fiona. They kept their promise and made relatively easy the parts Lis had been dreading the most. The girls accompanied her to the main office to collect her timetable, with Fiona even drawing a helpful map of the school on the back. Lis couldn't deny a swell of relief as Harry announced they were in the same tutor group.

Fulton High School served a number of Dales towns and villages, and as such had ballooned over recent years as new rural developments brought extra pupils. It was now an odd mix of grand gothic-looking towers with brand new annexes stuck onto the sides. Lis felt sorry for the building. Once upon a time, the school must have been imposing; now it looked like it'd had bad plastic surgery.

In many aspects, it might as well have been her old school: same lockers, same smell of urine by the toilets, same screams and cheers ringing through the halls, same faded Childline posters, same downtrodden faces. Lis prayed that something had to be *better* or at the very least, different.

Harry led her down an endless tiled corridor, called 'G Corridor', that clearly belonged to one of the original blocks; it had the look of a Victorian asylum. Harry was evidently popular; she smiled and waved at a number of girls with *very* straight hair and called coquettishly to an even greater number of Year Eleven boys. She pointed out which ones she liked, which ones she didn't like and which ones were simply 'losers' (unpopular geeks) or 'tossers' (popular – but no self-respecting girl would ever consider snogging one of them).

'OK, so this is G2, our tutor room,' Harry explained, stopping near the end of the corridor. 'We've got Mr Gray. He's really nice, and young too. If he wasn't a teacher, he'd be quite fit.'

Lis and Harry entered a high-ceilinged room, again part of the old building, with long narrow windows reaching almost the full height of the walls. Like her old school, the furniture had seen better days, but her new tutor cared enough to keep bright posters and displays on the walls. Seemingly, her form room was part of the languages faculty; various world flags and foreign vocabulary prompts were evident.

The classroom buzzed as Year Eleven pupils greeted each other after the mammoth six-week break. Girls exchanged air-kisses and boys gave each other manly back slaps or handshakes.

Maybe nothing ever changes, mused Lis.

Sitting in the furthest corner of the room were the redhead and boy from the weird trio on the bus. The girl had her head buried in a huge book called *Gravity's Rainbow*, while the boy leafed through some geeky TV magazine.

Without warning, Harry let out a high pitched scream. Lis whirled around, assuming she'd come under attack, but instead saw that Harry was simply thrilled at a new arrival to the classroom. Lis stared; she couldn't help it – the newcomer was a stunning girl with thick chestnut curls tumbling down her back. Tanned and slim, she had an air of confidence that was almost tangible. Lis felt a strange cocktail of envy and admiration. Time seemed to move more slowly around this girl as she strutted into G2, her glossed lips curling into a sexy half-smirk. She looked flawless, like something from *Vogue*.

Harry dashed over to the newcomer and threw her arms around her. 'Hi, babes!' She air kissed her friend. 'How was Thailand?'

'Fabulous, babe. Wish I was still there.'

The girl and her companion, a tall, thin Asian girl, quickly sat down in empty seats, crossing their legs in perfect synchrony.

Harry literally pulled Lis over to where they sat. 'Laura, Nasima. This is Lis London. She comes from Wales and she's new.'

Lis felt blood rushing to her cheeks. This Laura girl was obviously some sort of celebrity at Fulton High; self-assurance radiated from her as it would from a queen and Nasima had followed one step behind her, almost as if she were a subordinate. Lis realised she hadn't said anything in about three seconds. If she waited any longer they would think she was mental. *Quick! Say something! Anything!*

'Hi. Yeah, I'm Lis. Nice to meet you.' Not great, but it was a start.

'Hi, Lis. I'm Laura. This is Nasima.'

'Hi.' Nasima eyed her suspiciously through thick mascara.

'I said I'd show her around a bit,' said Harry, sliding into the row in front of Laura. 'Can she sit with us and stuff?'

Lis observed how Harry now seemed to be panicking. Maybe she and Fiona had made a terrible social mistake in allowing a newbie to join their hive without seeking permission from the queen bee.

'Duh, Harry, she can sit wherever she likes,' laughed Laura. 'Lis, ignore Harry; she's being a freak.'

'Thanks.' Again, Lis wasn't sure what to say in this supermodel's presence.

'I like your headband, it's well cute.'

'Thanks.' Lis paused. 'I keep saying thanks. Give me a minute; I can say other stuff too.'

Laura laughed. A sweet, musical sound that seemed to give Nasima permission to talk to Lis too.

'I have one just like it at home,' Nasima put in. 'I wish I'd worn it now.'

Lis leapt in while the going was good. It couldn't hurt to flatter these girls a little. 'Your hair is gorgeous without it. Mine would never go that straight.'

'My dad got me these amazing straighteners. I'll do your hair sometime,' offered Laura.

Lis didn't fancy the idea of being groomed, her mind conjured up an image of her lying before Laura like some sort of lap dog, but she was nonetheless glad of these tiny tokens of social acceptance.

At that moment, the third member of the freak-gang sauntered into the classroom. She had almost the same swagger as Laura but, while Laura's was confident, this girl's was defiant: a battle march. She cast a deadly glance at Laura as she made her way past.

'Urgh, could you not look at me, please?' asked Laura loudly. 'I don't want to catch "lesbian" off you.'

A dirty snigger ran around the classroom. The shy boy now seemed to actually hide behind his magazine, while the redhead rolled her eyes with obvious boredom.

The tall, punky girl stopped, turned and looked Laura dead in the eye, with no respect for her social rank. 'Yes, Laura,' she replied equally loudly. 'That is exactly how one catches "gay". You should wear an eye-condom next time.'

That got an even louder snigger. For a split second, Lis saw darkness flash across Laura's beautiful face and thought she was going to stand for a full-on fight. Instead, Laura simply turned back to her troops.

'What a total freak,' she said in a hushed voice.

The punk smiled and crossed the classroom to join her friends. It seemed that she'd actually come out on top.

'Who are those three?' Lis asked innocently, inwardly burning with curiosity.

'The lanky dyke is Kitty Monroe.' Laura glared at her enemy.

'And the ginge is Delilah Bloom and the gay boy is Jack Denton,' added Nasima.

'I went to primary school with them,' explained Laura. 'They were, like, quite normal then, but when we came here they just became bigger and bigger freaks.'

Disappointment filled Lis. Bitching. Name-calling. Was she back in Bangor? She squirmed in her seat, eager to get away. She'd rather die than sit alone, but did she have to endure three years of this? She certainly wasn't ready to try to enlighten them; they'd rip her to shreds.

Laura continued, 'Some people say . . . no, never mind!'

Nasima giggled behind her hand.

'What?' Lis frowned, intrigued.

'Well,' Laura leaned so close that Lis could taste her perfume, 'some people say they're witches ...'

'Oh!' Lis couldn't help laughing. 'Right! OK!'

'She's serious,' Nasima whispered. 'They go out into the copse and do spells and stuff!'

'I bet that's not all they do in the copse!' Laura cackled crudely.

'Seriously!' Harry added. 'You might as well know this right from the start. Hollow Pike is totally famous for witchcraft. We did it in History.'

'Swear down!' Laura's eyes flashed. 'When I was little my mum used to tell me all these scary stories about witches stealing children and taking them into Pike Copse. That place scares me half to death! I guess the witch tradition is alive and well, only instead of taking kids, they just make out and stuff!'

Lis was grateful when a handsome man in his early thirties entered. Mr Gray, she assumed. She was instantly taken with his bouncy walk and floppy hair. Despite his crumpled shirt and tie, Lis definitely found him attractive, a thought she planned to keep firmly to herself following her experience of 'Team Laura' so far.

The class reluctantly but obediently flopped into their plastic chairs as Mr Gray planted himself at a central desk.

'*Buenos dias*,' he greeted. 'And welcome back. Let's have a contest to see who doesn't want to be here the most!'

The class giggled and a few boys raised their hands and cheered.

'OK. Let's do the admin bit first. We should have a new pupil ... Have I got an Elisabeth London?'

Brilliant. The familiar burning crept back to her cheeks as

the spotlight swung onto her. Lis raised her arm a fraction. 'People call me Lis.'

'OK. Everybody, let's welcome Lis to Fulton.'

'Hi, Lis!' the class chanted dully.

Mr Gray smiled broadly at her. 'Every day's a party at Fulton High School, you'll be fine,' he said, the class laughing along, 'but if you do need anything, give me a shout, twenty-four/seven ... well, actually, seven/five tops!'

She nodded a silent thank you and Harry put an arm around her, claiming the new girl as one of her own. This gesture made her uneasy, especially when she caught the eye of the tall girl; Kitty arched a quizzical eyebrow that seemed to say *pick a side ...*

Following registration, Year Eleven pupils filled the corridors and congregated in an ancient main hall in the old part of the school. As Lis entered the room, she noticed that the door frame, like every doorway in the old building, was decorated with an intricate floral motif. It was beautiful and very, very old-looking. She ran her fingers over the carvings, feeling the smooth contours.

'It's mistletoe,' Harry chipped in. 'In the olden days, it kept witches from entering because this used to be a church school. Told you Hollow Pike had messed-up witchy history, but you wouldn't believe it.'

'Are you serious?'

'Yeah.' Harry nodded. 'If you don't believe me, look up!'

In the hall, beams arched high overhead, reaching up to a disturbing mural painted onto the ceiling. The colours were dark, rich, earthy reds; not unlike blood. Lis couldn't be sure, but the painting seemed to depict some serious fire-and-brimstone stuff: deformed hags at cauldrons, cowering from glorious avenging angels.

'Oh, my God!'

'I know, right?' Harry giggled.

With all the pupils together, Lis learned what it felt like to have two hundred and fifty pairs of eyes staring at her, and made her way to a seat as quickly as possible. The morning was moving too quickly, she needed a minute to catch her breath. Conversely, Laura was positively basking in all the attention she was getting, as pupils practically fell over themselves to greet her, speak to her, touch her, worship her.

A thick hush settled over the room as a door at the back of the stage opened. Out shuffled a strange little woman wearing some sort of long knitted shawl that almost dragged along the floor. She wore the thickest spectacles Lis had ever seen and had what could only be described as grey Lego hair. Although she was through with high-school bitching, Lis couldn't help thinking that it's never a good look when you can see a woman has a moustache from the back of a crowded auditorium.

'Welcome back to Fulton High, ladies and gentlemen,' said the woman on stage. She waited for silence. 'The office tells me that over the summer no one died and there was only one hospital admission. Excellent. This is excellent news.'

Lis's mouth fell open. Who was this woman?

'For our new or forgetful pupils . . .' she paused to laugh at her own joke, 'I am Ms Dandehunt, your fearless leader!'

Someone had put this woman in charge? Maybe there was a teaching shortage up here.

'Year Eleven. This is a very important year for you; you don't need me to tell you that. For some of you it will be your final year, for all of you it is your exam year. A year that will decide your future. Well, it will certainly decide whether or not we accept you into the Sixth Form here or whether you'll have to commute to Holmdale Sixth Form College which, believe me, young people, is a very dark place indeed!'

A knowing giggle ran around the hall and Lis made a mental note to Google Holmdale as soon as she got home. Despite her appearance, Lis noted that the other pupils seemed to respect Ms Dandehunt. She wasn't the most authoritative teacher in the world, but good feeling radiated from her, filling the room with warmth and positivity. In her own funny way, Ms Dandehunt had them charmed. Lis liked her.

'I have decided, Year Eleven, that this shall be a nice year,' the tiny headmistress continued. 'Yes, *nice*. A terrible, forbidden word that no English teacher encourages you to use, but I shall employ it regardless. I want our school to be a sanctuary of learning and love.'

A further snigger broke out.

'No, Jason Briggs, not *that* kind of love. A place where all pupils respect one another and work together in harmony. There is no room for unkindness, jealousy, prejudice or hate. Each day I want you to come to this school and ask the question, "Am I trying my hardest and am I being *nice?*". If you can answer yes to that question then step inside Fulton High, for you are most welcome here!'

As she nodded her square, grey bob, pupils began to applaud her rousing speech, a fitting start to a new school year.

'And now to our Thought of the Day . . .'

'Ignore that crusty old bitch.' Laura Rigg's voice poured into Lis's left ear like liquid velvet. 'Everyone knows I rule Fulton High. Welcome to my school.'

Boys

'So who were the witches?' asked Mrs Osborne with relish.

Lis knew the answer but she certainly wasn't going to out herself as someone who read books on the first day at a new school. Surviving registration, assembly and first-period Maths had left Lis almost drained. She'd politely listened to Harry's boyfriend troubles over morning break and was now sitting in English, listening to the teacher discuss a play she'd read years ago. She could barely imagine where she'd find the energy to get through lunch. If her life were a book, she'd call this chapter 'The Ordeal'.

'Oh, come on!' Mrs Osborne moaned, waving her copy of *The Crucible* at them. 'Didn't anyone read the book over the summer? Chloe, any ideas?'

'Erm, that slave woman, Tituba?' Chloe Wriggley frowned.

The mere mention of 'tit' caused Jason Briggs to almost fall off his chair in barely contained giggles.

From the far left of the classroom, doll-like Delilah Bloom raised her arm.

'Delilah?'

'There were no witches in Salem.'

'She'd know!' someone whispered behind Lis.

'Go on, Delilah.'

Lis sat up to take notice of the interesting new direction in which the lesson was heading.

'The whole point of *The Crucible* is that witches, if there were any, posed no threat to the community. The real danger was in the hysteria that took over,' Delilah explained.

Mrs Osborne smiled and nodded, although Lis sensed that many in the class were left trailing.

'Good points, Delilah, thank you. Good to know *someone* did the reading.' She addressed the whole class, '*The Crucible* was a metaphor for the way America treated suspected communists – a modern witch hunt. Can anyone think of any more recent examples where groups in society may have inspired the same suspicion or fear?'

Fear. Lis knew a thing or two about fear. She thought of her recurring nightmare. Her dreams were always the same, one minute it'd be something totally random like fretting about preparing a giant Christmas cake, and then, suddenly, without any chance to wake herself, the temperature would plummet and her hands would gradually submerge in the coppery waters of the stream in the wood. The *here we go again* sensation would kick in, but not until it was far too late and she'd resumed her doomed crawl through the forest, accompanied by the sound of her own screams.

Forcing herself back into the present, Lis focused on meticulously rearranging her brand new stationery. She lined up pointed pencils in length order, sliding her finger along the sharp graphite tips. She was safe in school where no murderous hands could reach her. She tried to refocus on the lesson – Mrs Osborne was suggesting that Islamophobia and hate crime were modern parallels of Miller's witch hunt – and suddenly noticed Delilah observing her from across the room. *Have I gone pale?* The absolute last thing she needed was to become 'the new girl who freaks out in English'; that really would take some living down.

Lis took a deep breath. Cool, calm, composed. New Lis™

was back on track. She sat up straight and started taking notes from Mrs Osborne's lecture.

As the class filed out of English, amidst a flurry of frantic text-message checking, Lis stole an opportunity to put her new social-butterfly wings to the test.

She fell into step alongside Delilah Bloom. 'I think we can assume we're the only two people to have read *The Crucible*!'

Delilah smiled a cautious grin, clearly on guard. 'I think that would be a safe assumption, yes.'

'Oh, well, maybe they saw the Winona Ryder film,' Lis suggested with a smile.

'There's absolutely nothing wrong with that version, darling. High camp!'

Lis loved the way Delilah spoke. It was wilfully eccentric, like she was channelling Oscar Wilde or something. 'Oh, I know, when I was little I wanted to *be* Winona and marry Johnny Depp. I used to watch *Edward Scissorhands* over and over on video!'

Delilah laughed heartily. 'Another high quality film. New girl, you have excellent taste!'

Like the Red Sea parting, the throng of pupils at the far end of the corridor separated to make way as Laura Rigg and her acolytes approached.

Delilah casually drew the longest pencil from Lis's fingers and used it to secure her wild red hair in a knot. 'You don't want to be seen talking to me, Lis. It won't do you any favours whatsoever.'

Before Lis had a chance to argue, Delilah strutted down the stairs and into fresh air.

Lis was surprised to find herself disappointed at the girl's departure. Was it that she really liked Delilah, or had she just been dreading lunchtime with the 'It Girls'?

She didn't have time to dwell on this as eight skinny, mini-skirted legs reached her position in the hall. She smiled as honestly as she could. She knew that half the girls in Year Eleven would kill to socialise with these pedigree creatures, yet she had a tight knot in her stomach.

'Hiya, you all right?' asked Harry, slipping her arm through Lis's own.

'Come with us for lunch.' Laura's intonation suggested a command rather than a question.

'Yeah, if that's cool?' Lis replied.

'Totally,' Laura replied. 'There are some people you need to meet.'

The weather had finally cleared up and hazy sunshine warmed the concrete outdoor areas of Fulton High, the drying buildings cracking in the heat. Lis was led through several communal quads full of pupils nibbling on sandwiches and apples. It seemed that each plaza had become territory for a different social clique: one occupied by childlike Year Sevens, another by the music crowd, balancing on cello cases while tuning guitars. Under a rain shelter, she spotted Delilah's trio lurking on the outskirts of an obvious 'geek' group. With them, but not with them.

As they left the school buildings behind and started to cross the rugby pitch, heading ever further from the canteen, Lis began to fear that, much like the girls at her old school, these new, stick-thin friends shunned any form of food during lunch break. Not wanting to say anything, Lis vowed to leave ten minutes to grab a sandwich before the end of break. 'Where are we going?' she ventured.

'We sit by the trees,' Nasima stated. 'The lads should be there by now.'

Oh, joy! She should have known there'd be boys involved. Lis didn't relish the idea of being 'fresh meat'.

'You can smoke in the wood, if you want,' said Fiona. 'Teachers sort of walk around, but they never look into the trees.'

Looking over the crumbling boundary wall, the trees in question were actually the edge of Pike Copse which so reminded Lis of the wood in her dreams. It seemed there was to be no getting away from her nightmare in such a small town.

She could hear the raucous laughter of 'the lads' from midway across the pitch. It sounded like the island of donkeys from *Pinocchio*. This didn't fill her with much confidence, although many of her closest friends in Bangor had been male so she was willing to give them a chance. The girls sloped down an incline much to the vocal appreciation of the gang waiting by the trees. Fiona instantly crossed to a tall, thin youth with far too much gel in his hair and launched into a tongue-filled display of affection.

Laura sidled over to Lis and grasped her hand, pulling her down to sit on the grass embankment. 'Make them come to us, obviously!' she whispered in her ear.

They didn't have to wait long for attention. Three young men threw their rugby ball aside and jogged over to where the girls sat.

Laura leaned further in. 'The one with the earring is Cam. He is so right for you.'

Lis could barely mask the look of horror on her face before the boys reached them.

'Y'all right, Riggsy?' asked the one Laura had identified as Cam. He had the broadest shoulders Lis had ever seen on a sixteen-year-old, and the dainty jewelled stud in his ear did nothing to soften his exterior.

Laura shot Cam her coy smirk. 'Yeah, I'm good. What's with the hair?'

He smiled broadly, twisting spikes with his fingers. 'Just somethin' new I'm tryin'!'

'It looks crap,' Laura retorted before nodding slightly at Lis. 'This is that new girl I texted you about, Lis.'

He looked Lis up and down before turning back to smile at his mates. 'She's mine!' he said, deliberately loud enough for her to hear. 'Nice to meet you, Lis. You are a very sexy lady.'

Lis stifled a laugh. How does one respond to that? 'OK. Thanks I guess.'

'I'm also very sexy. We should have sex.'

His mates laughed loudly as they threw themselves down on the grass.

'Cameron!' Laura punched him on a bulging arm. 'Why are you such a sex pest? Can't you just knock one out in your bathroom like everyone else?'

At that, Lis laughed out loud. Laura was fierce. She handled the boys as if she was one of them and Lis respected that. In fact, there was something quite masculine about Laura. Not physically, of course, but it was almost as if being queen of the school wasn't enough, she wanted to be king, too.

'Why are you so savage all the time, Riggsy?' Cam demanded.

'Because you're so boring and it amuses me!' She smiled sweetly. 'Now, try again with my new friend, Lis. She's not a piece of meat.'

Lis smiled, safe under Laura's protection. She couldn't stop staring at her new ally. It was as if Laura perfectly matched her idea of beauty, and when she was with her it made Lis feel more attractive too.

'Sorry, Lis. Welcome to Fulton. I'm Cameron and this is Ste and Bobsy. Is that better?'

'Much better!' Lis said, shaking his outstretched hand.

As the boys joined their circle, Lis was distracted by a newcomer striding down the slope. The new arrival was tall and slender, and Lis could just make out the curve of firm muscles underneath his shirt. But it was his face that held her gaze: square jaw and full lips, with ocean blue eyes looking out from beneath heavy, dark brows. Lis had always had a thing for blue eyes with dark hair. It was somehow otherworldly.

'That's Danny Marriott,' whispered Harry.

Gutted that she'd been well and truly busted, Lis gulped hard and realised her throat had become sandpaper.

Danny was approaching their group.

'He's so hot, isn't he?' Harry added rhetorically. 'He didn't used to be. He was like this big chubby geek and then all of a sudden he became gorgeous and joined the rugby team. Random!'

'Oi, Danny-Boy! Sit your arse down!' demanded Laura.

He smiled and it was so perfect, Lis stopped breathing. He shuffled into the group.

'How's it going?' he threw his rucksack down and sat cross-legged next to Nasima. 'I can't stay; I have to do homework for Physics next lesson. I forgot all about it. Bobsy, have you got your textbook?'

Bobsy started to rummage in his bag as Lis tried not to gawp at Danny.

'You're such a geek, Marriott!' Laura said and grinned. 'It's just not sexy.'

'If I mess up my GCSEs my dad won't get me the car on my seventeenth, remember?'

'Oh, yeah, bummer,' said Bobsy, handing over a dog-eared textbook.

Danny fixed Lis in his turquoise gaze. It was like a Caribbean wave washing over her.

'Hi, we haven't met. I'm Danny.' His voice was canyon deep but so gentle she had to strain to hear him.

'I'm Lis.' The words seemed misshapen and furry on her tongue.

Laura moved closer to him, stroking his arm. 'We've adopted Lis from Wales. How immense of you would it be if she could come to your shindig . . .'

Lis squirmed uncomfortably under Danny's gaze. Being around boys never usually fazed her. This was ridiculous! She barely dared to look him in the eye again in case some sort of sigh escaped her lips.

'Yeah, you should come. It's in a few weeks. My parents are going away for the weekend, so I'm having some people round,' Danny said.

'Cool, I don't think I'm busy,' Lis kept her eye line just short of his.

'Duh, of course you aren't busy!' Laura declared. 'It's not like you have any other mates yet, is it?'

The girls giggled and Lis managed an embarrassed semi-smile.

Danny seemed to roll his eyes as he got to his feet. 'Cool, I'll see you later then. Homework time.' Without any messing around, he strode up the embankment, heading back to the school.

Laura crawled nearer to Lis and Harry conspiratorially. 'That is so epic,' she whispered, 'you can pull Cam at the party!'

Lis frowned. 'Do I have to?'

'No, duh, I'm not a pimp! But you should, he's actually really nice.'

'What about you, Laura?' asked Nasima. 'Danny?'

Laura laughed, throwing back her curls. 'Maybe. Watch this space!'

And that was it. Game over. If Laura had her claws into Danny then it was finished before it had even begun. It was never gonna happen. And for some reason, Lis wanted to cry.

Stalking is a very strong word, but as the twenty-past-three bell rang throughout Fulton High School, Lis found herself stalking Danny Marriott. He was ambling down the slope that led to the bus turnaround with Cameron and Bobsy, the sound of their cheerful camaraderie drifting up to her location some thirty feet behind them.

She studied every inch of him: the way his backpack hung just above his perfect bum, his dimples, his almost coy laugh. She knew this was pretty shameless behaviour. Lis had always considered herself above this sort of nonsense. In fact, she'd been convinced that she didn't have the 'crush' gene. Turned out she was just a late developer. He was *divine*.

Some distance ahead she saw the little circus that was Kitty, Jack and Delilah heading out of the bus lane and towards the main road. What was more interesting was the reaction to their presence. As Kitty led their march, people almost dived out of their way like they had leprosy or something. Onlookers laughed nervously as they passed and, from such a distance, Lis could only imagine what people were whispering to each other, but one thing was for certain, Fulton High was scared of the trio.

Suddenly hands grabbed her shoulders and Lis let out a startled yelp.

'Guess who!' Harry squealed.

'Christ, you made me jump!'

Laura, Nasima and Fiona were close behind, fixated on something in the distance.

'Quick,' said Laura, 'you don't wanna miss this.' Laura took Lis by the arm and steered her towards the bus stop.

'What don't I want to miss?'

'You see the girl with the long ponytail?' Laura pointed to an aristocratic-looking girl waiting for the bus. 'That's Poppy Hewitt-Smith.'

Laura stopped the group as they reached the gate.

'Who's she?' Lis asked.

'She is the bitch that grassed me up for sneaking vodka into her barbecue before I went to Thailand. Her mum told my mum and I was grounded for a whole weekend!'

'She's well stuck up, too. Just because her sister's married to a Leeds United player.' Nasima tossed her silky hair back.

'OK,' Lis said, confused.

'Keep watching.' Harry giggled. 'The show's about to start!'

'How come?' Lis asked.

Laura's eyes widened, overflowing with fake innocence. 'This afternoon in Chemistry, I informed Connor O'Grady that Poppy had told Ms Dandehunt who started the fire in the boys' toilets. Let's just say he wasn't too happy.'

Lis was beginning to understand. Her heart began to beat a little faster and her cheeks burned. That sense of dread returned and the knot in her stomach tightened. *Something* was about to happen. Laura was claiming revenge, and Poppy, chatting to her friends, had no idea. Lis felt sick.

'Who's Connor O'Grady?'

'School psychopath,' Laura said, matter-of-factly. 'You don't mess. Seriously.'

Fiona stepped forward, camera-phone raised. 'Here he comes. Here he comes!'

A rugged youth with a zero crop pelted down the slope towards the bus turnaround. His hand was outstretched, carrying something that glinted in the lingering sunshine. Charging through the line of pupils waiting for the bus, he ploughed his way to Poppy, smashing onlookers out of his path. As her shocked friends began to protest, he clamped his hand around her thick ponytail and, with a flash of metal, it came away in his hand.

Lis took a step forwards as Laura and the girls howled with hyena laughter. Even from their safe distance, she saw Connor toss Poppy's severed hair into the overgrown wasteland beyond the bus terminal.

One of Poppy's mates shoved him aside, but he was already backing away, an ugly scowl on his face.

'You're a grass!' he spat at Poppy, before legging it out of the school grounds.

Poppy yelped. Her hands flew to her head, frantically feeling what hair remained. As realisation set in, she began to cry.

Lis's mouth fell open. 'Oh, my . . .'

'Oh, relax. It'll grow back. The bitch needed a trim anyway.' Laura wiped away a tear of joy. 'Did you get it all, Fi?'

'Every second! YouTube here we come.'

'Oh my God.' Lis watched Poppy crying.

'Gotta admit, that was pretty effing special!' Laura grinned, satisfied.

Harry shook her head. 'You're evil. Did Poppy even grass on Connor?'

'How should I know?' Laura tossed her hair over her shoulder. 'But maybe next time she'll think twice before she opens her horsey mouth to grass *me* up.'

As the others strutted towards the bus stop, Lis remained at the wrought iron gates feeling sick. She'd seen some things in Bangor, but this was a whole other level of cruel. Her new friends were monsters.

Shadows

Despite the generous heat coming from the wood burner, the terrace beyond Lis's bedroom was getting decidedly chilly as the evening closed in. The events of the afternoon weighed heavy on her mind. Lis had thought about it, and there was no way she could have stopped the attack on Poppy from happening. She hadn't even known what was coming, and Laura was unstoppable – not to mention nasty and vindictive.

That said, surely better to be in with Laura than against her? As long as she kept her head down and did as Laura ordered, Lis figured the queen bee would have no reason to sting her. She didn't like to admit it, but being around Laura today *had* made her feel more beautiful, more special. After all the crap she'd taken in Bangor, she needed that validation.

Sarah came out onto the terrace carrying a bottle of wine and two glasses. 'Oh, Lis, cheer up! You survived your first day. It'll get better from here on in.' Sarah poured Lis a glass of Pinot Grigio. 'You're only allowed this because it's your first day back. Do not tell Mum.'

Lis laughed, pulling her legs into her chest. 'I promise.'

'Anyway, babe, tell me all about this nightmare.'

As soon as she'd mentioned her bad dreams to Sarah, Lis had instantly regretted it. What sort of lame fifteen-year-old admits to having scary nightmares? It had been some sort of flashback to when she was eleven and Sarah had been the

37

ultimate confidante. Back then, the pair had watched old films in Sarah's room while Mum slept. Sarah, twelve years older than Lis, had always had the answers Lis needed and the movie sessions had inevitably turned into therapy.

'It's silly.'

'No, it's not. I remember when you were six and dreamt about putting all the farm animals onto a boat. Next day, half of Bethesda flooded! "Troubled Sleeper" the doctor said ...'

Lis sighed deeply and took a big mouthful of wine. She didn't especially like it, but it seemed like the kind of thing she *should* enjoy. 'OK, but you are going to think I'm properly mental.'

'Babe, I already do, so it's fine!' Sarah laughed.

'Cow!' Lis told her with a grin. 'Well, I first had the dream maybe a month ago.'

'Go on ...'

'It's always the same. I'm in this forest ... or maybe it's Pike Copse, I'm not sure,' Lis continued, 'and I'm in this stream, crawling along. I'm covered in blood and it's so cold. It's like I'm trying to get away from someone, but I don't know who. And it always ends the same way ... someone grabs my hair ...'

Lis detailed every aspect of the dream. She'd forgotten what an amazing listener her sister was, her kind eyes sympathising with Lis's endless nights of ruined sleep. Sarah listened and nodded, without interruption or mockery, until Lis had told her everything, including the bizarre real-life incident with the magpie in Pike Copse.

When she was done, Sarah reclined in her patio chair, processing the information. 'A stream of blood, eh? Are you sure you're not pre-menstrual?' she said, holding a straight face for as long as she could before bursting with laughter.

'No, you cheeky mare!' Lis rocked in her chair, laughing

too. Sarah had a gift for bringing humour to the direst situations.

'OK, seriously though, Lis. I'm sure this is just an anxiety dream. You were having an awful time at school, and then you made this huge decision to leave Mum and come to Hollow Pike. When I first moved here to look after Gran, I felt like a total bitch for months for leaving you and Mum behind – but I got over it. The nightmares are just your brain's way of working it all out.'

Lis absent-mindedly wiped her lip gloss off the wine glass. Her sister's words did make sense. 'You're probably right. Actually, I've not had the dream since I got here.'

'There you go! Try not to worry; that only makes things worse. As you settle in, I bet the nightmares stop altogether.' Sarah smiled brightly. 'A good night's sleep makes all the difference.'

Even though there was so much on her mind, the chat with Sarah calmed the busy thoughts. As Lis lay in bed that night, woozy from the wine, thoughts of Laura, Poppy, Kitty and Danny eventually began to fade away. A thick, empty sleep engulfed her.

Lis's eyes popped open. For a moment, she was disoriented, expecting to see her old bedroom in Wales. It felt like she'd been asleep for ages, but it was still pitch black outside, hours away from dawn. Why had she woken up? Wide awake, she looked down to the end of her bed, where the patio doors stood.

Pearly moonlight shone onto her crisp white bed linen and she realised she'd forgotten to draw the curtains over the French windows. For some reason, she now felt exposed and vulnerable, the eyes of the night on her body.

She wearily pushed the duvet aside and got out of bed to go and draw the curtains, but froze as a tall, angular shadow swept across the terrace. She recoiled, pressing her back to the cool plaster of the wall. *There was someone out there.* If she didn't move, they wouldn't see her. Screwing her eyes shut and holding her breath, she listened – listened for a movement, a footfall. *Nothing.*

She dared to open an eye. The long shadows of trees reached towards her door, but nothing moved. There's a reason films always portray branches as skeleton fingers, because that's exactly what they look like in the silent early hours. The shadow hadn't been merely trees, though, Lis was certain; it had been too quick. Someone had darted across the terrace. Only now doubt set in. What if she'd dreamed it? It wouldn't be the first dream she'd had that felt real.

Looking at her phone, the display read 12.54. Still the witching hour. Her head throbbed slightly as she recalled Harry and Laura's tall tales of Hollow Pike witches. It was funny, thought Lis, how everything seemed possible in the middle of the night. The fairy tales had been almost laughable at school. They weren't so funny any more.

She wouldn't sleep with those curtains hanging open. Lis forced herself over to the doors and looked out onto the terrace beyond, her heart refusing to beat steadily. The garden was silent, still and serene. What was wrong with her? Had she had too much Red Bull or something? Had it been the wine? She was so jumpy.

There was a sudden flurry of movement and Lis staggered back. Grasping the sturdy rim of her bed she saw it was just a bird. Another bloody bird. This one was huge, sleek and black all over, as if it were made from velvet. A crow or a raven – were they the same thing? She wasn't sure. It perched on the back of a terrace chair and watched her intently as she approached the window. Like the magpie, it was brazen, unfazed by her presence.

She'd never seen a crow this close up before. It was oddly beautiful, the curve of its beak elegant somehow. For a moment they sized each other up, the bird tilting its head quizzically. Perhaps the raven landing had caused the shadow to flash across the terrace. That *had* to be it. Lis was both vindicated – she hadn't imagined it, after all – and reassured.

Pulling the curtains over the windows, she returned to her bed, but she walked backwards, not taking her eyes from the doors. Just in case.

Party Hard

After a few weeks of struggling with surprisingly difficult maths, ploughing through a mountain of homework and surviving Laura's further transparent attempts to set her up with Cameron, Lis was starting to settle into her new home. Unfamiliar things were becoming routine. She could feel her nerves unclenching. Perhaps the move had been a bigger deal than she'd anticipated; no wonder she'd been so twitchy.

Since the ponytail incident, Laura had been, dare she say it, *nice*.

The weekend of the party – her first big party in Hollow Pike – came quickly. And it was at Danny's.

Her iPod played a selection of poppy dance tunes at full volume, but Lis was failing to get into the party mood. She knew Laura would have told Cameron he stood a chance despite her warnings to the contrary, and while his blatant attempts had their own special charm, the joke was starting to wear thin. Plus, every time Laura found an excuse to touch Danny – picking a bit of grass out of his hair, or brushing an imaginary eyelash off his cheek – Lis had to fight the urge to scream. The last time she'd had such a serious crush she'd been thirteen and fallen hopelessly in love with her ballet teacher who, on reflection, was probably gay.

Do I even want a boyfriend? Lis asked herself. She was starting to wonder if she was some sort of medical oddity. All fifteen-year-old girls are supposed to want a boyfriend, and Lis *had* dated boys in Bangor, but only because they'd asked and it was the done thing. But Danny ... Danny was something new, something special, and she had literally no idea how she could take it any further. With Laura hanging off him like a leech it all seemed so pointless.

She checked her reflection in the mirror. Getting ready was much easier with Sarah as style advisor. The other It Girls had taken a trip into Leeds to buy new dresses, but Lis had a wardrobe full of brand new Wales outfits to début in Yorkshire. Her new, sophisticated clothes were supposed to be mature, although she now worried the clothes were too grown-up: mumsy and dull. Tonight she'd been careful to select a demure look that would send a clear message to Cameron: plain, black skinny jeans with a simple grey vest and a pretty lace cardigan over the top. She tamed her brown waves into a chic knot and enlisted Sarah to help with make-up. It was a low impact disguise that Lis hoped would help her fly under the radar through this potentially tricky social situation.

She knew how important the party was – if she did something wrong at this event, it would haunt her for the rest of the year (or until someone else did something even more embarrassing). The night was bound to be full of pitfalls. There would almost certainly be alcohol. Should she drink any? If she did, how much should she drink? She hoped there wouldn't be any drugs doing the rounds. What if it was the norm to get involved? She'd managed to stay well clear of drugs at parties in Bangor, but she knew the day would come when she'd have to make a choice and stay resolute.

And then there were boys ... where to start?

She sighed as Sarah shouted up the stairs, 'Lis, your lift is here!'

With a final glance in the mirror, Lis sighed again. She was going to a party. Why did it feel like she was going into battle?

Harry's mum pulled up outside a large detached property on a brand-new housing estate, one of those where all the houses are identical and look a lot grander than they actually are.

'Right, you girls, behave,' she warned. 'Harry, I mean it . . . If you are sick, I will rub your face in it!'

Lis, Laura and Nasima lurched out of the back seat in a slightly undignified tangle of high heels and legs. Lis looked grossly under-dressed next to her glamorous companions, which was fine by her.

'I'll be back at midnight on the dot. Have fun,' Harry's mum said as Harry climbed out of the passenger seat and smoothed her tiny dress.

'I hope we're not early. You're dead if we're the first here, Harry.' Laura shot her friend a deadly look.

'Sorry, my mum wanted to be back in time for X *Factor*!'

'Sod it, let's get messy!' Laura led the posse towards the house.

They needn't have worried. It seemed that Danny's male friends had been there for some time – as evidenced by at least a dozen half-eaten takeaway pizzas lying around. The party was in the embryonic stage, but was nonetheless under way.

A group of boys Lis didn't know had set up camp in the lounge and were immersed in a football game on some sort of console, cheering loudly and rocking frantically, controllers in hand. Conflicting sources of loud music filled the house.

'Where's Danny?' yelled Nasima over the din.

'I dunno, but let's find him …' Laura stepped over a pile of spilled nachos and headed for the kitchen.

As they marched through the soirée, Lis popped her head round a door and found that the garage had been converted into a games room. Cameron and several others were gathered around a pool table. She quickly withdrew and followed the girls.

They pushed past some guy making an obvious move on a pretty Year Ten girl to find Fiona and her boyfriend, Lee, groping each other at a makeshift drinks station.

'Are you finished?' Laura loudly interrupted.

Fiona pulled away, lips red and make-up smudged. 'Hi babes! Y'alright?'

'Yeah, cool.' Laura was single-minded. 'Where's Danny?'

Fiona looked across the kitchen. 'He was here a second ago …'

Laura started to turn, but was rugby tackled by Cam, who bounded into the kitchen, almost knocking Lis and Harry to the floor. He swept Laura up in a massive bear hug, spinning her around.

'Riggsy!'

Laura pushed him away, yanking her dress down where it had ridden up. 'Jesus, did you forget your Ritalin? Get off!'

Cameron raised his hands. 'Sorry, Riggsy. Can't keep my hands off you!'

'Well, try harder or I'll get someone to break them,' she snarled.

'Christ, Riggsy, love, is it that time of the month?'

Laura picked up a bottle and for a moment Lis thought she might actually hit him with it but, luckily for Cam, Danny stormed in through the back door, surly and stressed. Laura calmed herself and gave him a kiss on the cheek, which Lis was secretly thrilled to see Danny pull away from awkwardly.

'Ste, mate, if you have to smoke ... garden, yeah?' he appealed to one of Cam's mates.

'Sorry, dude.'

Lis pulled herself onto the kitchen counter. 'You OK, Danny?'

'Hi, Lis. Yeah. Well, bit stressed. My dad gave a big speech about trust. If the house burns down ...'

'The next party will be your wake?'

'Something like that,' Danny replied with a grin.

'Well then, stress-head, let's get you a drink,' Laura interjected, suddenly bright and airy. She produced a hip-flask-shaped bottle of vodka from her handbag. 'Want some?'

Nasima followed suit, pulling an illicit bottle of rum from her own bag.

Danny waved a bottle of beer in Laura's direction. 'I'm all set, thanks, Riggsy.'

'Oi!' Cam punched Danny's toned arm. 'I'm the only one who's allowed to call her Riggsy. Isn't that right?'

'He can call me anything he wants. And, Cameron, it's nothing to do with you. Go away. Shoo!'

Lis was caught off guard by the tension between Laura and Cam. It was like someone had turned over two pages at once. Harry usually kept Lis well informed of all recent gossip, but she was missing something.

'Lis, what do you want to drink?' Nasima said, handing out plastic cups.

Lis thought for a moment. 'Vodka and Coke, please.'

'Good girl!' said Cameron. 'Get a drink down yer neck!'

Lis had used this strategy many times. She'd have her vodka and Coke and then refill with just Coke. If anyone asked, she'd tell them it was vodka and Coke; they were hardly likely to taste her drink, were they? She didn't like being drunk: the creeping dreaminess blurring her edges, losing control. It was too much like her nightmares.

With a loud bang, the front door swung open and half of Year Eleven seemed to spill into the hallway.

Danny took a huge step backwards, turning a sickly grey colour. 'I. Am. So. Dead.' He trailed after the crowd, trying to steer them into the garden, much to Laura's obvious dismay. Inside, Lis was glowing. The contest for Danny Marriott hadn't been won yet.

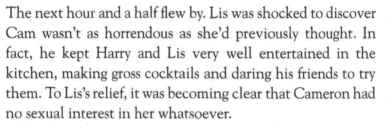

The next hour and a half flew by. Lis was shocked to discover Cam wasn't as horrendous as she'd previously thought. In fact, he kept Harry and Lis very well entertained in the kitchen, making gross cocktails and daring his friends to try them. To Lis's relief, it was becoming clear that Cameron had no sexual interest in her whatsoever.

Much to her continuing amusement, the more Danny ignored Laura, the more unpleasant she became: sulky, bitchy and sarcastic. She'd followed him around for most of the party with no pay-off until, eventually, she and Nasima headed upstairs for crisis talks in the bathroom. But that had been ages ago. Where were they now?

Lis excused herself and slid off the kitchen counter. She half needed the loo and half wondered where everyone had gone. The party was in full swing now: every hallway and room was crammed with dancing, drinking, snogging teenagers. Lis squeezed past a couple she knew from Physics who were engaged in a highly inappropriate embrace in the hallway, while a girl from her English class was hurling chunks into the downstairs loo. She circumnavigated the girl's feet and headed for the stairs.

Looking into the lounge, she was surprised to see Delilah,

Jack and Kitty sitting around a coffee table, talking amongst themselves. She wouldn't have thought they'd be remotely keen to attend Danny's party, but there they were in all their freaky glory. The group was even more striking out of uniform. Kitty was wearing some sort of Japanese school girl ensemble, while Delilah was wearing a tiny, sequinned gold dress that looked like it had come straight out of the seventies. Jack, by contrast, was wearing a very plain grey sweater and jeans, similar to Lis's own party camouflage.

Of course, no one else was anywhere near them.

As she scurried up the stairs, she thought she saw Kitty catch sight of her and give a trace of a smile, although she couldn't be sure. Lis made a vow to go say 'hi' after she'd used the loo.

The main bathroom was occupied, presumably by a livid Laura and her groupie, Nasima. A queue of annoyed girls had formed outside the door, the boldest demanding that they hurry up. Lis slid past and quietly slipped through a dark doorway, leading into what she hoped was the master bedroom. These identikit houses always had at least one en suite bathroom.

Out of respect for Danny's mum and dad, she crept across the plush carpet on tiptoe, not bothering to switch on the light in case the line of desperate girls made a run for the spare toilet. She quickly located the shower room and flicked the light switch.

A body lay on the bed.

Lis yelped, almost falling backwards into the lavatory. The form on the bed sat up swiftly, pulling a pillow from its head.

Danny stared at her from across the room. 'Oh, it's just you,' he said wearily.

'Sorry. There's a massive queue. I thought there might be an en suite in here ...'

He ran a hand through his thick hair. For Danny, the party was over. Lis knew the feeling. She'd learned on her fourteenth birthday that it's always more fun to be a guest than a host.

'No, it's cool.' He grinned. 'I thought Laura had caught me.'

Lis snorted. 'You noticed?'

'Well, yeah. She and Nasima have been following me all night. It's quite hard *not* to notice when you're being stalked.'

She slid down the wall and crossed her legs on the floor. Warmed by the glow from the shower room, Danny looked even more delicious. *There should be laws about boys being so attractive*, mused Lis, suddenly realising they were alone in a room with a sumptuous king-size bed. She felt her cheeks flush and prayed it didn't show in the dim light. She forced her nervous mouth to say something. 'You don't fancy Laura, then? She's stunning and she's clearly into you.'

Danny leaned back on the bed, resting on his elbows. 'Not really. She's, like, really, really pretty and stuff, but she's a bit scary.'

'No, really?' Sarcasm rolled off Lis's tongue. She mentally checked herself. This was a dangerous game. No matter how much she fancied Danny, this could all get back to Laura.

'Plus, Cam is still madly in love with her,' Danny went on.

She sat up straighter. 'Seriously? I didn't even know they'd been an item.'

Danny nodded. 'Yeah. She wanted to keep it quiet for some reason. He still likes her, so I'm staying well clear.'

'Fair enough. Bros before hos!' As soon as the words were out, Lis dearly wished she hadn't said them, but Danny laughed, revealing a beautiful smile. Lis beamed back.

'So what about you? Do you like Hollow Pike so far?' he asked.

She sighed and leaned her head back against the wall. Aside from her chats with Sarah, this felt like the first real conversation she'd had since arriving in the leafy town. 'Well, I've barely slept a wink because I've been having horrific nightmares, and then I crawl out of bed to go to school and hang out with a group of girls I don't really like, so it's not been a great start, no. Oh, and it hasn't stopped raining.' She had no idea why she was telling him these intimate details, but she couldn't stop herself. There was something about Danny that made her feel like she could be herself, be real.

'Well, that's no good!' He grinned. 'You know, sometimes I'm not that keen on all my friends either. Don't tell anyone … it can be our little secret!'

'Then why hang out with them?' she asked curiously.

'It's just easier.'

'Easier than what?'

'Easier than before. Back when I was Daniel, and not Danny, school used to be fairly rubbish. I'm not going to use the "B" word, but it was pretty crap. Then I joined the rugby team and all of a sudden I'm cool or something … I'm not going to argue, am I?'

Lis chuckled. 'Sell-out!'

'Totally!' He smiled once more. 'But it's true. I'm not going to complain that people aren't giving me grief any more. Anyway, you're one to talk – how are you finding being Laura's newest minion?'

He was dead right – she was no better than he was. She *did* relish the status Laura brought her, while at the same time being fully aware of what a bitch her friend could be. 'Tell you what: I'll ditch Laura if you ditch Cam!'

'Not that easy.'

'Tell me about it. The whole popularity contest thing. It's all crap. Why do we do it to ourselves?' She stood to leave, almost disappointed with him, and hating herself a little at the same time. Neither feeling outweighed the urge to crawl into his arms.

A commotion outside the bedroom turned both their heads.

'Who let the circus in?' came a cruel screech, unmistakeably Laura. 'Where did you park your broomstick?'

Danny bounced off the bed and headed for the landing, closely followed by Lis. They stepped out into a small congregation of classmates gathering to see a face-off between Laura and Kitty Monroe, who had seemingly forced Laura out of the bathroom.

Lis caught Laura's eye, very aware that she'd just emerged from a dark bedroom with Danny. Laura looked momentarily puzzled before turning back to Kitty.

'Well? Who let *you* in?' Laura repeated.

'I invited her,' offered Danny. 'We have English together. Back off, Riggsy.'

Kitty smiled innocently at Laura. 'Excuse me, I'm going to use the bathroom now if you'd be so kind as to move aside.'

Laura purposefully stretched her arms across the door frame. 'I'm sorry, Kitty. There's a no-dyke policy in this toilet.'

Lis groaned and tried to move forwards, but Nasima stopped her.

'Don't get involved,' she whispered. 'It's funnier to just watch.' She flipped open her mobile and started filming the altercation.

Kitty again smiled sweetly, although with the thick, black make-up, her grin had a twisted, manic edge to it. 'Laura, I'm not the one who's just come out of the toilet with another girl.'

Some members of the audience dared to giggle. Laura's

deathly glare soon shut them up. She moved closer to Kitty, invading her personal space.

'Oh, I'm sorry, Kitty. I know how much you want me and everything, but I'm not a dirty lesbian like you. You'll have to stick with that gypo, Delilah.'

For the first time, it seemed that Laura's blow had hit Kitty. She gave Laura a short shove that sent Laura stumbling back amidst gasps from the crowd.

'Laura, cut it out, please!' Danny pleaded.

But Kitty was on the offensive now. 'Laura, I wouldn't go near you if you were the last girl, no, *human*, on the planet. You're rancid. Toxic. Poisonous. People might be scared of me, but they *loathe* you.'

Laura flushed a deep red colour, scrambling for a comeback, but Kitty continued. 'If you don't believe me, ask anyone. They talk about you more than they talk about me and that's saying something. Ask Lis London. Better still, ask Danny!'

At that, Laura flew into a wild rage, expletives tearing from her lips. Her hands tugged at Kitty's hair, grasping her head and swinging her body into the wall. Danny shot forward, but it was impossible to intervene as Kitty responded by grabbing Laura's face in one big hand and pushing her down to the floor. Lis thought she saw Laura spit at her rival before slapping her squarely on the side of the head.

Kitty fought like a wildcat, scratching at Laura's hair and face, although Laura seemed to be the tougher fighter, curling her hands into fists and striking at Kitty's torso. Danny, and now Bobsy, stepped across the girls, trying to pull them apart, but it was no use as Kitty bombarded Laura with slaps.

Lis saw too late what was going to happen. As Laura advanced on Kitty, the top of the stairs grew dangerously close. Sure enough, Laura launched another frenzied attack and both girls teetered over the top stair. The following fall, rather than a television-style tumble, was more of a cringe-worthy bounce down the stairs for both girls. The pair rolled to an embarrassing halt, Laura's underwear clearly on show to the entire party.

Jack and Delilah ran from the lounge into the hallway.

'Bitch!' yelled Delilah when she realised what had happened, her voice the only sound other than the music as everyone else stared in stunned silence.

'Nice one, Riggsy!' Cameron's shout broke the silence.

A throaty scream exploded from Laura as she stood. Blood gushed from a split lip and she inadvertently smeared it across her face with the back of her hand. Without any further comment she marched out through the front door, a bewildered Harry trotting close behind.

Lis and Danny raced down the stairs to where Kitty was now sitting, her concerned friends at her side. Giggling and whispering, observers returned to the party, delighted with the night's entertainment.

'Kitty, are you OK?' Lis reached down to the taller girl.

'Yeah, I think so.' She checked herself for wounds. 'God, what a total bitch!'

'Well that's hardly headline news,' commented Jack in a shy voice.

'Let's go, this party was a bad idea.' Kitty hauled her lanky frame up.

Danny shrugged his shoulders as if the whole thing had somehow been his fault. 'I'm so sorry, Kitty.'

'You don't have to apologise for Laura Rigg,' Delilah stated simply. 'She's her parents' fault. They should have drowned her at birth.'

Kitty and Jack were already at the door.

'Wait!' Lis said, her heart in her mouth. 'I wanna come with you.'

Kitty turned back, a smile on her lips. 'Really? Defecting so soon? What would Laura have to say about that?'

'I . . . I don't care.'

'I think you do. We'll be in touch.' Kitty blew her a kiss and swept out of the front door. Delilah followed, leaving Lis on the stairs with Danny, but wishing more than anything that she could depart with Team Kitty. Lis couldn't ignore it any more, there was . . . *something* about them and she wanted a piece of it. As she watched the trio walk away into the night, they seemed so . . . *free*. Lis didn't want to be on Laura Rigg's leash for a second longer.

Aftermath

By the following Monday morning, the novelty of a new start in Hollow Pike had completely worn off and Lis felt school-sick. She'd lain in bed well past her alarm and was now running considerably late. She toyed with the idea of trying to convince Sarah she was ill, but knew her sister would only call upon her to make the mature, adult choice as to whether she was well enough to attend school, and then she'd only end up feeling guilty if she stayed home.

Cornflakes formed a dry, pulpy mass in her mouth, impossible to swallow.

Sarah shrewdly regarded her across the kitchen table as she fed Lis's little nephew, Logan. 'What's up, kiddo?'

'Nothing.' Automatic response.

'Don't believe you ...' Her sister smiled.

'I'm fine. It's just early.'

'Is it school?'

'Nope.'

'That Laura girl?'

Yes. 'Nope.'

'Your teacher ... Mr Gray, is it?'

Lis let herself laugh. Sarah wasn't going to let it go. 'Good lord, Sarah, everything is fine! Mr Gray is lovely! Satisfied?'

'He seems nice ... quite a looker too! Maybe I'll bob along to his adult Spanish classes ...'

'If you do, I'll emancipate myself from you!' Lis grinned. Sarah guffawed loudly as Lis ditched her soggy cereal in the sink and turned the tap on, squashing the cornflakes down the plughole.

After a second of processing the image before her, she took a step back. 'Sarah?' she said.

'What?'

'Look at this.'

Sarah heaved Logan onto her hip and shuffled over to the sink. 'What is it? And please don't put food down the sink, the drains get blocked.'

'OK, but look.' Lis motioned at the gurgling water.

'I'm looking. There's nothing there.'

'The water is going down the plughole the wrong way! It should be going anti-clockwise.'

Sarah looked at her with sisterly disdain. 'Ha! That's an old wives' tale. Or maybe it's magic!'

Lis's head snapped up at that. 'What?'

'You know – the whole Hollow Pike witch thang.'

'Did you just say *thang*?'

'Yeah, I'm still down with the kids.' Sarah winked. 'When Max and I first moved here, we went on this witch tour one Halloween. It's true, you know, there were witches in Hollow Pike. The town's supposed to be cursed or something.'

'But years and years ago, right?'

'Well, obviously. The tour was so naff, it was hilarious. We should go on it this year.'

Lis had dismissed Harry and Laura's talk as nonsense, but coming from her sister, the witchcraft legends were suddenly real. And fascinating. Sarah left the kitchen with Logan, leaving Lis to ponder the swirling water, spinning the wrong way down the drain.

Lis had missed the bus by a mile, so Max kindly offered to drop her at school and now the silver Transit van pulled up outside the main gates. She breathed deeply, adoring the smell of the van: varnish and wood chips.

'Are you sure you're all right?' Max asked, his big blue eyes prying for information.

'I'm fine. Promise.' She managed a feeble smile.

'OK. Have a nice day.' Her brother-in-law gave her a kiss on the forehead before she flopped out of the vehicle.

Once again the school was wrapped in a veil of fine drizzle guaranteed to turn her hair into a frizzy mess by the time she reached the safety of the corridors. She murmured a solemn farewell to Max and dragged her feet towards the entrance.

The huge ancient clock that dominated the main hall told her that at eight fifty-five she'd probably already missed the warning bell that prompted students to get to their form rooms by nine. She swung her bag onto her shoulder and wearily started for G2.

Her spider sense flickered. Something was *not quite right*. It was exactly the same feeling that had blighted her first day of school. But this was odd. The new-girl sensation should have left her by now, so why were people staring at her? Her hair couldn't be *that* frizzy! She'd left the party on Saturday night soon after Laura and Kitty had fallen down the stairs, so she was certain she hadn't done anything to embarrass herself.

Increasingly aware of others pointing her out or whispering, she hurried to G2 and settled herself into her seat next to Harry. To her horror, the hushed voices and sideways glances continued. Lis turned to Harry, who seemed

57

to be masterfully avoiding eye-contact. The paranoia boiled over.

'Harry, what is going on? Do I have something weird on me?' A sense of dread rose in Lis's gut and she started to wish she'd played sick for Sarah.

'Nothing, babe.'

'Then why is everyone staring at me?'

Harry shrugged and tried to pull an innocent expression. The effect was cartoonish and fake. 'I have no idea, babe. People must be talking about what happened at the party.'

Lis scanned the classroom. In their usual spots at the back of the class sat Jack, Delilah and Kitty, who sported a nasty yellowish bruise under her eye. No one was paying them any more attention than normal. This was ridiculous.

'Harry, nothing happened at the party! I was there for the fight, but that's it.'

As the 9 a.m. bell sounded, Laura and Nasima sauntered into class in their usual catwalk formation: Laura slightly ahead, flanked by her sentry. On passing, Laura gave Lis the most hateful look she'd seen in a long time.

Lis was baffled. What had *she* done to upset Laura? The strangest part was, despite the way Laura had behaved at the party, Lis hated the idea of Laura being mad at her. A tiny, residual desire to belong, to fit in with the popular girls still glimmered within her. Lis pushed that thought out of her head; she was so over that crap.

'Look, Lis,' hissed Harry. 'Laura told me what happened with Danny.'

'What do you mean?' Lis demanded. 'Literally nothing happened! I talked to him for, like, a minute.'

Harry scowled at her and turned away.

'Jesus, Harry,' Lis whispered emphatically, 'it's not my fault if Danny Marriott doesn't fancy Laura!'

With a sharp flick of her hair, Harry whipped around to face Lis, a nasty grimace on her face. 'Whatever. You're a liar and a slag and I don't like liars and slags. Now could you please stop talking to me or I'll tell Mr Gray you're bullying me?'

As Harry pushed her chair back to seek counsel with Laura, Lis felt herself gawping. What on earth had she done to deserve that?

Throughout Maths, Lis desperately tried to motivate herself by pretending she was some sort of future scientist who would one day need to know trigonometry. It didn't work. She still couldn't shake the feeling that the whole class was talking about her. She'd tried so hard since arriving in Hollow Pike, genuinely thinking she hadn't put a foot wrong, and now Harry's comments proved that she may as well not have bothered.

As her teacher spoke, she fought to hold back both tears and swear words. Was this what she'd moved away from Bangor for? More of the same? At least in Wales she'd held her head high right up until the end.

Slipping her homework into her bag, she rushed out of class the second the bell sounded. Following instinct, she ducked past Fiona and Nasima and headed straight for the outside quad, no longer caring about the rain's effect on her hair. She cursed her earlier vanity as if she'd somehow been infected by the values of Team Laura.

A new determination burned in her chest. She'd gone beyond feeling tearful and just wanted to know what the bloody hell was going on. She spotted her target under the shelter and marched over to where Jack Denton was sitting next to some of the other 'geek' males, peeling a satsuma.

'Hi, Jack,' she said, smiling broadly despite her rising fury. She reminded herself that Jack hadn't done anything wrong. Jack eyed her suspiciously and conversation in the group ceased entirely.

'Hello,' he replied, gentle as snow.

'Where are Kitty and Delilah?'

'I dunno. Loo maybe?'

She'd barely chatted to Jack. His softly-spoken nature made him almost impossible to read. Could she trust him? Something about his huge chestnut eyes reminded her of autumn and suggested a warmth inside. She looked around, only to see Harry coolly observing her as she moved across the quad.

'Could I have a word, please?' she asked Jack, unsuccessfully trying to keep a pleading tone out of her voice.

'A private word?'

'Please.'

The pair moved to the farthest corner of the rain shelter, and Jack continued to eat his satsuma as Lis explained her morning of paranoia. When she'd finished, Jack smiled and sat her on a damp wooden bench.

'OK,' he started. 'Well, the good news is you're not completely paranoid.' He had a light, almost musical voice and an accent, though, like hers, it wasn't a Yorkshire accent. Maybe he was from Newcastle? She wasn't sure, but she could see where the gay rumours had originated. Jack's voice was different enough to cause comment.

'Why not?' Lis asked.

'And if it's any consolation, it's all clearly made-up crap . . .' Jack continued.

'What is?'

And then he told her . . .

Exactly two minutes later, Lis stomped to the edge of the trees. Although her shoes sunk into the mud of the rugby pitch, her single-mindedness blinkered her. She smoothed back her hair, readying herself for a battle. Voices raged in her head, telling her to turn back, to avoid a confrontation, to seek the help of Kitty or Mr Gray.

Regardless, she powered on. They were sheltering under the trees, although none of the boys were there as far as she could tell, which suited her fine. It was just the four nasty bitches who weren't going to get away with it this time. She'd already left one school, and she wasn't about to let history repeat itself.

'Oh, fabulous!' sneered Nasima. 'Look who it is!'

Lis continued towards the girls. She paused just before them and drew a deep breath of humid air into her lungs. She was determined not to scream or shout, besides, she knew from the fight on Saturday that she didn't stand a chance against Laura.

'Laura. I want a word with you,' she said calmly.

Laura smiled and whispered something in Nasima's ear, causing the taller girl to giggle cruelly.

'I mean it, Laura. Do you need your cheerleaders for backup?'

Throwing her cigarette into a ditch behind her, Laura stepped away from the others.

Lis began in a low, even tone. 'You're making up rumours about me? How old are you, seriously?'

'You're well weird. *You* e-mailed *me*, you freak.' Laura was deliberately loud for the benefit of her audience.

'You're lying.'

'Poor cow. You must be bipolar or something.' The others were all staring now. Laura reached into her Louis Vuitton bag and withdrew a slip of crisp white paper. She handed it to Nasima who cast her pretty eyes over it while Harry and Fiona sniggered quietly behind their hands.

'Oh, you muppets can shut up!' snapped Lis. 'Give me that piece of paper, now!'

'You trying to start something?' asked Fiona.

Lis suddenly felt that coming to the most remote corner of the school grounds alone could have been an error. 'Just give me the piece of paper.'

'Do it,' said Laura. 'She sent it, anyway.'

Nasima held it out, then snatched it away when Lis reached for it.

'Seriously? Has it come to that?' Lis asked, rolling her eyes.

Nasima smiled and handed her the document. It was exactly as Jack had described. An internet print-out. An email from one lizlondon15@hotmail.com to Laura's account. It wasn't even her email address, but Lis guessed it had been enough to fool anyone seeing it this morning. She read on.

Hi Laura
Thanks for everything yesterday. I was so down and needed to talk. It's been so hard keeping it all a secret, I had to tell someone. Giving up my baby was the hardest thing I've ever done, but I know I've done the right thing. I couldn't have raised him all by myself without knowing who the father is. I deserve a fresh start in Hollow Pike.
You are such a good friend. Thanks for listening.
Liz xxx

'No one believes this,' Lis said coolly.

'You tell yourself that, Lissy love,' Laura said sweetly and snatched the paper out of Lis's hand.

Lis shook her head almost pityingly. 'Laura, that is the worst rumour I've ever seen. You'd think such an accomplished bitch might have been able to do better. I gave my baby up for adoption? How long did it take you to come up with that? What, you couldn't spell chlamydia?'

Harry stepped forward. 'You sent it, Lis. You can't deny it now.'

'Really? You fell for this? Laura sent it herself. That's not my email address, and she didn't even spell my name right!'

Laura's smirk slipped. A new strength blossomed inside Lis; Laura had apparently expected her to crumble a lot sooner than this.

Her rival took a cigarette lighter out of her bag and burned the paper by a corner until it fell to the floor as a black cinder. 'Who do you think you are anyway?' Laura's voice now quavered with fury. 'You think you're dead funny and clever. All shy and sweet. All "don't look at me; I'm just little Lissy the new girl", when you're actually a boyfriend-stealing whore!'

'That is total sh—'

'Really, Lis? So you *don't* think you're better than us? You *don't* think we're just all hair and boys?'

'That is exactly what you are!'

Laura laughed, a new, almost demonic quality to her now. Just for a second her eyes seemed jet black. She jabbed a pointed finger squarely into Lis's chest, pushing her backwards. 'I think you should shut your mouth. You are a stuck-up little snob and you have no idea who you're dealing with. I run this school, you got that? Now listen very carefully ... I am going to make you wish you'd never set foot in this school. You are going to have to come here every single day and I will be waiting for you. Every. Single. Day.'

Speechless, Lis shied away from the intensity of Laura's stare. Behind Laura, even her winged monkeys had been stunned into silence.

Laura seemed to have surprised herself. She stepped back, taking a breath and smoothing her blazer out. 'Better run along, Lissy. You don't want to be late for Spanish.'

Without another word, Lis turned and headed up the slope towards the rugby pitch.

'Oh, by the way, Lis, say hi to Mr Gray . . . I told everyone you're in love with him.'

Lis closed her eyes and started to jog. She would not cry in front of Laura.

She didn't go to Spanish. She had come off the pitch wet and barely able to breathe, and sought refuge in the library. Throughout her time in Wales, she'd told herself – no, more than that, *clung to the belief* – that none of it was her fault. Now the same thing was happening again. Only worse. So maybe it *was* her fault. Maybe there was something about Lis London that just said 'victim'. Christ, she was thinking about herself in the third person, a sure sign of impending mental collapse.

She pulled her legs up to her chest where she sat in the farthest corner of the library. Daphne, the elderly librarian, had set up some plump cushions against the water pipes, creating a warm nest to read in.

In her head, Lis wasn't a victim, she was mature and sophisticated. She read Italian *Vogue* and watched French cinema: cool stuff, god damn it! She wasn't the most beautiful girl in the world by a long stretch, but she thought she looked ... *acceptable*. But now Lis was forced to consider that, to the rest of the world, she wasn't cool, sophisticated or stylish. She was only weak. A target. Easy prey.

But why me? Her inner monologue raged. *What have I done to deserve any of this?*

'You skipped my lesson,' came the answer.

Mr Gray's shadow fell over her. She lowered her book and stared up at the towering figure. 'I'm sorry, sir.'

'Is it because you gave your illegitimate baby up for adoption?' he asked, his voice rich with humour.

Lis involuntarily snorted and Mr Gray sat down next to her. 'I don't want to be all "Cool Teacher", but you can talk to me if you like.'

'It's not true.'

Mr Gray laughed, rubbing his rough jaw. 'Well, obviously not! I think something like that might have come up on your school transfer records.'

Lis smiled a little, more at ease. 'You know Laura's lying?'

'Of course! Teachers know *everything*! Young people spend so much time saying we aren't listening. Believe me, we're listening to it all! We know who's seeing who, who's dumping who, who's *saying* they're seeing who but actually isn't. This is a small town – everyone knows everyone and most of us are related! It's better than *Perez*.'

Lis raised an eyebrow. 'I'm glad it's all so entertaining for you.'

He opened his hands – a peace gesture. 'I'm sorry. I didn't mean to make light of it, I just thought you could use some cheering up. We are aware that there are various problems with Miss Rigg at the moment.'

Lis let her head flop back onto the cushion. This was the

bit where he'd tell her how everything was going to be all right.

'I know what you're thinking ... that I can't do anything, that I'll just make it worse.'

Oh, this guy thinks he's good ... Lis thought.

Mr Gray carried on. 'You don't need to say or do anything. Like I said, we are all well aware of how Laura Rigg behaves and it's all being written down, recorded. Every last thing. Ms Dandehunt is gathering all the evidence she needs. You see, Lis, it's a delicate situation; Laura's mum is on the board of school governors ...'

'Oh, I see.'

'You have no idea.' He crossed his legs and leaned in for added impact. 'But listen, we are dealing with this. It will get sorted.'

Lis looked into his earnest green eyes. They were tired, but resolute. Her teacher believed he could help her. The gesture, if nothing else, gave her a tiny glow of hope. She had someone on her side. 'Thank you.'

'If you cut any more Spanish, I'll call your sister.' With that, he departed.

Lis inhaled and tried to think rationally. Laura and her groupies practically lived at the edge of the copse. That should be pretty easy to avoid. Lis knew they wouldn't be within ten metres of a calorie so heading for the canteen seemed a safe bet. She hauled her school bag onto a shoulder and started to make her way through the jungle of bookshelves.

Without warning, Kitty Monroe emerged from behind a bookcase and blocked her path. Lis let out a reflex yelp of surprise. Further down the aisle stood Jack and Delilah. How long had they been there? Had they heard her conversation with Mr Gray?

Kitty paused for a moment before smiling an electric, Cheshire Cat grin. 'Tonight we're going to plan how to kill Laura Rigg. Would you like to join us?'

Murder

A bus trundled up the hill to Upper Hollow, where the grand houses looked down loftily on the rest of the village. There was only one way to get there – through the copse, and long, wooden fingers scratched the windows of the bus, clawing at the glass. Lis leaned away from the talons, shuddering. Under the thick canopy of leaves it was so dark she could scarcely believe it was daylight.

It was crazy, but Lis could swear the rustling leaves were whispering her name. It was all in her head, for sure, but she found herself straining to listen. Her imagination was running wild. There was something about the copse – it was almost as if it . . . *wanted* her.

'Are you OK?' Jack asked.

'Yeah, fine,' Lis replied. 'The copse freaks me out a bit.'

'Oh, God, it freaks everyone out. All those fairy tales when we were little, plus – total rapist hotspot!'

Lis shivered, but she was enjoying Jack's company. Away from the rest of Fulton High School, Jack could not be more different. He'd barely shut up since she'd joined him on the bus.

'By the way,' he continued, 'I should warn you that Kitty's dad is the scariest man in the whole world.'

'Really? Why?'

'Wait and see!'

Lis had, of course, accepted Kitty's invite to the murder party. She assumed Kitty was kidding, but it almost didn't matter. The social lifeline thrown to her was too tempting to resist. From the second she'd seen them on the school bus, Lis had felt drawn to the trio. OK, the group weren't winning any popularity contests at school, but they had their own strange strength. They unsettled people – people like Laura Rigg. That was good enough for Lis.

'How long have you known Kitty and Delilah?' she asked Jack, distracting herself from the 'voices' in the trees.

'Oh, ages,' Jack replied. 'We went to primary school together, but we didn't really speak much until last year.'

'How come?'

Jack shrugged. 'I was scared of them, you know, because of the witch rumours, but then one day we got chatting in RE. After that I just wanted to be around them all the time – they get me, you know? I guess it was like destiny or something.'

Lis had to admire his kids' TV enthusiasm. She chuckled to herself.

'What's so funny?'

'Nothing. Just you.'

'Funny ha-ha, or funny strange?'

'Both!'

He laughed good-naturedly and poked her in the ribs.

The copse cleared and the bus rolled into Kitty's affluent neighbourhood. The houses were newer, grander and the fences higher. A few of the more ostentatious houses actually had statues on their front lawns, hiding behind locked iron gates. Who, in Hollow Pike, actually needed gated security was beyond Lis; surely it was the quietest, safest place in England?

'This is our stop,' Jack announced, ringing the bell.

The pair stepped off the bus and onto the damp pavement. Lis followed Jack, trying to get her bearings.

'Bitchface Rigg lives down there, and just around the next corner is Danny's place ...'

Lis's stomach flipped at the fleeting mention of his name, and she mentally slapped herself around the head.

'And that's Kit's ...' Jack gestured down a tree-lined cul-de-sac.

Kitty's house was just shy of mansion status. A huge perimeter wall occluded the whole estate, although Lis could just make out a long driveway leading to a substantial house.

'Good lord, are Kitty's parents royalty or something?'

Jack laughed loudly, 'Almost! Kitty's dad is like the sheriff or something.'

'What?'

'Seriously! He's the chief of police for the whole area, which is like being the biggest fish in a tiny, tiny pond ... but he's still the boss.'

'Is that why he's so scary?'

'Wait and see!'

Jack grasped her hand, practically dragged her up to the vast wrought iron gate and pressed the buzzer.

After a short pause, a timid female voice answered, 'Hello?'

'Hi, it's Jack and Lis for Kitty.'

With a hideous groan, the gate creaked open.

'Was that the maid?' muttered Lis.

'Her mum, who is not scary.'

The pair skirted around the edge of the neatly trimmed lawn in the centre of the semi-circular driveway.

'I'm a little bit scared of their house,' Lis confessed.

'Yeah, seriously, don't spill.'

Kitty appeared in the doorway. This was a dressed down version of her new friend: she wore a slouchy vest and a pair of cut-off, black skinny jeans. 'Hi. Come on in. Welcome to Monroe Manor.'

The interior was every bit as luxurious as the exterior and Kitty shuffled through the ground floor as if she was embarrassed by the grandeur of her family home. It was certainly in stark contrast to Kitty herself.

From the lounge a booming voice stopped the trio in its tracks. 'Is that more friends, Katherine?'

Kitty took a deep breath and Lis craned her neck to try to catch a glimpse of Kitty's father, but she could only see the top of a grey head emerging from a grand leather armchair.

'There are only four of us, Dad,' Kitty called back.

'No bloody weirdo music.'

'OK.'

She rolled her eyes and led them up the stairs. 'If you ever call me Katherine,' she hissed to Lis, 'it's all over.'

'Your secret's safe with me!'

After endless miles of plush carpeted stairs, Kitty led them into a converted attic room. This room *did* reflect Kitty. There was no bed; it was a sort of den. She'd hung sheer red fabric over the velux windows, creating a dark, warm cocoon. A tall vintage lamp draped in a gold shawl stood proudly in the corner, adding further enchantment.

Delilah was already sitting at Kitty's laptop, selecting *quiet* music. She gave Lis a friendly smile and a little wave of her fingers. The floor was covered in an old rug and all types of books, from tiny, battered volumes of poetry to massive coffee table books featuring photographers Lis had never heard of. Bits of homework were scattered around empty cups of tea, and the walls were papered with hundreds of eye-catching images. There were startling nudes, glamorous models styled as corpses, and one wall displayed an enormous Hello Kitty cartoon waving at the room. A broad grin spread across Lis's face. It was like being inside Kitty's mind.

Jack threw himself onto a battered leather sofa while Kitty crawled over to Delilah and embraced her from behind.

OMG – *they actually* are *lesbians!* Lis realised. Her mind flipped out – she'd assumed the lesbian rumours were as nonsensical as the witchcraft gossip. *Chill, Lis*, she told herself, *this is nothing you haven't seen on TV*. Lis once again forced herself not to stare and joined Jack on the sofa. So, she'd never actually met a lesbian couple before, but they didn't need to know that. Jack, meanwhile, was busy pulling a selection of clipboards and pens out of his rucksack.

'What on earth are those for?' asked Delilah, cosy in Kitty's arms.

'Well, if we're going to plot someone's death we should at least plan efficiently,' Jack told her. 'We don't want to make mistakes.' He unrolled a massive piece of white paper and pinned it to the wall.

'If we're planning to kill someone, why would we write *anything* down?' Delilah retorted.

Kitty snorted. 'Good point.'

'I second that,' Lis put in.

Jack pouted for a second. 'OK. Point taken. No notes at all!' He put the clipboards away. 'Lis, our rule is that anything said in Kitty's attic, never leaves Kitty's attic.'

'Seems reasonable.' Lis looked to Kitty and she smiled warmly. The air of menace Kitty had at school was nowhere to be found in the cosy loft conversion.

'That works for you too,' Jack continued. 'You can tell us anything you want. We won't say anything at school.'

'It's not as if anyone talks to us, anyway, is it?' Kitty added.

Lis smiled sympathetically. 'I want you to know, I'm not like Laura and the others. I never slagged you off.'

'We know.' Delilah smiled. 'We wouldn't have invited you here otherwise.'

Lis sat forward, feeling braver. 'I left my last school because I was being bullied. It got quite bad. I wouldn't do that to someone else.'

Jack pulled his legs up onto the sofa. 'You were bullied? But you're so pretty! And there I was thinking only the fat, gay kids got bullied!'

All four of them laughed uproariously, and Lis realised she hadn't laughed out loud like this in a very long time.

A few hours later, all four of them were sitting in a circle on the tatty rug. Night had long since fallen and the plan to murder Laura Rigg was well under way.

Jack's initial suggestions were hilarious and outlandish, involving the construction of various death contraptions for Laura to step inside, not unlike *Mousetrap*. Kitty and Delilah steered the conversation round to more realistic ideas.

'But how *could* we do it?' asked Delilah. 'How could we murder the most popular girl in school and get away with it? There has to be a way.'

'We could all provide alibis for each other,' Lis suggested.

'We could. They'd have to be airtight though,' mused Kitty. 'Maybe we could wait until someone's parents were on holiday, or something, so we could believably all be in one place at the time of death *and* make sure we could come and go without anyone knowing.'

Jack ran a hand through his mousy hair. 'My mum and Amber are always away overnight for Amber's dance contests, so that could work.'

Drawing tiny elaborate doodles on a notebook, Delilah

looked distracted but remained focused on the conversation. 'We wouldn't want to kill her anywhere near any of our houses, obviously.'

'And we can hardly follow her around, waiting for her to be alone in a dark alley,' Jack laughed. 'It's not as if we're inconspicuous.'

'Hmmm ... Maybe we could arrange for her to meet us somewhere?' Delilah suggested as she continued with her doodles.

An idea occurred to Lis. 'I'm pretty sure I have Laura's email address ...'

Kitty laughed. 'Nah, even from a fake account, they could trace where the email had originated.'

'Really? Forget it then.'

'No, it's a good idea. We could write a letter instead of an email. A print-out from a school printer wouldn't incriminate any of us as long as we didn't handle the paper,' said Kitty.

'We should totally write the note from Danny!' Jack said eagerly, popping up onto his knees.

Lis felt distinctly strange at the thought of dragging Danny's name into things. Although he'd have his own alibi, he'd no doubt be put through hell.

'No,' stated Delilah, to Lis's relief.

'I agree,' Kitty added. 'Danny's OK. I haven't got a problem with him.'

'Say it's from Nasima Bharat,' Delilah breathed.

'Good call!' Jack threw himself back onto the sofa. He was a bundle of energy, barely able to sit still for a second. 'Frankly, that bitch has it coming.'

Lis was drawn in to what was essentially a problem-solving exercise. How can you control all the variables surrounding a murder? The police, the body, the weapons? It was harder than any SAT question. She flipped her hair back and squinted in concentration. 'What about poison? Then there'd be no weapon.'

'Yeah,' said Kitty. 'Could work. But how would we get her to take it?'

'She's a teenage binge-drinking statistic! Spike her drink!' laughed Jack.

'Brilliant, Jack! Do you have any cyanide?' grinned Delilah.

'No, smart-arse, but I'm sure a load of Cillit Bang would do the trick!'

Lis rolled back onto the rug, looking up at the ceiling. 'She'd taste it straight away. She'd never drink it.'

'I dunno ...' Kitty said, not missing a beat. 'Have you ever tasted WKD Blue? Cillit Bang can't be much worse!'

Not for the first time, the group broke into uncontrollable laughter.

'OK, OK!' Kitty commanded the group to attention. 'So, what have we got so far? We send her a letter, maybe from Nasima, asking her to go somewhere ...'

'Right,' Jack confirmed.

'And then what if we make it look like an accident out in the copse or something? We could make it seem like she's been drinking. A blow to the head could look like she'd fallen over by mistake, and we wouldn't even have to work out how to dispose of the corpse.'

Corpse. Lis shivered. What a cold, inhuman word. They were talking about a human body. A dead, human body. *Laura's* dead, human body. *It's only a game*, she reminded herself.

'I like it. You're a genius!' Delilah finally left her doodle and kissed Kitty on the forehead.

'Wouldn't the police be able to tell it wasn't an accidental injury?' Lis queried.

'Probably not. There is no *CSI: Hollow Pike*,' Jack said with a grin.

Lis laughed. Despite the gory context, she couldn't remember the last time she'd had this much fun. There was such a glow in the room. From the limited time she'd spent with Laura and her girls, Lis doubted they ever had this type of uninhibited fun. With them, she'd been so wary of the other girls' judgement that she hadn't relaxed for a second. In Kitty's attic, Lis didn't feel judged for anything: her clothes, her hair, who she liked or didn't like . . .

'If we're going to fake an accident we probably shouldn't leave a note either, or Nasima will deny sending it and the police will get suspicious,' Jack pointed out. 'Maybe we could text her instead and then pry her phone from her cold dead hands?'

'That could work, although the police would certainly realise her phone was missing,' Kitty responded. 'Of course, there's no reason why one of us couldn't go with her into the copse while others waited there.'

'A trap?' Lis asked.

'Yeah,' Kitty continued. 'You could pretend to forgive her for the email thing and carry on hanging out with her. She'd follow you into the copse for sure.'

Lis hadn't expected such a pivotal role in the plot. She sat up, unsure how to react. The others looked at her expectantly, almost as if this was some sort of initiation test she was unaware of. 'Yeah. I suppose so,' she said finally, 'although I'm not sure I could convince Laura to come with me. I'm a terrible actress.'

'Anyway,' Jack started, 'donking her on the head's not good enough. I want her to suffer . . .'

The knife-like term *suffer* twisted in Lis's gut.

'I think we should maybe do it at half term. It would be

easier to convince her to come into the copse then,' Kitty suggested.

'Everyone knows that's where they hide all their booze and fags,' Jack added. 'It would be easy to get her to go there.'

Delilah snuggled in Kitty's lap. 'The trouble is, darling, dog walkers and stuff go through the copse until after dark. Someone would see – unless we used the old rubbish dump, maybe?'

Lis felt queasy. What had started as a game was beginning to seem a bit morbid.

'That's magnificent,' Kitty agreed. 'Throw her over the edge and the whole town would think the silly drunken girl had fallen to her death in a tragic accident.'

Lis remembered a time long ago when she and Sarah had gone walking on Anglesey. While running through sand dunes, free spirited, she'd come across a badly injured baby seagull. She could still hear it's shrill alarm call, crying to its absent mother for rescue. She recalled Sarah, older and wiser, reaching forwards to put the helpless creature out of its misery, certain it couldn't be nursed back to health. Even with the knowledge that Sarah was acting out of kindness, Lis had been unable to bear the thought of snuffing out a living creature's light, and she'd turned away, unable to watch.

Laura Rigg was no helpless creature, but Lis knew that when the time came to push her over the edge, she would still remember that seagull. She would not kill a living thing.

'What's wrong?' asked Jack.

Without even looking in a mirror, Lis knew she'd gone ghostly pale. 'We can't really kill Laura.' The words stuck at the back of her throat, coming out almost like a confession. How ironic: confessing that she *didn't* want to kill someone!

There was a second of silence and then the others burst into hysterical laughter.

'Oh, poor Lis!' Kitty managed through her tears of hilarity.

'Of course we can't really kill Laura! Can you imagine? "Hi, Laura, would you stand still while we beat you to death?"' Delilah asked with exaggerated politeness.

Jack gave Lis a little hug. 'We do this sort of thing all the time!'

'Plotting fiendish plans and terrible schemes!' announced Delilah in a theatrical deep voice.

'I am truly sorry, Lis.' Kitty smiled. 'Welcome to our twisted brand of fun! Too dark?'

Relief swelled inside. Lis shook her head, wondering when she'd undergone such a humour bypass. She hoped the others didn't think she was a total moron. It seemed that, whatever friendship group you were in, there was just a different set of rules to understand.

'Seriously!' Jack laughed. 'Can you imagine me in prison? I wouldn't survive an hour!'

Delilah collected up four cups, ready to provide fresh tea. Then she spoke softly, not facing the group, 'Joking aside, would you do it though? If you had the chance, would you kill Laura Rigg?'

The room went very quiet. Lis looked to the others; as the newcomer, she wasn't going to offer up her thoughts first and she already knew her own answer: no.

Kitty sat up straight. 'If I knew I'd get away with it, I'd kill her in a second.'

'Me too,' said Jack. 'I'd be doing the world a favour.'

All three now looked to Lis. She paused, trying to conjure a diplomatic answer. 'School would be a better place without her.'

A wave of guilt unexpectedly washed over her. For some reason, Lis felt that she'd just signed Laura's death warrant.

Belonging

The expression on Laura Rigg's face was priceless. Striding down the corridor alongside Kitty, Jack and Delilah, Lis spotted her nemesis near the lockers. People were staring – hell, eyes were hanging out of heads – but just as Lis had predicted, being part of the edgy tribe felt secure, bordering on powerful. She liked it.

Her new unit was almost the parallel of Laura's 'In Crowd'. They were the 'Out Crowd' – something which Lis decided was actually much cooler. Much like the In Crowd, Kitty, Delilah and Jack strutted around the school, now with Lis in tow. When Laura blew by, people took notice. Equally, when Kitty walked in, you couldn't ignore her. It seemed to Lis that Kitty and Delilah had realised that keeping their heads down didn't work; people were going to target them regardless, so they may as well have a little fun with it. If people were going to talk, give them something to talk about.

As they reached the lockers, Lis smiled, daring to push past Laura. She shared the burden of Laura's cruelty with the others and was less of a victim as a result. Maybe there was some mathematical formula for it: vulnerability times mockery divided by support, or something.

Recovering from her shock, Laura's face twisted into her usual smirk. 'Aw, that's sweet. The witches made a new friend!'

Lis stopped and turned to face her. If only Laura knew about their detailed plans to kill her. She wouldn't be smiling then.

'That's right, Laura, but I'm surprised you know what a friend is!'

Behind her she heard Jack laugh quietly.

Nasima weighed in, 'Maybe she's a lesbian too?'

Lis flexed her new-found bravery. 'Nasima, why are you always such a sheep? You're the only Pakistani pupil in our class. Don't you know what it feels like to be different?'

An angry look flashed across her face. 'Just because I'm Pakistani doesn't mean I'm a lesbian! That is well racist.'

Delilah stepped forward rolling her eyes. 'Don't waste your breath, Lis. If she ever had a brain cell it would have died of loneliness by now.'

'Losers,' Laura said bitterly. 'How's your pikey dad, Bloom?'

'He's fine, thank you, Laura,' Delilah replied sweetly. 'But how are you? Just between us girls, you're looking a little ... tired.'

Delilah's soft insult hit the target.

Laura's face fell like lead. 'Freaks!' With a swish of her chestnut locks, she strode away in the opposite direction.

'Nice comeback!' Kitty called after her.

Lis laughed and her new comrades laughed with her.

Later, Lis found herself at the back of a science lab with very little idea of what was going on. She excelled at English and foreign languages and, while her grades were always just-above-average in Science and Maths, it took an almost superhuman effort for Lis to stay on top of these subjects.

She was vaguely aware of what she had to do, but had

absolutely no idea why she was doing it. She was meant to be burning magnesium in a sealed container, but observed that everyone else seemed to be weighing their little pots. She cursed her daydreaming. As none of her new friends were in her set for Chemistry, she felt distinctly alone.

Plucking up the courage to ask Dr Maloney for assistance, she started to make her way around the workbench but was stopped dead by Danny Marriott. Her brain turned into melting toffee and she managed to formulate only a small coughing sound. He'd stepped into that important half a metre of personal space. It was accidental, but her heart pounded at the intimacy of his warm breath on her forehead.

'Sorry,' he said, stepping back.

Her brain desperately tried to reboot and think of anything sensible to say. 'That's all right. No worries.' She struggled to meet his turquoise eyes.

'You were about to do your experiment wrong.'

She smiled, blushing deeply at the same time. 'You were watching me?'

It was his turn to blush. Lis grinned further as he tripped over his words.

'Well, er, you were sitting right beside me. You looked miles away ...'

The simple fact that Danny had given her even a minute's thought warmed Lis a million times more than the array of Bunsen burners around her.

'You're right, I was daydreaming,' Lis admitted. Then she grinned. 'And I forgot you used to be a geek! Tell me, Danny, what am I meant to be doing?'

'Yeah, yeah ... keep it quiet. We're meant to be proving how a change of state won't affect the mass of the chemical components.'

Lis bit her lip and shook her head slightly. She squirmed,

not enjoying her ignorance in front of Danny.

'It's easy,' he continued. 'Weigh your little pot, then burn off the magnesium and your pot should still weigh the same.'

'Oh, I get it. Even though you can't see the magnesium, it's still there.'

'Exactly. The homework essay is all about car exhaust fumes. Our test shows how damaging the fumes are to air quality. If your pot doesn't the weigh the same, the test has gone wrong somewhere – probably the lid wasn't on tight enough.'

Lis smiled broadly as Danny's train of thought galloped away with him. She was reminded of her epiphany in Kitty's attic. She was pretty sure Danny couldn't talk like this around Cameron or Bobsy for fear of ridicule. Maybe that was where that little bit of sadness in his eyes came from.

'Are you laughing at me?'

'No, it's great! Cool, rugby team Danny Marriott is secretly Science Boy!'

He turned, looking around himself, now clearly paranoid. Lis knew the importance of concealing your cleverness only too well. Clever isn't cool.

'Don't worry. I won't tell anyone. I'm the girl who sold her imaginary baby on eBay, or whatever, remember?'

He stifled a laugh. 'Oh, yeah, I forgot about your secret past.'

'You didn't believe it, did you?'

'God, no! I thought that Laura had finally lost the plot. It was bound to happen sooner or later.'

Lis giggled quietly, aware that Dr Maloney was on patrol not far away.

Danny went on, 'But seriously, watch yourself around Laura. Her little mates are scared of her for a reason. I'm a bit scared of her myself to be honest . . . and hanging out with Kitty and Delilah won't help.'

Lis frowned. 'What's that supposed to mean?'

Danny's eyes widened. 'Don't get me wrong, I really like them. I went to primary school with them, but all those rumours . . . People say they worship Satan! Pretty dark stuff!'

Lis forced a smile to remain stretched across her face. Did Danny really believe that stuff? The cold possibility that Danny was no better than Cameron or Laura flitted through her mind.

'Are you serious?'

'Come on . . . They are pretty weird. If you hang around with them, people will take the piss.'

'I think that's the difference between you and me, Danny,' Lis stated calmly. 'I just don't *care* any more! I can't pretend to like someone as vile as Laura. You can hang around with those muppets if you like, but I'm out.'

Danny looked like a kicked puppy and she wondered if she'd gone too far, but at that moment, Dr Maloney drifted by. Lis grasped her beaker and headed off to find the weighing scales, leaving Danny hanging at the workbench, dumbstruck as she walked away.

School was a more comfortable purgatory now that Lis didn't dread break times any more, and the weekend came around with fantastic speed. Jack worked for a few hours each Saturday in Fulton at the dubious sounding Bagelicious and Delilah had explained that, to keep Jack from killing himself, they usually stopped by for a while to ease his boredom.

After they'd eaten, the girls trotted down the high street. It was a tragic scene. A number of the shops were boarded up entirely, while others stood in various states of ruin, with faded, chipped signs creaking in the wind. They had passed at least three bargain shops which proudly declared that all stock was 'Only £1!' (or in one case 'Only 99p'). Each of these stores had piles of tacky merchandise stacked up outside.

There seemed to be one large restaurant – an Italian called Luigi's – which represented every Italian racial stereotype known to man and looked like it hadn't been decorated since the eighties. There were also a disproportionate number of pubs for such a small town. So far, they'd passed The Cloven Hoof, The Slaughtered Lamb and The Green Man.

'That's why all the shops are so knackered,' explained Delilah, waving at all the pubs. 'Friday night is like Sodom and Gomorrah down here.'

'Sadly lacking the sodomy,' Kitty joked. 'Seriously, though, Friday night is Fight Night!'

Lis glanced around sadly. 'Aren't there any good shops?'

Kitty and Delilah said 'No' in unison and then doubled up laughing.

'Well, there's obviously Bagelicious. Classy place! Oh, and there is one quite nice coffee shop on the top floor of the book shop.' Kitty pointed across the street.

'Tomorrow we could go into Leeds,' Delilah suggested. 'My dad owes me some money.'

Kitty had some sort of family meal so she couldn't go, and Lis wasn't sure she could afford the long journey when she had so much homework to do. They talked about a trip for next weekend instead, and Lis was glad to feature in their future plans. It was reassuring.

There was one last stop on the tour. Kitty and Delilah had promised to save the best for last. They headed down a curving, cobbled side street that twisted away from the main shopping centre. Past a couple of olde-worlde looking shops, they reached their destination. This part of town felt more authentic. Here was a proper Yorkshire town with a baker, a blacksmith and some tiny second-hand bookshops. It was a shame more of Fulton wasn't like this. In fact, Lis realised, they had almost walked back into Hollow Pike.

'Oh, no. Look who it is,' Delilah whispered.

Across the street was Laura. God, she was the last person Lis wanted to see. Lis immediately tensed up, subconsciously hiding behind Kitty. Her foe was arguing with a handsome man who had closely-cropped silver hair and a Riviera tan, her father perhaps?

'Check out the domestic!' Kitty chuckled.

Although they were out of earshot, it was apparent that Laura and the gentleman were having a fiery disagreement. Laura looked hot and teary, even stamping her foot stubbornly at one point. She spat an insult into the man's face, but this was the last straw. With a heavy hand, he seized her arm and dragged her towards a midnight blue BMW parked in one of the side streets.

Even from where they were, Lis heard Laura scream a curse.

'Come on. Let's not get involved,' Delilah said and pulled Lis away by the hand, but in Lis's stomach there was now the familiar hybrid feeling of hatred and fascination she only associated with Laura Rigg. Heads down, they swiftly made their way along the cobbles.

'We're here!' Delilah presented a run-down looking shop with a grimy net curtain and a sign on the door reading 'Friends of the Church'. Lis guessed it was a charity shop, although what really caught her attention were the two terrifying mannequins in the window. One was bald and missing an arm, and you could still clearly see that its companion had empty eye sockets, despite the wig that covered most of its face. Both were wearing hideous floral dresses.

'You have got to be kidding!'

'No!' Kitty squealed. 'Wait and see ... It's amazing! I promise you'll find some buried treasures.'

The two girls took her by the arms and thrust her through the front door, a dainty bell signalling their arrival. The smell of musty old clothes and mothballs hit Lis in an invisible tsunami. She fought the urge to gag.

'You don't even notice the smell after a minute,' Delilah hissed, reading her mind.

The shop was in hazy darkness, only tiny shafts of light filtering through the filthy net curtains. Clothing hung off rails and junk was piled all around in recycled tea chests. Bric-a-brac was stuffed into any available space, while mounds of books filled every corner. Like the TARDIS, the shop was somehow bigger on the inside. Kitty was right, though – despite the smell, Lis found herself in an Aladdin's cave.

'Afternoon, ladies!'

All three jumped as a strange vision appeared behind the counter. The shopkeeper was hard to age; she was buried under a ton of bad make-up and a huge blonde wig. Lis's mouth hung open: this woman looked half human, half clown.

'Hello, Mrs Gillespie,' Delilah said politely. 'How are you?'

The figure waved a jewelled hand around the shop. 'You know how it is, darling. So much to do, not enough time to do it!'

The three girls nodded.

'You won't think I'm rude if I carry on folding scarves, will you?'

'Not at all.'

Mrs Gillespie slowly took a scarf from a teetering pile and

neatly folded it before selecting another. Lis doubted whether folding scarves would help rescue the shop from its current state of chaos.

Kitty took her hand and they slowly advanced to the back of the shop.

'You know her?' Lis whispered.

'Yeah, we shop in here a lot.'

'I know what you're thinking,' Delilah read her thoughts again, 'but if you look close enough there's some fabulous retro stuff here. All the desperate housewives were young and cool in the seventies and eighties and they're always having clear outs.'

'OK, I'll start digging!'

'Enjoy!' came Mrs Gillespie's shrill voice. Lis wondered if she'd heard every word they'd said.

Once again, her new friends had been spot on. In amongst some hideous fashion relics there were some cool pieces that suited Lis's new metropolitan style down to the ground. But the most fun part was the changing room: basically a corner behind a curtain. The three girls quickly organised a fashion show for each other. Taking it in turns, they would take armfuls of clothing behind the curtain. Some were genuine purchases, but mainly they chose the most grotesque, comedy-value items they could unearth. One second, Kitty would emerge from behind the veil in a giant peach bridesmaid dress, and the next Delilah would crawl out in a PVC catsuit. The eighties power-suits were something else! Lis laughed so hard her ribs ached.

'What do you think of this?' she asked, strutting around in a little red trench coat. It was the boldest blood-red she'd ever worn and, while it wasn't her normal style, she was feeling brave.

'So cute!' enthused Kitty. 'Very "rainy day in Manhattan"!'

'You *have* to buy that!' Delilah agreed.

'Excellent!' Lis smiled, basking in the sunshine of friendship.

As Delilah and Kitty searched for a winter coat for Kitty, Lis broke away and started to look at the books and gifts. Most of the stock consisted of ancient crockery or glass ornaments that looked a lot like they had been cleared out of dead pensioners' houses, a thought that made Lis uneasy.

She ran a finger across a stack of dusty books topped with three copies of the *Spice Girls 1997 Annual*. At the very bottom of the tower was a huge hardback entitled *An Occult History of Hollow Pike* by Reginald J. Dandehunt. Any relation to Ms Dandehunt? Lis wondered. She pulled the heavy tome out, careful not to let the whole pile tumble down. How many Dandehunts could there be in such a small town?

Sitting cross-legged on the floor, she set the ancient book down in front of her. Turning to the publisher's page, she could see that the book had been published in 1922. It was an heirloom! Lis grinned at the pencilled price of £1.75. She wondered what it would fetch on one of those BBC antiques shows.

She made a mental note to ask Ms Dandehunt if her granddad had been called Reginald, and then started leafing through the book. Lis adored old photographs – as a child, she had genuinely believed that the past had been black and white. She immediately recognised Hollow Pike village. From a distance it looked almost unchanged by time: the copse, the winding roads, the cobbled streets. What was noticeably different were the people: they stood in front of old houses and shops with blank, austere faces.

Apparently it was true, Hollow Pike did have a supernatural history. She flicked to a page entitled *Early*

Witchcraft – The Reformation and Beyond. No photos here, only curious paintings and etchings. They showed hags shoving chubby infants into a bubbling cauldron, laughing as they did so; boils and plagues; whole fields of dead cattle – all supposedly a result of witchcraft. One image showed nude women – witches – dancing around fires.

Flicking further in, the book grew darker still with drawings and etchings of pentagrams and goat-headed demons. Sinister words like 'blood rites' and 'sacrifice' jumped from the page, and there were haunting images of animal offerings and strange altars where crones stood entwined with gleeful demons. Lis remembered enough from RE to know how Christianity had demonised pagan practises, but the images disturbed her nonetheless. Her eyes lingered on a more recent photograph of four hooded figures, standing arms aloft, worshipping some unseen deity. But what brought the sting of tears to her eyes was the background: a tiny stream was clearly visible in the picture. It was the stream in Pike Copse. The stream in her nightmares.

'What you looking at?'

At Kitty's voice, Lis slammed the book shut. 'Nothing,' she said instinctively, ramming the book onto the nearest bookshelf.

'Cool, do you like this coat?' Kitty modelled a huge brown fake fur.

'Gorgeous!'

'I know! Are you finished? I'd best head home soon.'

Lis nodded, quickly forgetting the book and its sinister contents. 'I just need to pay for my jacket.' She picked up the red coat from where she'd left it and headed for the cash desk, where the eccentric Mrs Gillespie was still folding scarves.

'Hi. I'd like this, please,' Lis said.

The old woman continued clawing through the scarves, apparently unaware of her presence.

'Hello, Mrs Gill—'

'You're new,' Mrs Gillespie stated, reaching over and taking the jacket from her.

Lis smiled nervously, trying to remain as polite as possible. 'Yes, I just moved here from Wales.'

Through spidery lashes, Mrs Gillespie eyed Lis with suspicion. Her piercing green eyes burned into Lis's own and her ruby mouth grew tight. Without warning, the woman reached out a thin arm and grasped Lis's hand. Cold rings pressed into her flesh. 'I've heard about you, Lis London.'

Lis pulled her hand away sharply. 'How do you know my name?'

Mrs Gillespie's face shook with intensity. 'The birds are your friends, but beware the trees!'

'What?' Christ, the woman was mental.

'You don't know, do you?' Mrs Gillespie went on. 'Well, listen up, young lady ... *your dreams are a warning!*'

Tears suddenly stung Lis's eyes. The woman couldn't know about her nightmares – that wasn't possible. 'I don't know what you mean.'

Mrs Gillespie relaxed, smiling once more. 'Very well. That'll be three pounds fifty then, please.'

Lis quickly fumbled in her purse for the money as Kitty and Delilah arrived at her side.

'Are you OK?' asked Kitty.

'Yeah, fine. Let's go.' Seizing the jacket, Lis turned and ran out of the shop, stumbling onto the cobbled pavement outside. She sank down onto the cold, stone step as Delilah followed.

'Lis? What's up? Kitty's just paying for her coat.'

Lis looked into her friend's concerned face and told a lie.

'I'm OK. That smell was just making me feel sick. Sorry.'

'No worries,' Delilah replied sympathetically.

On the contrary, Lis's head was now full of nothing *but* worries.

Tired

The dream was back with a vengeance and it had evolved. It would start the same as always: Lis crawling, exhausted, through Pike Copse, struggling for breath. The trees, the birds, the distant screams were all there, as was the moment when her assailant drove her face into the freezing waters of the stream.

And then she would wake up, cocooned in her still, silent bed. She would roll over to try to return to sleep, only now Mrs Gillespie would be lying in bed next to her. Yellow teeth revealed in a snarl and red painted nails reaching for Lis's face . . .

'Liiiisss!'

And then Lis would wake up for real.

A week of broken sleep became full scale insomnia. Although her body was exhausted, fear prevented sleep, and, by the following Monday, Lis could feel the sleep deprivation beginning to affect her health. Weak and dizzy, she felt somehow separate from reality, like a hologram.

What had Mrs Gillespie meant by calling her dreams *a warning*? Lis wondered if the nightmare was a taste of things to come, but then told herself that that was impossible. She also reminded herself that Mrs Gillespie was a fruit-and-nut-case who couldn't possibly be talking about *her* dreams, because it was also impossible for her to have known about them.

God, she needed a good night's sleep.

And yet she drifted into school, hoping tedium would squeeze out the strangeness of her encounter at the shop. Lis was in luck; she received a cold, hard dose of reality as soon as she entered the gates. Laura hadn't lied – she was waiting, just as she'd promised. She and her hags were draped around the railings: gargoyles protecting their lair. Nasima spotted Lis and turned to whisper something in Laura's ear. A shadow of a smirk crept across Laura's perfectly glossed lips as she stared at Lis, and she drew a perfectly manicured nail across her elegant throat.

Adopting a classic victim stance, Lis put her head down and scurried past before the spider could lunge for the fly. She cursed her own weakness. If she wasn't her, she'd probably pick on her! Lis wished she'd caught the bus with the others instead of having Max drop her off; at least there was strength in numbers.

Somehow, registration and first period drifted by easily like a hazy summer cloud. She was *so tired*. She *had* to sleep tonight. She'd read all sorts of things about what happened if you didn't sleep for too many days: hallucinations, anxiety attacks, spontaneous fits of sleep, blackouts. Lis knew she couldn't be far off. She hadn't slept for more than thirty minutes in over forty-eight hours.

Second-period Spanish. At least she had the whole gang to keep her afloat in this lesson. They sat in the corner at the back of the classroom, farthest away from Mr Gray at the front and Laura near the windows. But Spanish oral practice was dull and the classroom was way too hot. *Maybe I could sleep here*, Lis thought. *Would Mr Gray even notice?* Across the room Laura had artfully arranged her blazer into a pillow and had her head down, pretending to repeat the lines to Harry.

'*Me duele la cabeza*,' Jack announced. Spanish with a Geordie accent sounded extra special.

'My head hurts,' repeated the translation on the CD.

'Your turn,' Jack prompted, but Lis remained slumped in her corner, her eyes aching.

'You do it,' she mumbled.

Kitty turned round from the row in front and pulled her headphones off. 'What's up?'

Lis leaned forward, every movement a triumph in her current state. 'I'm not sleeping too well.'

Delilah looked concerned and paused the CD. 'Why not? What's on your mind?'

'Nothing. I suppose I'm just a "troubled sleeper".'

'My dad knows some amazing homoeopathic sleeping remedies,' Delilah said. 'I'll get him to dig you something out.'

'Thanks, Delilah, but I'm sure I'll sleep tonight,' Lis told her.

'My mum swears by three Nytol and a glass of Chardonnay,' Jack put in, pausing their own CD.

Kitty spoke. 'Bad dreams?'

Lis froze. A knowing glint sparkled for the briefest moment in Kitty's blue eyes. Impossible! This was her paranoia again. Kitty had asked a perfectly reasonable question given the context. Regardless, Lis wasn't ready to share the full horror of her nightmares with her friends yet. Would any of them understand her horrific recurring dreams? She feared she was too freaky, even for them.

'Something like that,' Lis muttered, cutting the conversation short.

Kitty's gaze held suspicion for a second and she opened her mouth to speak.

'Kitty!' Mr Gray yelled. 'Turn around and get on with your practice, please.'

Kitty rolled her eyes and pulled the headphones back onto her head. Lis leaned back as Jack continued his butchery of the Spanish language.

'*Me duele la espalda.*'

'My back hurts,' the CD responded.

'*Me duele el brazo.*'

'My arm hurts.'

'*Me duele* . . .' His voice grew quieter.

Lis jumped. Something freezing cold washed over her feet. There must be a leak or a flood . . . or blood. Looking down, she saw deep, purple-black liquid rushing up around her ankles. Time slowed to a crawl and she turned to Jack, but he was gone. They were all gone. Lis was alone in a deserted classroom.

Angry winds somehow blew through the walls, and the posters and displays of G2 faded to be replaced by the familiar criss-cross lattice of branches against the night sky, the tree canopy locking her in its cage. Pike Copse. Once more Lis heard the branches whispering her name in their monotone: '*Lissss*', the final phoneme hissed like a serpent.

The classroom dissolved to nothing. Lis realised she'd fallen asleep in class. Oh, God. She was asleep in class! She looked around the forest, now standing knee-deep in a bubbling stream of oily blood. This was different though, new. She'd never ever been *standing* in the stream before. She had to wake up. Lis screwed her eyes tight shut. *Wake up, Lis. Wake up, right NOW!* she told herself. She opened her eyes but, instead of Jack, she saw something else that she'd never seen in the nightmare before: herself.

About six metres ahead she could see her own slender body locked in the futile crawl through the brook, her long brown hair matted to her soaking back.

'Lis!' she screamed. That was weird, calling to herself. 'Stop!'

She started to wade through the blood, or water, or mixture of both, towards her doppelgänger. It was exhausting, forcing her legs against the current. Instinctively she knew she had to reach herself, warn herself about the inevitable conclusion the nightmare always reached. Maybe this time she could break the cycle.

'Lis!' she called again, but her clone failed to respond. Lis quickened her pace, trying to jog through the stream, the sharp pebbles shifting underfoot. As she drew closer, she now saw that she was wearing her school uniform. She'd never noticed that in her previous visits.

Two metres away. 'Lis, for God's sake!'

She stumbled, toppling forwards into the icy water. Steadying herself, Lis saw that she was just a metre away from her other self.

Her hand now moved as though it were not hers. She watched as her fingers glided forwards of their own volition, reaching towards her own drenched hair. In the same instant she became aware of a solid object in her right hand. Her fingers were gripping a leather handle of some sort. Connected to the hilt was a deadly-looking blade, the edge waved and engraved with an intricate pattern of circles and some sort of writing. Lis couldn't read the inscription, though. It seemed to be in old English – beyond anything she could understand.

Her left hand made contact with her other self's thick, dark locks, her fingers weaving into the dripping strands. Lis pleaded with her hands to stop, but they had a sinister mind of their own. Her hand tightly gripped the hair, tugging the head back.

But she wasn't clutching her *own* head any more. It was Laura Rigg's.

Her eyes snapped open and she found herself looking into Jack's grinning face.

'Rise and shine, sleepy he—'

A scream and a crash from the other side of the room cut him off. Laura had *also* awoken with a start, throwing her entire body back, as if waking from the worst nightmare imaginable. Her chair toppled backwards and she tumbled into the table behind, dragging the CD player onto the floor with her.

The room was stunned into silence. Lis stood as Laura lay squashed in between chairs, table legs and CD player. No one spoke for about three seconds and then Bobsy tentatively tried a laugh.

'Nice one, Riggsy!'

Mr Gray darted forwards from the group he was working with. 'Robert, be quiet. Laura, are you OK?'

Harry pushed herself out of the way and reached down to help her friend up.

'Get off me!' Laura screeched.

Mr Gray pulled the table back as a dishevelled Laura clambered to her feet. 'Laura, let me have a look at y—'

'Don't touch me!' she snapped. 'I'm fine!'

'Laura, just let me make sure you're OK ...' Mr Gray began.

Without another word, Laura pelted out of the classroom. There was another second of silence, followed by some nasty, hushed giggles from the rest of the class, including Kitty and Jack.

'That's enough!' Mr Gray snapped. 'Get back to work.'

Lis couldn't move. She was still at her desk, her eyes fixed on the spot where the whole scene had played out. Laura had been in her dream. How? Why had the nightmare changed now? Mrs Gillespie's words echoed in her mind: *your dreams are a warning.*

'Child, that girl act like she on crack!' Jack sniggered.

Kitty could barely hide her hysterics behind her hand. 'What the bloody hell was that all about?'

Delilah also suppressed a grin. 'And the award for best actress in a dramatic meltdown goes to . . .'

Lis didn't think it was very funny. It wasn't very funny at all.

Laura, Laura, Laura. That girl had filled Lis's head from the moment she'd met her. It seemed that now she couldn't even avoid her in her dreams.

Another night of fractured sleep followed. Lis couldn't even close her eyes. She lay motionless, gazing out of the French windows at the stars shining brightly in the cloudless sky. It was as if Mrs Gillespie's bonkers message had caused real life and her nightmares to merge. There was no escaping Laura now. Lis recognised it all too well. It was Gwynedd Community College: the Sequel. This was only the beginning. Being scared – scared of Laura, scared of her bitches, scared of school. And Lis knew her lies would follow: lying to get out of school, fake illnesses, truancy. She wasn't sure what the third stage was. That was the point at which she'd run away to Hollow Pike.

But Lis couldn't let it happen again. Something had to change if she was to end the pattern, refuse to be the victim this time. Maybe she'd have to take charge. It made Lis feel sick with fear, but tomorrow she was going to have to face Laura. The nightmare in class must have meant something. The way Laura had freaked out, it was almost as if they'd had the same dream. No, that was ridiculous, another thing for Lis's impossible list. But after the histrionics in class, Laura did seem more human, more fallible. She'd made a total fool of herself. Whatever it was about, Lis couldn't be scared of her any more. Confronting her had to be worth a shot.

Perhaps *that* was the message from her subconscious – fight fire with fire. It was time to stand up to Laura Rigg.

Tuesday morning and there was only one place Laura would be at 8.45: the edge of the copse, having a final fag before the school day started.

Sure enough, Lis spotted her as she made her way across the rugby pitch. Laura was alone and smoking, almost hidden on the outskirts of the trees. She was sitting cross-legged in an armchair the lads had dragged out of the fly tip in the copse, writing in a pretty notebook covered in dainty apricot flowers.

As Lis grew nearer, she barely recognised the girl in the chair. *God, Laura looks tired!* Lis thought.

Despite a valiant effort with hair and make-up, dark circles surrounded Laura's eyes and her cheeks were hollow. It was strange seeing her without her band of cronies, too. She seemed frail. The freak-out in class must have really shaken her up. Lis approached with caution.

As soon as Laura spotted Lis she threw her journal down, a look of bitter distaste on her face. 'Look who it is, the Skanky Bike of Hollow Pike.'

'Give it a rest, Laura,' Lis said calmly. 'I only came to talk to you and to see how you are after what happened yesterday.'

'Relax, Lis. It was hardly an event. I had the PMT from hell, so what?'

'So ... I wanted to make sure you were OK. After that email thing I—'

Laura shook her head, a grim smile carved into her face. 'Oh, is that what this is about? Well done, Lis, revenge is yours; I made a tit of myself in front of the class. Now could you please piss off? Your face offends my eyes.'

Lis sighed. 'Look, I just wanted to say, I know how you feel and I hope we can at least co-exist at Fulton High. I'll stay out of your way if you stay out of mine. I don't want to fight any more.'

Laura sprang off her threadbare throne. 'Oh, get over yourself. You don't know anything about *how I feel*. You really think I give a tiny rat's ass about what happened yesterday? This is me we're talking about, not you. Every girl in the school wants to be me and every guy wants to *do* me. I think I'll survive. You, on the other hand, might not. I told you I'd make your life hell. Well, nothing's changed. You're still just the weird new girl, and I'm still queen of this place!'

Lis folded her arms, not budging an inch. She had to reclaim her place in this school. 'Then what's wrong? You look like a wreck.'

'Thanks. As if I'd tell you, loser.'

Anger bubbled inside Lis. *Take a deep breath and count to ten.* 'Laura, believe it or not, I'm actually trying to be nice and sort stuff out. I don't even know what I did to upset you. Is it about what happened with Danny at the party, because if it is—'

Laura interrupted, a hint of desperation creeping into her voice. 'I'm warning you, stay away from Danny.'

'Oh, come on! How am I meant to avoid him? That's insane!' Lis snapped.

'Screw you! You only turned up like a month ago – you don't know what it's like here and you don't know me! I bet you think my life is pretty sweet, right? Nice house, nice clothes, nice friends? Well, guess what? It's all crap! And sometimes I want to run away and never come back to this stinking town,' Laura paused for breath and Lis actually found herself starting to feel sorry for her. 'Danny and I were fine until you showed up,' Laura continued. 'We even talked about leaving Hollow Pike together.'

Lis's lips parted in surprise. 'Really? But I didn't think Danny fancied—' she broke off, realising that what she'd been about to say would have just sounded bitchy. But it was too late.

Laura laughed cruelly. 'What? And you think he fancies *you*? As if! He told me he thought you were a freak, just like Kitty and Delilah. If you think Danny Marriott would ever touch you, you're even more deluded than you look.'

'That's not true!' Lis gasped.

'You go anywhere near Danny and I'll mess you up. That's a promise.'

A thought occurred to Lis. 'If Danny isn't interested in me, then why do I have to stay away from him?' she asked coolly.

Laura finally boiled over. 'Because you're a slut!' she screamed.

Lis's sympathy burst like the most delicate of bubbles. 'You know what? I almost felt sorry for you, but now I think you deserve everything you get.'

Lis turned away.

Laura was stunned for a moment and then shrieked, 'You're a dead girl walking, Lis London!'

A cold, searing wind rolled across the rugby pitch and the branches of Pike Copse dipped and swayed, reaching down towards Laura like gnarled hands as Lis walked away across the field.

Revenge

Frustration churned away in Lis's stomach well into first-period English. Twisting her pencil around and around, she let Mrs Osborne's monotone ramblings about Abigail in *The Crucible* drift straight over her head. She saw Delilah taking detailed notes and banked on her friend sharing them with her.

How had her meeting with Laura gone so wrong? They were supposed to be peace talks. Lis wasn't sure if her desire to make peace was born out of pure human kindness or if it was just the ultimate way to beat Laura in their turf war; to show Laura that despite everything, she was the bigger person. Either way, she'd failed on an epic scale.

Halfway down the rugby pitch she'd sworn a private oath never to talk to Laura Rigg ever again. She was so cruel, she dragged everything and everyone around her down. Lis had never felt like this before. Hate is a strong word, but she was pretty sure this was it. Lis *hated* Laura Rigg.

There was only one person in the world she wanted to share this new bitterness with: Kitty, the only person she could think of who probably loathed Laura as much as she did.

'So what do you think?' asked Kitty. 'Jack: straight or gay?

Discuss. He's playing it very close to his chest and we don't wanna ask ...'

For the second time in two weeks Lis abandoned a lesson – this time last-session PE – at Kitty's suggestion. Kitty assured her she hadn't participated in PE since Year Nine and no one seemed to miss her. They drifted through the copse, walking the long way to Kitty's house. Jack and Delilah were trapped in Science all afternoon, and it was nice to have Kitty to herself for a bit. With honey sunshine streaming through the branches and the birds twittering merrily, the copse was no longer the stuff of nightmares.

'I'm not sure,' Lis replied, glad of a diversion from her worries about Laura, 'either gay or in love with Delilah!'

This time Kitty laughed. 'Yeah, you're probably right! I wish he'd hurry up and come out though. What's he waiting for – a written invitation?'

Lis shrugged. 'The right time I suppose. It can't be easy. It's not like Hollow Pike has a thriving gay scene!'

'Yeah and his mum's a bit of a psycho.'

Lis bit her lip to stop herself from passing comment on Kitty's own stern father.

'What's the story with you and Delilah?' she asked instead. 'I haven't been brave enough to ask.'

Smiling wistfully, Kitty reached the fly tip in the centre of a sheer rock basin and flopped onto a busted sofa. Water from the brook trickled over the edge of the cliff, creating a fairy tale waterfall. 'There's not much to tell to be honest. We've been friends since we were about ten. Year Six was when it all changed. Delilah moved back to Hollow Pike from down south and it was so weird – straight away I knew I wanted to be her best friend. It was instant, like, *boom*! I don't really know what it was that made us any different to anyone else, but people started treating us like a circus sideshow.'

'Maybe it's a puberty thing.' Lis joined her on the damp couch.

'Maybe. Who knows? Whatever it was, we just sort of clung to each other for dear life. At first emotionally, because it was so awful, and then the physical stuff sort of followed all by itself. It seemed like the logical thing to do when you really like someone.'

'Well, I think you make a lovely couple.'

'Thanks. I'm not sure I'd call us a couple, though. We've never had to clarify what we are. We both fancy boys as well as girls, and she can be a bloody nightmare. She flirts constantly, she's never ever on time, she's clingy – but she's the only person who really gets me.'

Lis shot her a sly smile. 'Sounds like L O V E to me!'

Kitty laughed again. 'Quiet, you! Time will tell. I wouldn't know what to do without her, that's for sure. I'd be lost. We both would.'

Lis drew a deep breath, tasting the sweet, rich, earthy aromas of the forest. Kitty had widened the boundaries of conversation and now it was her turn. 'Kitty . . .'

'Yes?'

Lis wondered where to even begin. 'I think I'm sort of going through something at the moment . . .' The words tried to cling to the back of her throat.

'Something? You think you might be gay, too?' Kitty asked with a grin. 'Is everyone in Hollow Pike gay or what?'

'No, not that!'

'What then?'

'How do you know if you're going mad?' Lis sighed.

Kitty raised a quizzical eyebrow. 'What?'

'I mean it. Like mental illness.'

Kitty frowned. 'What makes you think you're mentally ill?'

she asked. 'I think you're very brave for mentioning it, but you don't seem crazy to me.'

'A few things.' Lis couldn't meet Kitty's gaze. 'I'm having these messed-up nightmares. I haven't slept for nights.'

Kitty's face wrinkled. 'What are the nightmares about?'

'You're gonna think I'm mental – but they're about Laura. She's totally screwing with my head. I can't stop thinking about her. I went to try to sort things out with her today but I just feel worse.'

'Well,' Kitty said with authority, 'I suppose you have two options. You can approach it either like my mum or like my dad.'

'OK. Go on.'

'My mum's amazing strategy is to stick her head in the sand and act like nothing's wrong with the world. She retreats inside her head and hopes the problem will just go away.'

'Does it work?'

'Have you met my mum? She's a nervous wreck.'

'Well, what about your dad?'

'Hit it with a stick.'

'I beg your pardon?' laughed Lis.

'I'm serious! My dad was the head of the riot squad for years! His philosophy is that you either stand there waiting to have a bottle thrown at you, or you strike first and hit them with a stick.'

'Does that work better?'

Kitty nodded. 'Yeah. You might upset people in the process, but at least you're facing your problems. Actively doing something. My mum hides, but her issues *don't* go away by themselves, and you can't let Laura Rigg rule your life.'

'But I *did* stand up to her, Kitty, and look how far that got me.' Lis sighed. She'd run away from Wales and now she was retreating into the arms of her sister or friends when things went wrong. 'What do you think I should do now?'

'I've said it before, I'll say it again. Kill her.'

'Kitty,' Lis pulled at a leaf on an overhanging branch, 'that's not helpful.'

'But just think,' Kitty said with a grin, 'you'd be rid of her once and for all.'

'Drop it.'

Kitty laughed and made a thoughtful humming noise.

'What?' Lis demanded.

'OK, how about this? We can't kill Laura, but what if we give her a taste of her own medicine? Come up with something to get her off your back for good?' Kitty flashed Lis a devilish smile.

That sounded promising. A life in Hollow Pike *without* Laura and *with* her new friends and Danny. That would be paradise. 'I could be up for that ... what did you have in mind?'

Kitty beamed at her. 'Babe, you will not regret this ...'

Later that same evening, Lis stood outside the local Budgens in Hollow Pike, her hands shoved deep into her pockets. She tried to distance herself from a cluster of Year Nine girls who were trying to lure passers-by into buying cigarettes for them. Classy.

Twilight had fallen early, and even though the streets were still busy, everyone was in a rush to get home before darkness came. Lis hopped from foot to foot trying to keep warm. Right on time, Laura Rigg stepped off the bus and crossed the street to join her. She was still in her school uniform, save for the Ugg boots she'd put on her feet.

'Didn't you get the message this morning?' Laura snarled when she was close enough.

'Hi, yeah, sorry. I wanted to try to sort things out.' Lis tried to smile sweetly at Laura, although it didn't come naturally.

Laura pouted for a second. 'Go on, then. Your text said you wanted to talk about Danny. Have you said something to him? He wouldn't return my texts today.'

Lis noticed that Laura seemed twitchy about this fact. 'No, I haven't seen Danny all day. Do you wanna come back to mine? It's freezing out here.'

Laura shrugged. 'Whatever. Where do you live?'

'Just through the copse.'

Laura nodded. 'What did you wanna talk about anyway? I've gotta be home by nine thirty; my mum's being a total bitch at the moment.'

Lis led them down the urine-scented alleyway at the side of the corner shop that led to the car park. At the back of the car park was the gate into the recreation ground. There were some Fulton pupils climbing all over the swings, laughing and joking as they knocked back cheap lager.

'I'm glad you came. I wanted to put the fight behind us,' Lis said as they gave the play area a wide berth and headed towards the dark trees of Pike Copse. 'I never meant to fall out with you and nothing happened with Danny, I promise.'

Laura eyed her with distaste. 'I know. Danny wouldn't piss on you if you were on fire.'

That stung, but Lis kept her cool. Laura's reign of terror could be over forever if she could just keep up the act for another few minutes. 'Laura, I'm trying to make things better. I liked being friends with you. You're clearly smarter than Nasima and that lot. I thought you'd at least listen.'

Laura seemed to soften at the compliment. This was easy, much easier than Lis had ever thought it would be.

'Whatever. Look, I only came to talk about Danny. You need to get it into your dense head that it's not gonna happen with you and him.'

The wild hoots and jeers of the lads in the play area were distant whispers now, the chattering of the wind through the trees much louder. The black copse loomed before them. By day, the trees were just trees, but now, at dusk, they were a single, swaying entity.

'That's what I'm trying to say,' Lis said, suppressing the anger inside. 'Friends are more important than guys. I'll stay away from Danny if you stop giving me grief.'

Laura thought about it for a moment. 'Yeah, but if I see you with Danny again, I'll cut you, I swear. Oh, and you can't hang about with that dyke Monroe – you know, she properly tried to tongue me once. Seriously. She's *obsessed* with me.'

Lis fought the urge to punch her there and then. Kitty was twice the friend Laura was. 'OK, I promise, scout's honour!'

'Yeah, I bet you *were* a girl scout too!' Laura grinned.

They reached the stile into the copse, Lis stepping over first. Laura hung back on the other side, seemingly reluctant to set foot in the wood.

'What's up?' Lis asked.

'Nothing. I just hate the copse when it's getting dark,' Laura replied.

'Scared?' Lis knew full well that Laura was scared. She'd remembered their first conversation in G2 – Laura's mother and the bedtime stories that had terrified her as a little girl.

'Uh, yeah. You've heard the rumours, right?' Lis could tell that Laura wasn't kidding. Her mouth had formed a grim line.

'What? Witchcraft and stuff?' Lis asked lightly. 'That's all crap, though! And, anyway, it was hundreds of years ago – like in the Dark Ages!'

Laura climbed over the stile. 'You're not from Hollow Pike, though. You don't know the stories. I grew up on them. Everyone here did.'

'Laura, my sister's house is like five minutes away. I think we'll be fine!'

'Whatev.' The beautiful girl looked around apprehensively, surveying the winding forest path. 'You lead the way then.'

Lis set off down the trail. Somewhere overhead a crow cawed loudly from high in the trees. Black, winged shapes darted through the forest canopy and, in the gloom, they could easily be mistaken for bats. Lis sensed Laura's nerves but refused to feel any sympathy. It served her right; she had it coming. 'So what stories should I be scared of?' Lis asked her.

'When I was little, my dad used to tell me stories about children who went into the copse and never came out. They just vanished,' Laura said. Twigs crunched underfoot as the trees closed up around them, blocking out the dying light.

'You don't believe that, do you?'

'No . . . Maybe . . . I don't know. Everyone knows the stories. You just keep out of the woods after dark.'

Lis laughed. 'Big, Bad Laura Rigg, scared of the—' She stopped and turned, hearing a noise behind her. From out of the shadows, a dark figure had emerged onto the path. A pair of strong arms seized Lis and she screamed. Laura shrieked as another figure appeared from behind a tree. Both attackers wore long, rough brown robes, hooded like a monk's gown. A third hooded figure charged down the path towards them.

'Laura!' Lis yelled, her scream ripping through the forest. 'Run!'

Run

Laura backed across the forest floor, evading the hooded figure who stalked towards her.

'Laura,' Lis screeched again as the figure that held her produced a mean-looking dagger from his sleeve, 'run!' As Lis said it, her captor plunged the dagger into her stomach and she doubled over, gasping for air. She flopped to her knees, clutching her wound as the hooded man jerked the knife out of her torso.

Laura sobbed, her hands at her mouth. Then, as Lis toppled over into the dirt, she turned and fled, heading away from the hooded trio on unsteady feet. Lis and the dagger-man blocked the way they'd come – so Laura ran deeper into the copse.

The three robed figures stood over Lis's body, watching Laura vanish into the indigo darkness. Within seconds, they could no longer hear her footsteps stomping through the leaves.

'That was genius!' said Jack, pulling off his hood.

'Did you get it all?' Lis asked, sitting up.

'Yep!' Delilah pulled back her hood and switched the digital camera off. 'Laura Rigg, starring in *Soil Your Pants!*'

Kitty poked at the retractable blade Jack was holding, a bargain from the joke shop on the high street. 'That was priceless! Lis, you were amazing, I will never forget the look on her face. Did you see it?'

'Not really, I was too busy pretending to be dead. Can I see?' She took her camera from Delilah and played it back. The action started, showing a jerky, grainy Lis and Laura strolling down the path, talking about how spooky the woods were. Then the battery sign flashed up and the screen faded to black. 'Crap,' Lis sighed. 'I'll have to charge it when I get home. At least it lasted for the filming.'

'I can't believe it worked!' Jack laughed. 'Now all we have to do is threaten to put this on YouTube if Laura doesn't leave us all in peace. She'll be putty in our hands. You won't ever have to worry about her again, Lis – none of us will! Man, I love blackmail!'

Kitty looked ahead anxiously. 'We should get out of here. If Laura calls the police, we are in deep, deep trouble.'

Nodding eagerly, Jack started to back out of the copse. 'We should split up, just in case.'

'Yeah, and lose the robes!' Lis urged, clambering over the stile.

'Give them here. I need to put them back in the drama studio before Mrs Osborne notices they're gone.' Delilah stuffed the robes into her rucksack.

'Ring when you get home, yeah?' Lis said. 'I'll email you the video.'

'Epic!' Kitty gave her a kiss on the cheek. 'Call as soon as you're home.'

Kitty and Delilah set off in one direction, towards the play area, while Lis and Jack went in the other, towards the main road. It was fully dark now, and Lis was so high on adrenalin that she didn't see the raven watching her from the crumbling wall of the copse.

Less than a mile away, the tallest trees of Pike Copse stood, enveloped in the thickest night silence – until a scream rang out through the serene woods, echoing across the valley. The scream, not playful or coy, spoke only of terror. A girl was in great danger. Trees shook and the woods sprang to life. Birds took flight, fleeing the scene. The copse was suddenly wide awake.

Heavy footsteps pounded the damp earth. More screams, pleading now: '*Stop! Leave me alone!*' The brittle crack of sticks and twigs. The crunch of autumn leaves. Desperate fingers snatched at branches and reeds. More feet pounded across the soil – a chase! It had been a long time since the copse had last seen a hunt, a return to the days of blood.

A girl fled, running with such intensity her legs burned inside. This wasn't the kind of run used at races on sports day, this was the dash of prey. A race for survival, a predator close behind. Her breath came in short raspy bursts as her lungs heaved painfully. There was no air left in her body to scream for help and there were no saviours in sight. She spun unsteadily, searching for the hunter. She couldn't go on, so she crouched behind a tree, cocooned in a network of roots. She clutched her chest, barely able to breathe yet too scared to make any sound. Her filthy feet were bleeding from where she'd lost her shoes in the chase. Her tights were torn and her hands raw. She strained to listen. Should she run again? Or should she stay hidden?

Fear drove her. She ran. But after only three paces, she tripped and fell, tumbling down a steep incline. Skeleton tree hands tore at her face and body. Barely recognisable as human, the girl looked feral in her fear. She rolled to a halt, groaning. A freezing sensation crept up around her legs. She was in water.

Everything hurt: limbs, skin, nails, hair. With an exhausted moan she started to haul her body out of the stream, using weeds, but she found herself sliding back down in the slippery mud. She sobbed uncontrollably, pleading, wailing at the flock of birds that flew up, occluding the moon.

'Help me!' she screamed pitifully. 'Someone ... please ...' *Please God, help me ... I'll be better. I'll try harder. I'll be nice.*

She clambered onto her knees, not hearing the footsteps behind her. Too late, something flashed in her peripheral vision. Hands reached out, yanking her up by her hair. Rough fingers grasped her with vice-like strength, and then another flash: moonlight gleamed off a curved silver blade. As she was lifted clean off the ground, feet kicking uselessly in the air, she screamed: a primal scream from deep within her gut.

It was the last noise Laura Rigg ever made.

Part Two

And if they seek to know some secret . . .
they learn it in dreams from the devil,
by reason of an open, not a tacit,
pact entered into with him.

THE MALLEUS MALEFICARUM, 1486

The Next Day

At 8.12 a.m. Lis saw the first police car. It hurtled past her, siren wailing as she made her way to the school bus. Her red trench coat was the only splash of colour on an otherwise monochrome morning.

She'd risen and dressed for school with a spring in her step. Would Laura even dare to show her face at school today? She must have realised by now that she'd been punked. Smiling to herself, Lis made her way to the bus stop. Laura deserved everything she'd got. Lis knew Laura had savoured *her* fear at school, well, last night they'd turned the tables. It had been Laura's turn to be scared.

For once, Lis was on time for the bus. Today she boarded the vehicle with greater confidence than ever before, ready to take on the world. She saw Harry and Fiona whisper as she went past, but didn't even think of entering into an argument. She wondered what Laura had told them. When she'd spoken to Kitty last night, her friend had reported that no one had called the police.

She joined Jack on the back seat. Ste and Cameron made some sort of comment as she walked by.

'God,' Jack said, 'will they ever get bored?'

Lis smiled, not willing to let them bother her. 'Probably not. They're not going to change. But you know what? I don't care any more; they can't hurt me if I don't let them.'

He laughed. 'Right on, sista!'

'Jack, today is day one! A new beginning!'

'Amen to that!'

At 10.15, midway through English, Lis asked to use the bathroom, although in truth she merely wanted to check her texts to see if there was anything from Kitty or Jack – or even from Laura herself.

Excusing herself from class, she observed the rows upon rows of pupils as she drifted through the corridors. All these people – and, after last night, she felt she had found her place among them. She was no longer an outsider, but an insider; she belonged with Kitty, Delilah and Jack. She giggled again at the memory of Laura's face. Where was she? She couldn't wait for the punchline – when Laura saw her alive and well. Her phone found the network, but there were no new texts waiting to be read.

Leaving the girls' bathroom, Lis drifted back towards her lesson, but was stunned to see a police officer heading into Ms Dandehunt's office. The fluorescent yellow jacket was unmissable. She took a detour; the long way back to B8 would take her past the head's room. Slowing to get a good look, she saw two officers, Ms Dandehunt, the deputy head and the school receptionist gathered around the gigantic desk in the centre of the room. Lis couldn't hear what was being said, but through the thick glass she could see that Ms Dandehunt had turned a sickly shade of grey. As the head pushed her chair away from her desk, she knocked a potted plant onto the floor.

Anxious not to be caught, Lis hurried back to English and slid into her seat. Leaning close to Delilah, she whispered as quietly as she could, 'There's something going on. There are two policemen in Ms Dandehunt's office. You don't think it's because of what we did, do you?'

'No, it's probably nothing.' Delilah shrugged. 'The school has a police liaison to deal with the naughty boys!'

'No, it looks more serious than that. I saw Ms Dandehunt's face; she looked pretty sick.'

'Hmmm. Oh, well, the way gossip travels around here, I'm sure we'll all know about it by the end of break.'

Lis smiled, oblivious to the majestic black bird perched just beyond the classroom window. She was being watched.

At 10.38, just before the break-time bell rang, Nasima Bharat was called out of English by the school receptionist. Looking confused and slightly concerned, she exited the room and was led away down the corridor.

'Nasima!' yelled Ste Mangano. 'Been a bad girl, eh?'

'Thank you, Stephen, that is quite enough!' barked Mrs Osborne.

This time Delilah turned to Lis. 'Curiouser and curiouser!'

At 10.47, Lis paused at a water fountain. After a moment, she realised she was standing in a steady stream of teachers and staff members flowing into the staff room. While it wasn't especially surprising that teachers would use the staff room, it *was* unusual to see all of them going in at once. Something was seriously wrong, she could feel it. Even the teachers didn't seem to know what was going on. Lis guessed it must be

connected to Nasima's disappearance from English. The girl hadn't returned to class.

Rachel Williams, a cool, quirky girl from Lis's Art lessons, paused alongside the water fountain.

Lis greeted her quietly. 'What do you think's going on?' she asked.

'Well!' Rachel announced, clearly relishing the gossip. 'Danielle Chung told me that Nasima Bharat's dad has cancer or something. We think that maybe he's died.'

Lis frowned. 'Oh, that's sad. I wonder if that's what it is.'

As she said it, she saw the same police officers from Ms Dandehunt's office now following Mr Gray into the staff lounge. *Would the police really need to be here if Nasima's dad had died?* she wondered. It was tragic, yes, but surely no reason for a police presence.

'I don't think that can be it,' she half muttered to Rachel, but she was already drifting down the corridor.

10.53 and frustration was starting to simmer in Lis's belly. She couldn't find Jack, Kitty or Delilah anywhere. She'd been to their usual spot under the shelter and not only were they absent, but no one had seen them all break. Sometimes Jack went to the snack shop in the canteen. It was worth a look.

By now the whole school buzzed as gossip spread like wildfire. Everyone had seen the police or knew someone who had, and everyone was speculating. You didn't even need to eavesdrop, the rumours were everywhere: *Jason Briggs has been caught with . . . Apparently she's told police that he mugged her, seriously!* Lis did her best to block it out.

A fork of lightning split the sky, drawing 'oohs' from awestruck pupils. Strange to see lightning without rain. A storm must be on its way. Looking to the heavens, Lis failed to see an oncoming Danny. Their shoulders clashed, almost knocking Lis over. He grabbed her and she stumbled into his strong arms.

'Ow!' The noise was a reflex more than an indication of pain. Lis steadied herself.

'Sorry!' they said together.

Danny's face was milk white, a deathly, unnatural shade. He moved her out of the way to continue at his hectic pace, but Lis caught his hand.

'Hey, are you OK?'

'No, I'm not.' He looked at the floor, avoiding her gaze. 'I have to go.'

Lis kept hold of his hand. 'Danny, what is it? You look awful.'

He looked up and, on seeing the pain in his usually tranquil eyes, Lis dropped his hand. He opened his mouth but no sound came out.

'What is it?' she repeated.

He frowned and a single tear pooled at the side of his nose. He caught it with the back of his hand before it could tumble down his cheek. 'Cam's mum called him,' Danny said, carefully controlling his voice which threatened to tremble. 'Laura was murdered last night.'

'What?' Lis gasped. She felt as though a sonic boom had hit her. No. Just, *no*. She was hearing things. Oh, hang on a minute, was this Laura's way of getting them back? 'Are you sure?' she asked Danny.

'They found her body in the copse this morning.'

'No, this is a joke, right?' she whispered, although Danny's face was all the proof she needed. Laura was dead. The entire playground felt like a wildly spinning carousel. This couldn't be real. She'd wake up in a second. But she didn't. Why wasn't she waking up? Lis reached out, leaning on the nearest wall to hold herself up.

The first drop of rain fell, hitting the concrete with a thick splat. Like a drop of blood.

'Look, I have to go find Harry and Fi. They don't know yet.' Danny turned and ran.

Lis struggled for breath. Kitty. Jack. Delilah. They couldn't have . . . *What had they done?* It was meant to be a joke! She had to find them.

A fierce wind picked up and the rain fell urgently now, joining the dots on the slabs. More lightning pierced the sky, which seemed to hang impossibly low, dense cloud closing in around the school. Lis burst into a sprint, heading straight for the canteen, barging past a group of Year Eights who cursed her loudly, but she was moving too fast to hear what they said. She became the storm, levelling anything that stood in her way.

Then the texts started to arrive. All around her, text alerts sounded before faces fell in shock and horror and disbelief. The fire was catching, spreading, burning out of control.

Almost falling up the stairs, Lis tumbled into the dining room, scanning the sea of students shovelling sandwiches and crisps into their faces. There was no sign of her clan. Her wet hair was plastered across her face. A couple of Year Nine girls giggled at her dishevelled state, but Lis had no time to dwell on it. She headed back out of the door. Where else could they be?

Lis prayed she was wrong. It had been a wind-up, nothing but a silly game. But now Laura was dead for real.

She stood for a second, letting the rain hit her face. It washed over her and she felt her shirt sticking to her hot skin. She took deep breaths, staving off the very real possibility that she might vomit in a public place. Opening her eyes, she saw the briefest glimpse of Kitty entering the old G Block by the boys' toilets.

'Kitty!' she yelled, ignoring sideways glances from the students all around her. 'Kitty!'

Her screams were lost in the hungry thunder and she started to run as fast as she could across the concrete. Pushing through a group of Year Seven pupils struggling to come in from the rain, Lis just spotted Kitty charging up the stairs to the top corridor.

'Kitty!' she yelled, desperate not to lose her, but judging from the dark, determined look on Kitty's face, her friend was also on a mission. Had she heard the news too? Or had she been the first to know? Either way, Kitty failed to stop.

'Move!' Lis demanded of the little girls in her way. She squeezed past them and reached the stairs. Kitty was nowhere to be seen.

Feedback shrieked through the halls as the ancient PA system hissed into life. Lis's hands flew to cover her ears.

'Attention, all pupils. This is Mr Raynor.' It was the deputy head, 'There will be a whole school assembly in the new gymnasium in ten minutes. On the first bell, Years Seven, Eight and Nine will make their way to the gym. On the second bell, Years Ten, Eleven and Sixth Form will follow.'

He started to repeat the simple instructions, but Lis was already on her way to the gym. Her friends had to be there.

11.17 a.m. Unfortunately, nobody seemed to have followed the bell system. The gymnasium was chaos. Teachers desperately attempted to shepherd their classes into some sort of order, with younger pupils at the front and the Sixth Form at the very back of the hall.

This was the first time Lis had been in the gymnasium. It was brand new and still had that pristine polish smell, although, as it filled with soaked students, the scent of rain and sweat was taking over.

Amidst the madness, Lis could clearly see Jack and Delilah already sitting cross-legged on the floor at the other side of the hall. She waved frantically at them, but through the hordes of milling pupils, they failed to see her. Scanning the hall, Lis couldn't see Kitty anywhere. The six-foot, mixed race girl with a purple Mohican stood out at the best of times. She plainly wasn't in the hall.

'Lis,' called Mr Gray, who looked more stressed than she'd ever seen him, 'can you sit down next to Millie, please?'

She opened her mouth to protest, she *had* to get to Delilah and Jack.

'Lis. Just sit down. Now!'

It was no use. Fighting the urge to scream in frustration, Lis flopped down next to Millie Carpenter.

Laura Rigg was *dead*. She had thought of that girl almost every hour since she'd met her in G2 on her first day. Now she would never see her again. Laura Rigg. Lis screwed her eyes shut and pressed her hands to her face. The darkness behind her eyelids flickered, interspersed with the gruesome images she herself had conjured during the murderous meeting in Kitty's attic. Kitty, rock in hand, standing over Laura's body, laughing manically. Jack holding her head under the black waters of the creek. Delilah giggling as Laura choked on a poisoned alcopop.

'That's enough!' boomed Ms Dandehunt, who was standing on a gymnastics table at the front of the hall, directly below a basketball hoop. The police officers stood just to one side of her, along with Mr Raynor. She raised a microphone to her lips. 'Quiet. You know I don't enjoy shouting, Fulton High.'

The hall quickly fell silent. By now, everyone was desperate to hear the news.

'I am afraid I have gathered you here to deliver some devastating news. A teacher should never have to say this; I don't even know where to start. It is with great sorrow that I must tell you that last night a Year Eleven pupil died in the most tragic circumstances.'

A gasp ran around the auditorium. Some turned to friends, a question on their lips. The texts hadn't reached everyone, then.

'To prevent gossip and further distress, I will tell you now that that pupil was Laura Rigg.'

The hall roared to life. Lis sat still and silent as everyone around her exploded with every kind of shock and emotion. Lis put her hands over her ears. Between the noise in her head and the noise in the room, she couldn't bear it.

'Quiet, everybody, please! This is a very serious matter.' Ms Dandehunt's face was iron, entirely different to the cuddly creature Lis had experienced in assemblies so far. 'I will not have speculation or rumour spreading. I understand many of you are distressed at the loss of your fellow pupil. Laura was a dear friend to many of you.'

Lis looked over to Delilah and Jack. They were statues, eyes fixed on Ms Dandehunt, neither moving nor speaking.

'We have never had such a tragedy at Fulton High School before. I'm afraid I have no reassuring speech, no soothing words. All of us will need support at this dark time.' Her voice softened. 'We have experienced a great loss today. Some of us may have lost people before, others maybe not. But now, more than ever, we need each other, for strength, comfort and love. This is a very, very sad day. Spare a thought for

Laura's friends and think about her family. Out of respect for them, this will be a day of quiet reflection and school will be closed.'

No one in the audience, not even the most obnoxious Year Nine boys made a sound at this news. Even the wildest teenagers knew where to draw the line.

'Spend the day with your families and friends. Reflect on how lucky you are. Or think about Laura and how special she was. Fulton High School won't be the same without her.'

School would be a better place without her. That was what Lis had said in Kitty's attic, and now her words haunted her.

'But before you go back to your form rooms, some very important people from the North Yorkshire Police need a few minutes of your time.'

Ms Dandehunt passed the microphone to the female officer who climbed onto the gym table next to her.

'Hello, Fulton High School, my name is PC Jacqui Briggs. I'm your school liaison officer. Most of you have met me before at some point in lessons.'

Lis again looked over at Delilah and Jack, who were this time subtly trying to get her attention.

Jack seemed to mouth 'O.M.G.'

Delilah parted her hands and mouthed, 'Where's Kitty?'

Lis shrugged.

'I am so very sorry, guys,' PC Briggs continued. 'This must be a huge shock. It's the worst possible thing when someone dies, but it is especially dreadful when it's someone so young. I know a lot of you knew Laura and will want to talk to your parents and friends, but there are a couple of messages from us before you can go.'

Lis noted that Delilah now seemed to be highly agitated and Jack was trying to calm her. She longed to be with them and know what they were saying. Did they look guilty? She couldn't be sure.

'We need you to be extra sensitive and careful right now, guys. There will be a police investigation, and we will need your help with that. We'll be talking to some of you in the next few days as we gather information. I'm sure you'll do everything you can to be as cooperative as possible. You can also help us by staying well away from Pike Copse. Thank you, Fulton, that's everything for now.'

The room once again erupted into chaos as pupils clambered over each other to reach their friends. Teachers tried their best to establish calm, but with little effect. Lis witnessed some Year Eleven girls collapse into each other's arms. A number of classmates looked around dazedly, unsure of what to say or do. Lis just stood there, numb to it all. Suddenly it felt as if there were too many colours in the room.

She saw Delilah rush from the gymnasium, closely followed by Jack. Her head told her to chase after them, but her feet would not move. And that's when she realised that tears were flowing freely down her face.

Q & A

Lis went home and slept for the rest of the day. Darkness came. She heard her sister and Max talking quietly outside her room, but she remained in hibernation under her duvet. Later still, Sarah tapped on the door and entered bearing a cup of tea and a cheese toastie, but Lis still hid under the duvet. Under the duvet Laura's murder wasn't real.

She slept all night and when the vanilla light of dawn flowed through her curtains, she rolled to the wall and kept her eyes shut.

She dozed, dreaming that Laura was alive and well and her death had been only a nightmare. Sweet relief. Each time she woke, Lis experienced the gut-wrenching prospect that one of her closest friends might be a cold-blooded murderer. It was agony.

Her mind ran over and over the conversation she and Laura had had at the edge of the copse. She remembered Laura's haunted eyes, so full of secrets. What had she known? What was she caught up in? Whatever it was had led to her death. Worse still, did Lis's own friends have the answers? So many questions; it felt as if they were tearing her brain to shreds.

Lis herself had wished Laura dead. *Be careful what you wish for.*

It was nearly noon when Lis woke up hungry. Heavy rain battered the patio doors and the growl of thunder echoed sporadically.

Was there any possible way she could opt out of today? Lis groaned and kicked back the duvet. No, today she had to find her friends. Difficult questions badly needed asking.

Slipping on a plush white dressing gown, she crossed the hallway. At the top of the stairs she heard voices floating up from the kitchen. Sarah was chatting to Logan and he babbled back to her. It was so normal, so real, so comforting.

Shocked to see Lis enter the kitchen, Sarah looked up from the newspaper she was reading. 'Hello, stranger!' She smiled warmly. 'How are you?'

Logan was playing happily on the floor with a set of plastic cups. His little hands and tufts of soft, fair hair somehow cracked Lis's shell. Crossing the kitchen, she swept her nephew into her arms and held him close.

'Lis?' Sarah said gently.

'I'm fine. Really. I just needed to sleep.'

'I'm the same when I'm down. Everything always seems better in the morning, though.'

Lis felt tears pricking her eyes and she kissed Logan's head, breathing in the scent of talc and baby lotion.

'Do you want something to eat?' Sarah asked.

'Yes, please,' Lis said. 'I'm starving! Do we have any fruit? I have a craving for fruit, ice-cream and pancakes.'

'Done, done and done.' Sarah rose from her chair. 'You stick the kettle on.'

Lis replaced Logan, who was beginning to wriggle, and quickly filled the kettle. Leaning against the counter, her gaze fell on Sarah's newspaper. It took her a second to realise the face on the front cover was that of her former best friend/worst enemy.

Sarah turned back from the fridge-freezer, her arms full of eggs and ice cream. She paused, realising why Lis had frozen.

'Oh, God! Lis, I'm sorry! Don't look at that!'

Lis shook her head. 'No, it's OK. This all really happened. I'll have to get used to the news, won't I?' She slipped into a chair at the big family table and took a deep breath before starting to read.

North Yorkshire Police are continuing their largest ever manhunt today in the search for the killer of Hollow Pike schoolgirl Laura Rigg, 15, whose body was found in Pike Copse, near Fulton, yesterday morning. A spokesperson refused to comment on growing speculation that this was a ritual-style killing. Police are questioning a number of witnesses, including Laura's parents and school friends, although they stressed that no arrests have been made at this early stage.

'It's sad how people always think it's the parents,' Lis commented, reading the subtext. 'How sick is that?'

Sarah sat beside her and rubbed her hand. 'I know, but that's the world we live in. You should have heard the conversations in the post office yesterday. So much gossip.'

Lis remembered the public spat Laura and her dad had shared in town. Surely it wasn't significant, though? Surely it had just been a teenage diva moment.

'What do you think they mean by "ritual-style killing"?' Lis murmured.

'I've no idea, hon. I dread to think.'

The story continued on page three. No further information was given on how Laura had died and, although Lis didn't want the gory details, the words 'ritual-style killing' had tapped into her own fears. Rituals might involve hooded capes and ceremonial daggers – the things she and her friends had had that night, inspired by what Lis had seen in Mrs Gillespie's book.

What was more depressing were the pupils who paid their respects to Laura, no doubt for a fee, in the cheesy tabloid. There was a picture of Laura with Poppy Hewitt-Smith, the ponytail victim. Lis knew that Poppy and Laura had despised each other, and yet there they were, smiling in ink. *Like sisters* read the quote under the picture. The photo looked about two years old. Yuck, Poppy was a vampire, feeding on Laura's death. Lis slammed the paper shut and threw it across the room where it tumbled into the recycling box.

'You OK?' Sarah asked.

'Yeah. I suppose it'll get easier.'

Sarah poured the tea. 'Well, there is one thing, Lis . . .'

'Go on.'

Placing the tea next to her, Sarah started mixing the pancake batter. 'Well, while you were sleeping, we had a phone call from the police.'

'What?' Lis exploded, nearly dropping her tea.

'Don't fret!' Sarah said quickly. 'They're talking to most of your class – just gathering information about the last few days. They said it was absolutely nothing to worry about.'

Oh, if only that were the case, Lis thought.

Two hours later, Lis looked across the car park. Sheets of rain bounced off the tarmac, yet she could still make out the shape of the police station in the distance.

'Right. I'm ready.' She sighed.

'Are you sure?' asked Max in his broad Yorkshire accent. As Sarah was with Logan, Max had left his site to accompany Lis. 'You know we don't have to go today. They said "in your own time".'

Lis turned and tried for a smile. 'What's the point in waiting? Might as well get it over and done with.'

With Max holding a mighty golf umbrella over both of them, they sprinted through the downpour. Lis had never seen rain like it. Even in the short dash, they were both drenched by the time they fell through the automatic doors.

Fulton Police Station was a local affair, but it had that strange council vibe: tatty posters curling at the edges and leaflets littering torn vinyl chairs. Lis sat, pulling at some exposed seat padding, while Max spoke to the officer on the desk. This place was almost as chaotic as the gymnasium had been. It was obvious the regional station didn't have the capacity to handle something like this.

'Lis, we've got to wait through here.' Max beckoned her through a security door and she found herself in an almost identical waiting room. She wondered if the whole station was like an Escher print where she'd keep going through doors only to discover the same room behind each one.

'I need the loo,' Lis said, feeling increasingly nervous.

'OK, pet, I'll wait here.'

Lis left the waiting room and searched the long corridor, looking for the ladies'. She turned a corner and saw the lavatories next to a tall, brown coffee machine. Suddenly, she heard a familiar voice.

'Do you have any idea how embarrassing this is?' It was

Kitty's father. He had close-shaven grey hair with a neat beard to match, and the darkest mahogany skin. He was maybe even taller than Max, who took some beating in the height stakes. He towered over a terrified Kitty, who was pressed against the vending machine. Her friend had been crying, and was without her trademark make-up. She looked very young. Lis quickly ducked back around the corner, but remained within earshot.

'I'm sorry. I should have said something sooner,' Kitty said. The pair were speaking in low voices.

'Do you think?' her father raged. 'Do you bloody think?'

'What else can I say? I'm sorry!' There was none of the usual coolness in Kitty's voice.

'Katherine, do you think you get some sort of special treatment for being my daughter?'

'Well, clearly not!' Kitty sobbed bitterly.

'Don't get bloody clever, young lady!' he snarled. 'Now, are you sure there's nothing else you want to add before you go? Because if I find out you've "forgotten" something, I will have you arrested and that is a promise!'

Lis winced at the grilling. It was painful to listen to so Lis could only imagine what it would feel like to be on the receiving end. Jack was right: Kitty's dad *was* the scariest man ever.

'That's everything,' Kitty said. 'We had a fight at Danny's party. It wasn't even a proper fight. She was taking the mick out of Delilah, so I slapped her and we both fell down the stairs. Dad, I promise, that's everything. It had nothing to do with what's happened!'

Her father paused for a moment. 'Right, get out of my sight.'

Lis heard their footsteps approach. She promptly resumed

her walk, trying to look as casual as possible. Kitty and her dad almost crashed straight into her.

'Lis!' Kitty said, astonished. 'I tried calling you a hundred times. Your phone was off. I—'

'That's enough,' snapped her father. 'Go home, Katherine. I'll speak to you later.'

Kitty looked from Lis to her dad, choosing not to argue. 'Call me later, OK?' she said to Lis and left quickly.

Kitty's dad turned to Lis. 'Right. It's Elisabeth London, isn't it? I'm Inspector Keith Monroe. I've got you down as my next appointment.'

Lis and Max were led into a room marked 'Interview 1'. A female officer sat quietly at a desk in the sticky little room. The only sound was the streaming rain beating against the single window pane.

'This is PC Alison Price, my colleague. She'll be taking some notes while we chat,' explained Inspector Monroe, gesturing to them both to sit. 'Try to relax, Elisabeth, you're not in any trouble.' He was full of Yorkshire charm now, but Lis couldn't forget the way he'd treated Kitty.

'Everyone calls me Lis,' she mumbled.

'Fair dos. Right, Lis, we need to gather as much information as we can about Laura's last few days. We've spoken to all her friends at school and your name came up. That's why we'd like to speak to you.'

Lis nodded slowly. Under the table, Max gave her hand a supportive squeeze.

'Now we need to know anything at all you can tell us, love. It might not seem important but you never know when something might be a smaller piece of the big puzzle, do you see?'

'OK,' she practically whispered. She cleared her throat noisily. 'What do you want to know?' Her heart was pounding so loudly in her chest Lis felt the inspector must be able to hear it. Guilt, guilt, guilt, banging away. Had Kitty, Jack and Delilah confessed to their little game? She recalled how Delilah had insisted they write nothing down so there'd be no evidence. Why would they then go and tell the police everything? But then it had all been hypothetical, at least to her. Now it was real. Just answer the questions, she decided.

'Right. Something that's come up a few times is that Laura had upset quite a lot of people at your school. Is that true?'

Be honest. Don't waffle. 'Well, yeah. She could be really mean, I suppose.'

'How was she mean?'

'Well. Uh . . . she was rude to a lot of people. And unkind. Really unkind.'

'Was she unkind to you?'

Oh, Christ, she saw where this was heading. Max again gave her hand a rub. *Just be honest*, Lis told herself. She hadn't done anything wrong. She'd had nothing to do with Laura's *actual* death. *Theoretical* death was another matter entirely. 'Yeah. She told everyone that I came to live with my sister because I'd given my baby up for adoption, or something. It's not true, but it was still embarrassing.'

'You didn't say anything, love!' Max seemed shocked.

'It's not the sort of thing I enjoy sharing, Max.'

He let a long breath out through his nose and fell silent once more.

'Was that the end of it?' asked Inspector Monroe.

'Yes. I talked with Mr Gray, my form tutor. He said it was being sorted out with Ms Dandehunt. Laura was picking on half the school. It wasn't just me!' Anger started to rise inside her. Did they really think she'd killed Laura over some stupid prank? Of course, it had been that email that had prompted her to plan Laura's death, but that was different.

Monroe relaxed in his chair. It was a physical apology of sorts. 'Lis, we weren't trying to say you'd done anything. We just need every side of the story. We've already chatted to Mr Gray. He said exactly the same thing as you.'

Lis nodded, feeling calmer.

'Do you know anyone who would want to hurt Laura?'

Anyone who met her. 'No.' She paused. 'I don't know.'

'Well, which is it?'

Lis stared, unblinking, at Monroe. 'Was Laura nasty? Yes. Did she upset lots of people? Yes. Can I think of a single person who could be evil enough to actually *kill* her? No.'

On the last word, her voice broke into a sob. It was true. Did she really think that Kitty, Jack or Delilah could have murdered Laura? She *had* to believe they were innocent. *But what if they weren't?* It felt like acid, burning at her insides.

Monroe observed her shrewdly for a moment and Lis held her breath. He finally looked away, seemingly accepting every word she'd said.

Damp and tired, Lis dragged herself up the stairs to the side door. The drive back had been eerily silent, with none of her usual banter with Max. As soon as they entered the house, Lis headed for her bedroom, wanting to seek refuge under her duvet again. She only got as far as the lounge.

'Elisabeth May London, what's going on?' Oh, Sarah meant business if she was bringing out the middle name. Logan looked at Lis accusingly too – what did he know? He wasn't even one year old yet!

Lis slumped on the sofa. 'It was awful, Sarah.' She could hardly find the words.

'Why?' Sarah demanded.

'She did fine,' Max said from the kitchen. 'You were very brave, pet.'

'So what's up?' Sarah wanted to know.

'I ... I ...' Could she really tell her sister? What if she dragged Sarah into her problems? What if her friends *weren't* innocent? Did she really want to put Sarah in the firing line? 'I just ... I mean, there's a murderer out there! It could be anyone!'

'You silly sausage! What happened to Laura has nothing to do with you.'

At that point, an uncontrollable sob wracked Lis's body. She shook as it found its way out.

Sarah regarded her, her face full of concern. 'If there's something going on, Lis, you know you can tell me, don't you? You can tell me anything, babe.'

Lis nodded, not daring to speak in case all the events of the last weeks spilled from her lips.

'It's just me, your sister. We don't need to tell Mum or Max,' Sarah continued in a low whisper.

But Lis couldn't do this, not to Sarah. 'I'm fine. This Laura stuff ... it's like the nightmares. Only this time I don't wake up.' Her voice cracked.

Sarah carefully placed Logan on the rug and came over to her, wrapping Lis in her arms.

'You're not too big for a hug, you daft thing.'

Lis curled into her sister's embrace, drawing in a lungful of her comforting scent.

'What do you want to do, babe?' Sarah asked gently. 'Watch

a DVD? Go do some shopping maybe? I'm all yours. I've neglected you!'

Lis straightened up, tucking her hair behind her ears. How much could she risk telling Sarah about Laura, the woods, the rituals, the rumours about her new friends being witches? And what about the nightmares, or '*warnings*' as she'd been told – visions of what was to come. 'Sarah. You know the stories about Hollow Pike?' Lis began.

Sarah shrugged. 'Which stories?'

Lis squirmed in her chair. 'You know ... about the copse and ... the witches ...'

Sarah laughed heartily, throwing her blonde hair back, but seeing the concern on Lis's face she quickly pulled herself together. 'Oh, sorry, honey, I thought you were kidding.'

'No.'

'It's all ancient history, babe!'

That wasn't good enough. 'But you've heard the stories?'

Sarah's forehead creased. She knelt next to Lis, taking Lis's hands in her own. 'Lis, look at me. There's no such thing as witches.'

Lis nodded, but another tear rolled down her pale cheek.

Her eyes snapped open. Her sleep had been warm and fulfilling, yet she had suddenly woken up. Why? Sitting upright, Lis pushed her hair back from her face and peered into the moonlight that was shining through the translucent curtains.

She could hear talking in the distance. Sarah and Max? A quick glance at her mobile confirmed the time as 1.15 a.m. Maybe little Logan was having a bad night. She strained to catch the conversation.

And then she realised it wasn't Sarah's voice. Or Max's for that matter. The speaker was talking in a hoarse whisper and Lis still couldn't hear what was being said.

Suddenly, something tapped against the terrace door: three short, sharp knocks on the glass. Recoiling, Lis pulled the duvet up around her face and flattened her back against the bedhead. Once more there were strange shadows on the terrace, and this time there was no way that she was imagining it or that it was just a bird. She slowly edged down the bed towards the door, wary of any quick movements that would alert whoever was out there to her presence.

'Lis . . .' The word came through clearly this time, freezing Lis to the spot. She dare not even blink.

'*Lis!*' The tone was more serious now. Threatening.

The door handle rattled as an unseen hand tested it on the other side. Shadows flickered, followed by frantic scrabbling against the glass.

'*Let us in!*' hissed a second voice, angrier than the first. Lis recognised that voice: Kitty.

They'd come.

Lis's hand hovered at the door handle, trembling and uncertain. Who was she about to let into her room – friends or killers?

Who's There?

'For crying out loud, Lis. It's only us!' a Geordie accent lamented. 'It's freezing, will you please open the bloody doors?'

There was something about Jack's voice that prevented it from carrying even a whiff of menace. And, besides, she desperately wanted to ask her friends some questions. She needed to know the truth. Lis twisted the key in the lock.

Three cold, unimpressed friends stood huddled on the patio. 'Are you going to let us in, or not?' Kitty said sulkily.

'Come in,' Lis said. 'But my sister and Max are just upstairs ...'

'Dear God, what do you think we're going to do?' Kitty snapped, pushing past her.

'Keep your voice down!' Lis whispered.

Jack and Delilah flopped onto her bed, making themselves at home, while Kitty leaned back insouciantly on the chaise longue, as though she were Cleopatra or something. Lis perched on the desk chair, an outsider in her own bedroom.

'Well?' Lis demanded, struggling to control her shaking voice. It was like someone had left the cage door open and the lions had escaped. She'd have to tread very carefully.

'Well what?' Jack asked.

Lis's eye's widened. 'You know what! Did you do it? Did you *kill her?*' OK, not *that* carefully, then.

Her three friends looked at one another and rolled their eyes.

'Of course we didn't,' Kitty said, as if she were stating the obvious. 'Did you?'

'*What?*' hissed Lis.

Delilah propped herself up on her elbows. 'Be fair. The dastardly revenge plot was your idea, too.'

'I wanted to blackmail her, not kill her!' Lis protested.

'Where do you think we've been all this time?' Kitty asked. She jabbed a finger in Lis's direction. 'Googling you to see if you'd escaped from some Welsh mental institution!'

'Are you serious?'

'Lis.' Jack tilted his head. 'You were just as much a part of this as us.'

'That is so not fair!' But then she realised that it *was* fair. She *had* been in it every bit as much as them. She'd been there, plotting and planning, playing along with the prank. She'd wanted Laura to pay. Maybe she wasn't as lily white as she liked to imagine.

Kitty sighed. 'Look. After we punked Laura, I went back to Dee's and Jack headed home. We don't know where *you* went. Any one of us could have headed back into the copse, but I sure as hell know it wasn't me or Dee.'

'And it wasn't me, ask my mum,' Jack added.

'Well, it wasn't me. You can ask Sarah!' Lis said vehemently.

Delilah stifled a laugh. 'So none of us are going to confess to murder? There's a shocker!'

Jack moved to the edge of the bed. 'What did you tell the police? Did you tell them about our plan to get Laura off our backs? Did you tell them what we did?'

Lis pouted. 'No. I'm not completely stupid.'

All three of them exhaled deeply, clearly they'd been every bit as tense as Lis.

'So if we didn't kill her, who the hell did? Pretty dark, right?' Kitty's white teeth gleamed in the gloom of the bedroom.

Lis shrugged, feeling a massive sense of relief; these people weren't killers, they were her friends. Her only friends for that matter.

'Have you shown anyone the video?' Delilah asked.

It took her a second to process what video Delilah was actually talking about. 'Oh, no. I haven't even watched it myself. When I got home from the copse, Sarah asked me to bath Logan. I guess I forgot all about it.' Lis swivelled the chair around and rummaged under the pile of homework on her desk to retrieve her pink and silver camera.

'We should delete it right now,' Jack urged. 'If anyone ever sees that, we're as dead as she is.'

'OK,' Lis replied.

'Wait! We should at least watch it first,' Kitty said. 'Come on, this is the last home movie she'll ever star in – someone ought to see it.'

'Kitty, this isn't a game,' Lis snapped.

'CTFO. We watch it once and delete it,' Kitty said.

Lis opened her laptop. The white-blue glow of the monitor filled her dark bedroom and the group gathered around the desk. Lis retrieved a USB cable and plugged the camera in. It pinged back to life as the PC began to charge it.

'OK, give me a sec.' She navigated the desktop, opening the right files. 'Here it is.'

The film started, grainy and shaky. Delilah was no budding Spielberg, that was for sure.

When I was little, my dad used to tell me stories about children who went into the copse and never came out. They just vanished, Laura was saying, although it was difficult to hear her over the rustling leaves and Delilah's breathing. In the clip, Lis and Laura were two blurs moving through an even blurrier setting.

You don't believe that, do you? Lis remembered saying that. Why had she agreed to the trick? Laura wouldn't even have been out there in the copse if it hadn't been for her.

No . . . Maybe . . . I don't know. Everyone knows the stories. You just keep out of the woods after dark.

Big, Bad Laura Rigg, scared of the—

What followed next was a mess. As Delilah moved, the image shook so much that there was no recognisable picture. It was like *The Blair Witch Project* on acid. Screams and yells could be heard over footsteps and muffled struggling. She saw herself fall over when Jack pretended to stab her. As Laura sprinted off into the black abyss of the copse, the camera steadied in time to see Laura fade from sight. And fade from life.

'Oh, God,' muttered Delilah, even paler than normal. She seemed genuinely upset.

'We shouldn't have done it,' Lis said quietly, as a tear ran down her cheek.

'How could we have known?' Kitty snapped, too loudly. 'It was just a joke!'

'Wait,' Jack leaned over her shoulder. 'Can you go back a bit – to where Laura runs off?'

Lis turned to the computer and moved the cursor to the time bar, sliding it back an inch. 'Here?'

'Yeah. Play it.'

She pressed *Play* and again watched Laura tumble awkwardly into the shadows.

'Pause!' Jack ordered.

'What?' Kitty was irritated, which Lis took to be a sign that she was feeling guilty.

'Look ...' Jack rested his finger on the screen. He was pointing at a tree just to the right of where Laura had fled.

'What am I looking at?' Delilah asked for everyone.

'Can we swap seats?' Jack edged Lis off the computer chair and took control. 'Keep your eyes on that tree.'

He backed up the video about three seconds and pressed *Play*. Although it was poor definition, something on the bark of the tree moved, a pale spider creeping out of sight. If you squinted, it could be a hand. A human hand.

Lis leaned further in as Jack played the clip again. Maybe it was nothing. Maybe it was a leaf catching the last of the light. She glanced at the others. There was a look of horror on Delilah's face and a look of puzzlement on Kitty's. The more they watched the video, the more the spider really did look like a pale hand resting on the tree. And that meant only one thing ...

There had been someone else in the woods that night.

In Memoriam

The water was black, impenetrable, rushing over her body and threatening to sweep her away. The stream flowed faster than ever. It was so cold it hurt.

Lis continued her search. She was no longer crawling, but pushing through the water, scanning and searching. 'Laura!' she screamed, her voice reverberating through the copse. 'Laura!'

There was nothing in the brook. Her hands found only stones and weeds. Damp green tendrils wrapped themselves around her fingers as her search grew more frantic. 'Laura!'

She stopped. She wasn't alone. Looking beyond the stream, a figure flitted between the trees, engulfed in shadows. *There was someone else in the forest.*

Pond weed entangled her wrist and Lis pulled her arm out of the stream. It wasn't weed. Thick, matted chestnut hair was knotted in her fingers and Laura's face floated to the surface of the water, swollen and blue. Dead eyes stared up at her and Lis could only scream.

'Lis . . .' said the corpse, without moving its lips. *'Lis!'*

Lis jerked forward, almost head-butting Delilah in the face as the redhead gently shook her awake.

'Lis, you need to wake up.'

Lis pushed the duvet back, rubbing her eyes. 'Yeah. What time is it?'

'Keep your voice down,' Jack reminded her from inside his nest of bedding on the floor. 'It's just gone six.'

Kitty was already up and hovering at the door. 'We need to get going if we're going to be ready for school.'

Lis shook the last of the nightmare from her mind. 'We can't go to school today.'

'We *have* to!' Delilah said. 'It's the first day back and it's Laura's memorial thing. We have to act normal.'

Lis wasn't convinced. 'But what about the video? There's a killer out there!'

'Isn't that better than one of *us* being the killer?' Kitty pointed out.

'Kitty, I really think we should take the video to the police.' Lis clambered out of bed and listened at the door. It seemed that Sarah and Max were still sleeping. She didn't know how well Sarah would react to a secret sleepover.

'Are you high? If we take that video to the police, my dad will actually kill us dead. There is *no way* we can let anyone know that we were in the copse.'

They'd already been through all of the arguments at 2 a.m., but Lis still didn't know what to think. They'd been standing just metres away from someone in the woods. They'd watched the clip over and over and over, and every time it looked more like a hand – the hand of someone lurking just out of sight.

'The thing is ...' Delilah whispered. 'If we saw them ... then *they saw us*!'

The room fell silent. Delilah was right. Jack was shocked. Kitty was speechless.

Lis spoke first. 'Do you guys believe in the witch stories?'

Kitty seemed relieved at the change in topic. 'Honey, we *are* the witch stories.'

'I mean it. Laura was properly scared of the copse. Even

Sarah has heard the legends. You don't think that witches ...'

'... that witches killed Laura?' Jack smiled for the first time that morning. 'I wish. Hollow Pike is begging for a bit of supernatural fun. We could be the UK's answer to Forks!'

Lis took a deep breath and dropped onto the bed. Now was the time to open up, she was certain of it. 'I'm serious. Ever since I decided to come to Hollow Pike, I've been having these messed up, extra twisted dreams. Dreams where someone is trying to kill me. Dreams about Laura. Dreams about Pike Copse. Mrs Gillespie said my dreams were, like, warnings. What if there *is* something evil in Hollow Pike?'

Well, at least they didn't laugh. Quite the opposite. Delilah moved to Lis's side and took her hand, giving it a supportive squeeze.

'I'm with Jack,' Kitty said tenderly. 'Some*one* killed Laura, not some*thing*. Mrs Gillespie is as mad as a box of frogs. Don't listen to a word she says.'

'And dreams are only dreams,' Delilah added.

A huge weight lifted from Lis's shoulders. A problem shared was, in this case, a problem quartered. If Hollow Pike didn't have a killer at large, it would be a pretty cool town. 'So what do we do?'

'We stick together and we don't utter a bloody word to anyone. The police will catch the killer. It's not our problem.' Kitty was so confident that Lis drew strength from her. Spiking her hair, Kitty opened the patio doors to make their getaway. 'Let's haul ass. We have a Laura Rigg memorial to attend. I'm gonna need Red Bull.'

'Pupils returned to Fulton High School today, although police are no nearer to catching the killer of schoolgirl Laura Rigg. There is mounting pressure on the North Yorkshire Police to make an arrest . . .' The journalist's massive back-combed hair was unmoving, even in the angry winds whipping across the entrance to the school.

Lis kept her head firmly down as she crept onto the premises. It was quite an eye-opener: her school looked like a film set. There must have been seven TV trucks, each with their own crew and cameras.

'This is a bit surreal,' Jack muttered, as they slipped past a film crew.

'Dalí surreal,' Delilah agreed.

It took Lis a moment to work out what was wrong with the scene, and then the penny dropped. Nothing had changed. Year Seven boys kicked a football around, swearing loudly at each other's errors. Girls huddled together checking text messages. A group of Year Eight lads snatched girls' bags for the ensuing chase. Year Ten girls sat on their boyfriends' knees. A clique of indie kids stood listening to their individual iPods.

Laura was dead, but everyone else lived.

'Come on,' Lis said as they arrived at the main entrance. 'Let's get this assembly over and done with.'

The most recent school photograph of Laura Rigg stood proudly at the centre of the stage, surrounded by a huge wreath, smiling sweetly at the room. The picture had been altered to greyscale. *Is black and white sadder?* Lis wondered. *Is colour disrespectful?* Laura's serene smile was peaceful and beautiful, so unlike the real Laura whose features had so often seemed spiteful and twisted.

Lis and her friends squeezed in next to Rachel Williams, who had come prepared in her best black funeral outfit instead of uniform. In fact, most of Year Eleven seemed to be treating the assembly as the official substitute to Laura's actual funeral, which was apparently delayed while the police carried out their investigations.

Cameron Green was sitting very quietly with his friends, his face looking as if it were carved out of stone.

'I don't know how he dares show his face,' Rachel whispered. 'You know the police questioned him for nearly twelve hours. People are saying he did it . . .'

Lis said nothing.

The mood was dark and sombre. It seemed that mourning Laura was the new 'in' thing to do. Lis was acutely aware that most of the room had actively hated Laura, yet here they were, sobbing into handkerchiefs and resting heads on friends' shoulders. Guilt and disgust mixed in Lis's stomach. As bad as she felt about planning Laura's death with her friends, she wasn't now about to herald her as some sort of saint. Turning her head, she saw Nasima Bharat wailing gently in Danny's arms, her elegant hand stroking his neck. Lis snapped her head away as jealousy tore through her body. This was so inappropriate. Danny and Nasima, though? Seriously? Laura would have *loved* that.

Base instinct won out and Lis chanced a further backwards glance. To be fair, Nasima looked genuinely devastated, but did she really need to hang off Danny quite so much? Suddenly Danny looked in Lis's direction, squarely catching her eye. Lis whipped her head back, but she'd been busted.

Thankfully, Ms Dandehunt and Mr Gray entered the hall, hopefully drawing Danny's attention away from her. A lectern had been erected next to the image of Laura and Ms Dandehunt took to the stage.

'Thank you for coming into school today, Year Eleven. We are all still mourning Laura and that will take some time. Sometimes it is possible to find comfort in normality; in these turbulent waters it is my hope that Fulton High School can be a lighthouse for all of us. Some of Laura's friends wanted to do a special assembly about a special girl, and I think it is a touching way to remember Laura. So enough from me and over to the choir who are going to sing some of Laura's favourite songs . . .'

The choir sung beautifully, although Lis suspected that choral versions of Lady Gaga songs, while thoughtful, weren't entirely appropriate. Poppy Hewitt-Smith (tabloid favourite) had written a dreadful poem entitled *Our Friend*. Lis resisted the urge to stand and walk out at that point. Harry Bedsworth was the last of Laura's 'friends' to take the stage. Without any make-up, she looked like Caspar the Friendly Ghost, her white hair blending with her face.

'I wanted to say a few words about Laura,' she started quietly. She took a deep breath. 'You know, Laura could be a real bitch.'

A horrified gasp ran through the crowd. Lis turned and saw Nasima now sitting bolt upright, mortified.

'Oh, come on, you all knew her,' Harry continued, but she was barely holding it together now, her voice trembling. 'She could be so mean. I was, like, one of her best mates and she was mean to me all the time. She constantly took the mick out of all of us.'

Ms Dandehunt and Mr Gray edged towards the stage. Were they going to actually pull Harry off?

Behind her, Lis saw that Laura's friends, Cameron, Fiona, Nasima and even Danny, looked massively uncomfortable, their eyes not daring to meet Harry's.

'The thing is, even though I loved her, sometimes I used

to wish that Laura was dead.' At that Harry's voice broke into a sob. 'You don't know what it was like! It's all my fault!'

Her wails reverberated around the room. Lis felt tears pricking her eyes. She wiped them away. Self-absorbed, she'd imagined she was the only one Laura had affected. Apparently not.

'That's why I wanted to do this memorial,' Harry finished. 'Because I'm so sorry! And I'm going to miss her so much!' Harry dissolved into a flood of raw, real tears. Mr Gray tentatively climbed the stage steps and embraced his student. She buried her face in his chest as he walked her quietly off stage.

Ms Dandehunt quickly took the microphone. 'Year Eleven,' she began, catching Lis's eye. 'I think what Harry said is very important. When someone dies, we might feel a little bit guilty because maybe we rowed with them, or thought negative things about them, but that's human nature. We are what we are. None of us are to blame for this tragedy.'

Lis was overwhelmed by a fresh urge to cry. Instead, she clutched Jack's hand.

'I think it's time the choir sung us out. It's a difficult day for everyone.'

Memorial over, all Lis had to do was survive an afternoon of Art and she could fall into bed. Harry's outpouring had been oddly cleansing. Maybe this searing guilt she felt was normal after all.

'Lis!'

She looked around and saw Danny weaving his way through the crowd of mourners towards her.

'Lis, hey! I was hoping to catch you. Can I have a word?'

Lis became aware of three pairs of eyes watching them intently. Kitty, Jack and Delilah were choosing not to take the hint. 'Sure,' she told Danny. 'I'll catch you guys in the shelter?' she said pointedly to her friends.

Jack and Delilah could hardly contain giggles, while Kitty grinned. 'Be good, London!' she said.

Her friends headed off, glancing over their shoulders. Lis's cheeks flushed.

'You sticking around this afternoon?' Danny asked. 'Some Year Elevens are allowed the afternoon off, apparently.'

Despite her shock at Danny seeking *her* out, Lis remained collected. 'Yeah. I just have Art. Should be easy enough.'

'Are you heading for the canteen?'

'Yeah.'

'Cool, can I come?'

She smiled, continuing to walk. He seemed nervous. 'Are you sure Nasima won't mind?' Lis asked.

'Nasima?' Danny repeated, looking confused. 'Oh, right! I guess that assembly got a bit heavy. She was upset, that's all.'

'Ah, OK.' She chose to accept the sketchy excuse. 'Poor Harry, her speech took some balls.'

'For sure,' he agreed. 'She was right though. I've felt sick with guilt since Laura died. Like I could have saved her somehow.'

Lis dared to give Danny's arm a tiny squeeze. She hoped it seemed platonic. 'You can't blame yourself. We don't know what happened to her. It's for the police to sort out.'

'I know. It's just that I sort of rejected her. Twice, actually. Maybe if I hadn't . . .'

'That's crazy talk—'

'I know, I know! I know all of these things, but it's like I can't get the voices out of my head.' He drifted off and sat on the steps outside the cafeteria. Rubbing his hands on his trousers, he seemed to be searching for words.

Lis sat next to him. 'What's up?' she asked gently, not wanting to appear nosy.

'Nothing. It's just that this seems really wrong.'

'What does?'

'Well, I'm trying to ask you out.' Danny glanced at her for a split second and then looked away. 'But it seems really awful to do that with all this Laura stuff going on.'

Lis's eyes almost fell out of her face. In a moment, her skin had become hotter than she could stand. Had she heard right?

'You want to ask *me* out?' The idea that rugby team pin-up Danny Marriott was interested in freaky Welsh new-girl Lis London was plain ridiculous, to her at least.

'Yes. Well, if you want. I'm not sure where we could go. Maybe into Fulton or something? I've been wondering how to ask for ages. I've never really asked anyone out before. I mean, I've pulled, obviously, at parties and stuff, but that's not like this ... I was worried I'd make a mess of it. Every time I speak to you I seem to say something really bloody stupid and—'

'Danny?'

'Yeah?'

'You're babbling. Before you *do* say something stupid, I'll just say "yes"!'

He smiled and looked at her properly. His eyes made her heart beat so fast she had to look away.

'Really?' he asked.

The broadest smile broke out on Lis's face, matching his expression. All the toxic thoughts in her head briefly vanished as she bathed in the yellow sunshine of this moment. 'Yes, really!'

Danny raised an eyebrow, 'God, now I'm really nervous! I'd sort of thought you'd say no.'

'Well, sorry to disappoint you!' Lis laughed.

'No, no. It's good. It's awesome! I can't wait. When are you free?'

'Any time,' she said far too quickly. *Well done, Lis, way to play it cool.* 'Well, I don't think I have too much on . . .'

With a violent jolt, her phone vibrated in her bag.

'Hold that thought,' Lis told him, reaching for the device.

The display read INCOMING CALL. NUMBER WITHELD. REJECT? ANSWER?

It was probably Sarah calling from the landline or something. 'Hello?'

'Hello, Lis.' The voice sounded distant, but vaguely familiar.

'Hello? Who is this?'

'It's Mrs Gillespie, dear. From the shop.'

Danny, seeing Lis's confused expression, frowned. Lis wanted to be far away from him; she didn't want him to hear this conversation.

'How did you get my—'

'Never you mind,' Mrs Gillespie interrupted. Then she paused. There was a moment's silence. 'I know what you and your little friends have done . . .'

The Legend of Hollow Pike

Lis pounded on the door so hard it rattled in its frame. Even if she put the glass through, she wasn't going to stop knocking. She must have looked ridiculous – a fifteen-year-old girl in school uniform so eager to get into a charity shop. Why was the bloody door locked anyway?

Peering through the filthy window, Lis tried a different approach. 'Mrs Gillespie, it's me, Lis London!' she called.

She pressed her ear to the grimy glass and listened closely. Sure enough, after a few seconds she heard unsteady stilettos totter towards the entrance. Red fingernails drew aside the net curtain and Mrs Gillespie glanced out before unlocking the door. 'That was quick,' she said.

'I came straight from school,' Lis replied. She was reminded of how hideous the old woman was. This time she was wearing some sort of oriental robe with a turban perched on top of her nasty wig. It must have been the height of glamour in the thirties, but now it looked like a Halloween costume. The aroma of gin and cigarettes drifting from her was equally repulsive.

'You'd better come on in then. You can't stand in the street all afternoon.'

Stepping aside, Mrs Gillespie let her into the dank shop. Lis hugged her arms to her body, not sure of what to do or say.

'Don't just stand there, girlie, come and sit down!'

In the front section of the shop was a sort of tea party set-up: a dainty round table with three antique looking chairs. A stained, yellow lace tablecloth hung over the table.

'This is where we take our afternoon tea. Would you like a cup, deary?'

Lis tentatively sat on one of the chairs. She couldn't imagine who the 'we' referred to, as the shop was entirely empty.

'No, thank you,' she said quietly.

Mrs Gillespie poured herself some tea from a Charles and Di teapot and held the cup to her withered mouth. 'Now, are you going to own up?'

'I don't know what you mean,' Lis stared down at the tea set, unable to look at the strange woman.

'I think you know exactly what I mean.'

Lis shook her head, sensing the onset of panic. Should she confess the whole sorry prank? The murder game? 'I ... I—'

'You stole my book,' Mrs Gillespie snapped.

What? Lis blinked hard to check she wasn't imagining things. 'What book?'

Mrs Gillespie slapped her thin, veined hand on the table. 'You jolly well know which book – *An Occult History of Hollow Pike*!'

So this was nothing to do with the prank? Lis felt an overwhelming sense of relief. Her mouth formed a small circle. 'Oh, I didn't take it!'

'Well, it was one of your rotten friends then.'

'I ... I don't know. If they did take it, they didn't tell me.' *Could they have stolen it?* Lis wondered. Then again, why would they want a book about witchcraft? And they'd have mentioned it that morning when she brought the subject up, surely.

'I want that book back. It's not for sale.'

'It was on the shelf, though,' Lis pointed out. 'What's so special about it anyway?' She felt much more relaxed now that she knew this was a) nothing to do with Laura and b) nothing to do with her at all.

Mrs Gillespie watched her like a hawk, beady eyes glaring over her china teacup. 'Don't tell me you haven't heard the stories. I saw you looking at the book.'

Lis remembered her dream for a second, but pushed it away, clinging to Kitty's certainty that the killer was just your everyday, run-of-the-mill murderer with no supernatural connections. 'I've heard *fairy tales*.'

Mrs Gillespie's thin red lips parted to reveal her yellow teeth. 'Ha! How old are you?'

'Nearly sixteen.'

'So naturally you know everything there is to know? It's interesting that the young are gifted with such certainty. I find myself becoming a more *un*certain woman, the older I get!' She cackled at her own joke.

Lis frowned. This was a waste of time. 'I don't get it.'

'Of course you don't! How could you?' Mrs Gillespie was suddenly more serious. 'There's more than you could ever know in the woods, Lis. A town full of ghosts.'

'What? Are you saying Hollow Pike is haunted?'

Mrs Gillespie seemed to consider this. 'In a way, haunted by the past. Its own past. Bad things happened here. Very bad things. People were hunted down, tortured and killed: drowned or burned. Hollow Pike is a mass grave.'

Lis could tell that she wasn't joking. This, to her at least, was real. 'Who was killed?'

'The witches. A long time ago, people would come to Hollow Pike with their sick, with the infirm or barren. The families that lived in the forests and hills would help with remedies and potions. People said they were powerful healers. But then a couple of children vanished. People fell ill and cattle died. Coincidences. Bad luck. But everybody wanted someone to blame.'

'So what happened?' Lis asked curiously, wondering if the story could be true.

'They were burned. In the early seventeenth century the witch-finders rode into town, calling themselves the Righteous Protectors. They came from the church. Not just God-fearing folk, but fanatics. It was like they had a fever of hate. They thought witches would bring about a return to the dark times, the fall of God. The women were taken from their homes and the Protectors tortured them for hours until they confessed. Some of them were drowned in the river, some were burned in the village.'

'That's awful.' Lis could almost hear their screams.

'Yes, it is. All those people who died – their blood is at the roots of the trees. Some people say the town is cursed but, of course, you said it yourself: curses are the stuff of fairy tales.'

Lis did think that, didn't she? But, ridiculous as it sounded, the moment her mum had driven into Pike Copse, Lis *had* sensed something strange. The air had felt heavier, the sky had darkened, the wood had seemed frighteningly *alive*, and the magpie had stared at her as if it knew who she was. Admitting these things seemed a step too far, though. Things like that belonged to books and films, not the humdrum life of Lis London. 'There's no such thing as magic or curses.' She stood to leave, swinging her bag onto her shoulder. 'Look, when I see them I'll ask my friends about the book. If they've got it, we'll bring it back.'

Someone had taken the book. Interesting. Laura's had been a *ritual-style* killing, or so the papers said. Maybe the killer had needed the book for tips or something.

Mrs Gillespie rose and slid over to Lis, brushing a stray curl out of her eyes. 'Lis, you look tired. How are you sleeping?'

Lis flinched and moved to the door. 'I'm sleeping fine,' she said reflexively. It was becoming her mantra. She looked into Mrs Gillespie's face, trying to find the kind old lady behind the make-up.

'Really? Some people are privy to special dreams, you know.'

'Yeah, well not me.'

'Are you sure?'

'I'm nothing special, seriously – ask anyone.'

Mrs Gillespie smiled. Lis thought it was probably her version of a sweet smile; it was unsettling to say the least.

'Before you leave, I'd love for you to meet the children.'

'OK,' Lis said reluctantly, but wanting to be polite, 'although I'd better be getting home soon.'

'It'll only take a minute, dear. We live right above the shop.'

Lis followed Mrs Gillespie through a narrow side door and up some perilously steep stairs.

'The children will be so pleased to meet you, Lis.'

The smell hit Lis the second Mrs Gillespie opened the creaking door to her flat. Her hand flew to her mouth as she fought the urge to gag; she'd never smelled anything like it.

Stepping into the dingy room, the cause of the odour was immediately apparent: budgies. Dozens of the brightly coloured birds covered every spare inch of the grimy flat. At first Lis was mesmerised by the spectrum of colour: blues, greens, vivid canary yellows, deep magentas. It was beautiful. Lis counted twenty birds lined up along the curtain rail. More were in the sink, pecking at the tap for drops of water. But bird seed was spilling from every surface. And, looking down, Lis saw her feet sinking into a faeces-encrusted carpet. Her stomach reflexively kicked, vomit spilling into her mouth.

'Babies! Look who it is! It's that nice little girl, Lis, I was telling you about.' Mrs Gillespie had the broadest grin on her face as an incredible green specimen landed on top of her wig.

The room was filled with chirps and whistles. So many birds chirruping together sounded like screaming. But then, one by one, the little creatures ceased their song and a thick silence fell. They regarded Lis with fierce curiosity. One brave individual fluttered over to her to get a better look. Lis backed towards the door as another attempted to land on her shoulder. She didn't understand – why had the birds stopped singing? Had she upset them?

She reached the exit, almost falling backwards down the long wooden stairs.

'Now isn't that interesting?' Mrs Gillespie said with a smile. 'You passed the test.'

'What?' Lis gasped. 'What test?'

'"Nothing special", you said, but there's more to you than meets the eye, isn't there?'

'I don't know what you mean!' Lis replied, desperate to leave.

'You will – soon enough.'

The birds started singing again and Lis's vision swam. She needed to get away from the noise and the smell. 'I'm sorry! I have to leave,' she murmured. 'Thanks for everything.'

Taking the stairs two at a time, she reached the shop and then the cool, fresh street in seconds. She drew clean, sweet air deep into her lungs, expelling the stench of the squalid flat.

The old woman was mad – worse than mad. Kitty was

right, she shouldn't listen to a word Mrs Gillespie said. Lis ran down the cobbled street, putting the hideous woman and her mysterious words as far behind her as she could.

The Watcher

That evening, Lis found herself alone in the lounge. Shattered parents, Sarah and Max had retired to bed early, leaving Lis alone in front of the widescreen TV. She aimlessly channel-hopped, trying to avoid news coverage of the ongoing investigation into Laura's murder. According to today's bulletin, the internet was to blame.

Lis had soaked in the bathtub for over an hour, but she was sure the odour of Mrs Gillespie's flat still lingered on her skin. She felt dirty, and it wasn't just the flat. Facts and fiction were starting to blur. Fact: Laura was dead; someone had nicked a book from Mrs Gillespie; Lis had had a few bad dreams. Fiction: there were once witches in Hollow Pike; Laura's murder was connected to the witchcraft; Lis's dreams were a message from the great beyond. She needed to ditch the fiction, it was threatening to drive her as mad as Mrs Gillespie.

Lis swung her legs off the leather sofa and wandered to the sliding doors that led onto the front balcony. The chill night air was biting, but she embraced it, hoping it would help clear her head. Frustration crackled through her body.

When did everything get so confusing? Just a few short years ago, Lis's life had been nothing more than ballet lessons and prize guinea pigs at the Bangor fair. Hollow Pike was supposed to be her fresh start, and although she had met some of the coolest people in town, she'd never felt this sort of fear before. Every time she closed her eyes she saw that silver hand on the tree in the copse.

Everything that had happened in Bangor, the daily feeling of dread she'd experienced on her way to school, it all suddenly seemed lightweight and inconsequential. It was just regular high school bullying: teasing, name-calling, people spitting at her. She almost longed to return. Sure, she hated everyone at school, but at least there she could pretend that none of this had happened. No one in Wales had been murdered.

A flicker of movement far below on the street drew her attention. A figure ducked down the gravelled alleyway on the opposite side of the road. It was a private, narrow lane that led to the old cottage where the neighbours lived.

The silhouette seemed to pause, looking up at the balcony. Lis waved jovially, guessing it was just Mr Carruthers, the old man from the cottage, putting the recycling out or something. But the shape didn't wave back. Instead it lingered in the shadows away from the street lights, motionless, watching.

Lis leaned over the rail, squinting to get a better look. The observer was so shrouded in darkness, it was impossible to even determine whether it was a man or a woman. Whoever it was stood mannequin-still, head slightly tipped to one side, as if they were sizing her up. Watching her. Watching her like the figure in the copse.

Something brushed against her skin and she shrieked, turning to find that Sasha had squeezed out through the gap she'd left in the door.

'Jesus!' she yelped, grabbing the dog's collar with one hand. 'You scared me to death!'

She turned back to the night. The crooked lane was empty now. The watcher was gone.

Before retreating to bed, Lis checked that every window and door in the house was securely locked.

The cafeteria stunk of chips and vinegar as Lis sat, stiller than a garden gnome, at the table with her friends. She'd bought a vegeburger, but couldn't bring herself to even raise it to her lips – her appetite appeared to be on an extended retreat.

'That was all it was? Someone nicked a book?' Jack shoved a chip in his mouth.

'Yeah, but a book about *witches*,' Lis hissed.

'Lis, you have got to relax, sweetie …' Delilah reached over the table and stroked her hand.

'Seriously,' added Kitty.

Lis leaned in close. 'There's more, though. Friday night, and this is going to sound insane, but I think there was someone watching my house.'

Her friends looked sceptical. 'Are you sure?' Kitty asked.

'Well, I thought it was the old man who lives down the road at first, but I don't think it was. This … figure … just sort of stood there, staring at me.'

'You're hot. Own it.' Jack laughed.

Lis had to laugh too at that. 'Doesn't it bother you in the slightest that there's a killer pottering around town?'

'No.' Kitty shook her head. 'Anyone who *met* Laura wanted her dead. Frankly, it's a surprise someone didn't bump her off sooner. Now, Lis, for the love of Baby Jesus, LET IT GO!'

A magical sparkle tone from Lis's handbag announced the arrival of a text message. She pulled out her phone and flipped it open. Danny. Damn, she'd forgotten all about Danny.

Hey, Lis, how's it going? U still wanna do somthin next week? D xx

'What is it, Lis?' asked Jack, peering over her shoulder.

Eyes fixed firmly on the message, Lis placed the phone on the greasy table carefully, as though it might disappear. 'It's Danny, asking about our date. He wants to do something over half-term.'

Big mistake. Her three friends exploded like a mockery bomb.

'Lis and Danny sitting in a tree ...' Delilah sang.

'Lis Marriott ... Lis London-Marriott ... Lis Marriott-London ... Ooh, sounds like a hotel!' laughed Jack.

'Oh, shut up!' Lis snapped, although she couldn't keep a smile off her face. After so many weeks, the others knew exactly how she felt about Danny. The murky fog of Laura's death lifted from the room.

'Sorry.' Kitty laughed. 'We're only teasing because you're making such a song and dance out of it!'

'Oh, I know! I can't explain it ... I mean, I've been with other guys—'

'Oh, yeah?' said Delilah suggestively, prompting hysteria from Kitty as Jack made an obscene gesture with his tongue.

'That's disgusting!' Lis laughed. 'I didn't mean it like that! It just never happened like this before. In Wales, either I wasn't keen on the guys I went out with or they weren't keen on me. This is the first time where the boy that I really like ...'

'Likes you back!' Delilah declared happily.

Lis grinned. 'I don't know why, but he seems to be pretty keen.'

'Oh, I can't think why he likes me with my luscious long hair or Bambi eyes or amazing boobs!' simpered Jack in a faux little-girl voice.

'You can sod off!' laughed Lis.

This was the most relaxed Lis had felt in some time. It felt nice, as if the last few weeks hadn't happened.

'So, are we to assume that Danny Marriott would be your *first*?' Delilah asked pointedly, calming the raucous table.

'You would, er, assume correctly.' Lis stumbled over her words a little. 'Last year in Year Ten, four girls in my class got pregnant. I'm not judging, but that's not what I want, so I'm being picky.'

'Good for you.' Jack nodded. 'Last year Gemma Cutler gave birth to a baby on the toilet ... everyone totally judged her!'

The four dissolved into peals of laughter, the girls rocking in their seats uncontrollably.

'OK, Jack. For that one, you are most definitely going to Hell!' Lis giggled.

Jack didn't reply, instead he reached across the table and grabbed her phone.

'Excuse me! What are you doing?'

'I'm replying to Danny!'

'No, you bloody aren't!'

'OK, you do it.'

All faces looked to her.

'I'm not sure whether I'm going to go on the date or not,' Lis confessed.

'Lis, why not?' Kitty asked, eyes wide. 'You've been obsessed with him since you got here. This is your big chance.'

She sighed. 'Don't get me wrong, I want to! It's just ... with all the murder stuff going on ...'

'Which is exactly why you *have* to go on the date!' commanded Jack.

'Why?'

'Keep calm and carry on and all that. You are allowed a boyfriend!'

Kitty and Delilah smiled encouragingly, signalling their agreement.

Jack went on. 'You have got to go out with Danny. You are the only one of us with a shot at a normal relationship!'

'Er, excuse us?' Delilah gestured at herself and Kitty pressed together on the canteen bench.

'Pipe down, I didn't see you two on the Pride march!' Jack said sternly.

'Really? Were you there?' retorted Kitty.

Jack shot her an evil look with a tiny wry smile on the side. 'OK, sorry! But it proves my point ... just because we're all freaks doesn't mean you can't have a nice normal boyfriend. Besides, Danny is lovely. And hot.'

Lis felt the corners of her mouth curl up a little. She'd never had friends like this. Friends who wanted to see her flourish not fade. Their eager faces were like mirrors in which she could see herself more clearly.

'Well? Are you gonna text him or am I?' Jack demanded.

'Should I?' Lis asked.

Three heads nodded enthusiastically and three mouths beamed as she tapped her reply into the phone. Like it or not, she was going on a date with Danny Marriott. And, just for the record, she liked it!

First Date

The nearest cinema to Hollow Pike was on a fading 'entertainment complex' on the outskirts of Fulton. Drizzle hung in the air as Lis waited outside the main lobby, wrapped in her red trench coat and Sarah's old scarf.

Maybe it was the promise of a week off school, or perhaps it was the time she was spending with her friends, but Lis was actually sleeping peacefully. Neither Laura nor Mrs Gillespie troubled her dreams. The tiredness was losing its grip on her and she felt better than she had in ages. She was ready as she'd ever be for her date with Danny.

How are people under legal driving age meant to have an old-fashioned date? The thought of meeting Danny on the bus had just seemed rough, so she'd agreed to meet him outside the cinema instead. Max had dropped her off early, Danny was late and Lis was starting to feel highly visible and increasingly vulnerable.

What if this date was just some sort of elaborate prank? It crossed her mind that the offer of an evening alone with rugby team Adonis, Danny Marriott, might be too good to be true. Were Danny and his friends hiding in the bushes, filming her on mobiles, ready to post on YouTube?

This was a big mistake. She'd stupidly allowed herself to believe that she was an ordinary girl, entitled to first dates and first kisses and boyfriends. Glancing at her phone for the millionth time, Lis resolved to give Danny another ten minutes before accepting that she'd been dumped even *before* the first date.

'Lis!' Danny pelted around the corner, red faced and flustered. 'So sorry I'm late!'

Lis, you're a paranoid mentalist, she told herself as he reached her position at the cinema entrance.

'That's OK. You're not that late,' she lied, confirming how much she must like him.

He hovered at her side, possibly unsure whether to kiss her. Leaning in towards her face, he gave her arm a rub before apparently mentally chastising himself and zooming in a second time to plant a dry kiss on her cheek. 'I left my wallet at home. I had to go back! Anyway, you OK?'

'Yeah, I'm cool,' she replied, immediately wondering if *cool* was still an acceptable term. 'Come on, or we'll miss the trailers.'

'You like the trailers?'

'Yeah. Sometimes they're better than the film!'

Danny smiled *that* smile, and Lis's heart fluttered. Now that he was here, her nervousness had reached epic levels.

'Nutter! Come on then!' Danny said.

They stepped through the double doors and into an olfactory assault of popcorn, body odour and tinned hotdogs. It was a long time since this place had seen a lick of paint. They crossed the chewing-gum-matted foyer to where a messy queue had formed in front of the box office.

Lis was genuinely thrilled to be seeing the exceptionally brutal sequel to *Hacksaw – Hacksaw: Torn 2 Pieces*. The first film had been unintentionally hysterical, but had also had its moments of terror. Earlier, Jack had questioned whether this was a suitable film for a first date, what with one dead girl and a killer on the loose, but Lis suspected Danny would be only too pleased to offer a shoulder to hide behind!

A life-sized cut out of the film's satanic clown, Mr Jinkie, dominated the foyer. A nervous rush ran up Lis's spine. It was ironic that she craved a good scare even after the last few days.

'I'm getting the tickets, OK?' Danny said, trying masculine confidence on for size.

'Perfect gentleman. I'm impressed,' Lis said and smiled. 'But I'm getting the popcorn, no arguments! Or are you a pick 'n' mix kinda guy?'

'In here? Can you imagine the fingers that have picked that mix? No thanks!'

Lis laughed a full, chesty laugh. So far, so good. In fact, being with Danny was surprisingly easy; it felt somehow natural.

'Popcorn it is then!' Lis decided.

The queue moved quickly and they were called to a sealed perspex booth containing a spotty, overweight guy with greasy hair stuffed under a cinema-chain baseball cap, and a name tag that said he was 'Gary'.

'Hi,' Gary said, his face devoid of any enthusiasm.

'Hi, mate,' Danny replied. 'Can we get two for *Hacksaw* please?'

Gary's bored expression barely flickered. 'ID.'

The smile fell from Danny's face. It was common knowledge that the run-down movie house let pupils into pretty much any film they wanted. It was the only reason to come to this dump rather than get the train into Leeds.

'What?' Danny asked.

Gary leaned forward a fraction. 'I said ID! I need to see some ID; *Hacksaw*'s an eighteen, mate.'

The film was due to begin in three minutes and there was still a queue of customers waiting to get in. Lis heard the couple behind them sigh loudly in impatience.

'We're both eighteen. Sorry, I left my ID at home,' said Danny, playing it cool.

'I didn't say *she* needed ID. I said *you* needed ID.'

'Oh. Well, I'm eighteen, honest.'

'Date of birth?'

He mumbled his birth date to the assistant. *Jesus, it's a good thing his Science is good, because his Maths stinks*, thought Lis, grimacing.

'Nice one, mate. That makes you seventeen,' said Gary.

'No! It makes me . . .' Danny did the calculation too late. 'Oh, OK.' His face turned red and he couldn't meet Lis's gaze, even as she took his hand in hers. She swore she could actually see his ego bruising.

He leaned closer to the ticket agent. 'Look, mate. You've just let half my year at school in. Don't be shifty!'

'Are you telling me how to do my job?'

'Not at all!'

'I hope not, you little turd.' Lis flinched at that. 'You've got three options: show me some ID, piss off, or I can do you two tickets for *Castle of Imagination*. What's it to be?'

Castle of Imagination was a new 3D animation about unicorns. No thanks.

'I think we'll piss off, actually,' Lis said before Danny could respond. 'There was no need to be so rude. I see your name is Gary. I might give your manager a ring tomorrow. Thanks.' She smiled sweetly and dragged the shell-shocked Danny towards the exit.

'Oh my God. That was so embarrassing,' Danny groaned, unable to look Lis in the eye. 'You must think I'm the biggest loser ever.'

'No, I think *that* guy's the biggest loser ever. You just need to work on your mental maths.'

Danny managed a weak smile as they passed into the fresh air of the car park. 'Yeah, what was his problem anyway?'

'He's probably a twenty-two-year-old virgin who still lives with his mum!' Lis laughed. She let Danny's hand go and turned to face him. 'Don't let him bother you, he's just jealous.' With every ounce of confidence she had, she rose up on tiptoe and gave Danny a gentle kiss, just brushing his lips. He'd looked like he needed it. A wide grin spread across his face: mission accomplished!

'Well, if he was jealous, it's only cos I'm with such a beautiful girl,' Danny told her.

Lis roared with laughter. 'Oh, that's really slick!'

'Thanks.' He returned the laugh, this time taking her hand. 'Well, the film's out, so how about dinner? If we cross the car park there's an amazing steak house. It has the best food, like, in the world!'

She frowned sympathetically. 'Danny . . . I'm vegetarian!'

He slapped a flat palm to his forehead. 'Kill me now! Shall I just call a cab?'

'No!' Lis grinned. 'You weren't to know. I have a better idea . . .'

'Is that Garlic Bread or Garlic Bread *Extreme?*' asked the surly waitress, a student Lis recognised from Fulton High Sixth Form.

'Oh, I think Extreme. Lis, can you handle Garlic Bread Extreme?' Danny grinned.

'Extreme is my middle name, baby!'

'Extreme it is!'

The waitress rolled her eyes and slouched away from the table. A children's party consisting of at least ten nine-year-olds occupied the next booth, and the kids were repeatedly running past Lis and Danny in a bid to get to the ice-cream machine. Pizza Factory was such a classy place – Delilah had worked there last summer, apparently, but quit after less than a week because she couldn't take the screaming kids.

'I am so sorry about this.' Danny leaned across the Formica table. 'This is so not the evening I had in mind.'

'It's fine,' Lis told him for the fiftieth time. 'Actually, this is maybe better.'

Danny laughed. 'I seriously doubt that!'

'I mean it. We can talk here. We couldn't have done that at the cinema.'

'True. So what do you wanna talk about?' he asked, his sapphire eyes sparkling more than ever. Lis took that to be a sign he was enjoying himself, despite the dayglo restaurant.

'You,' she replied honestly. This was the first time in what felt like decades that she hadn't been preoccupied with dead girls and nightmares.

'Me?'

'Yeah. Everyone knows all about me – I'm the weird Welsh new girl. And that was before Laura's stunt.' She stopped herself as soon as Laura's name crossed her lips. This wasn't the time or place to get onto her. 'But what about you?'

'What *about* me? There's really nothing to know.' He raised his palms, a wide-eyed open book. Almost.

'As if! No one's that straightforward.'

'Oh, really? What's *your* secret?'

Lis frowned involuntarily and for a second she wondered if he somehow knew. No, it was just paranoia again. 'Don't change the subject. We're talking about you,' she chided.

'OK, but there really isn't much to know ... I have four sisters and I'm the only boy.'

'Wow, your house must be hormonal fun!' Lis laughed.

'Tell me about it! And I'm the youngest, so I'm a constant target. But it's cool. Helena and Abby have moved out now, so it's not as mental as it used to be.'

'You think your parents kept going 'til they had a boy?'

'That's exactly what they did!' he laughed. 'I'm the blessed boy-child! Must have been a big disappointment there ...'

Lis sensed the walls coming down a little. So far, Danny had been on full entertainment mode, like a TV presenter or something, now he suddenly seemed more real.

'What makes you say that?' she asked.

'I don't know. I'm just not sure I'm what my dad wanted in a son,' he mumbled. 'God, this is depressing. Let's move on!'

'No, I know what you mean. I'm not sure my mum gets me much either.'

There was a moment of silence and suddenly they were the only pair in the whole world, the noisy restaurant slipping away.

'I suppose that's the trouble with kids ...' Danny murmured, 'you never know what you're going to get.'

'Is that why you joined the rugby team?' Lis asked in a low voice, hoping she wasn't being too bold. 'To please your dad?'

'Totally! I only did it cos he promised he'd let me go to this massive *Star Wars* convention in London if I did.'

'Hold on a sec, that *is* too much information!' Lis laughed.

Good-naturedly, he returned her humour, 'I know, right? But, anyway, it turns out that I'm really good at rugby *and* really enjoy it. Random or what?'

'That is fairly random, but it's great that it suits you, and your dad.'

'You'd think, wouldn't you? Nah, he just found something else to give me grief about!' Danny frowned. 'Christ, I'm not really doing much to impress you tonight, am I?'

'Danny, I moved two hundred miles to live with my sister! My family life is hardly picture perfect. Hell, I haven't even *seen* my dad since I was eleven.'

'Lucky you!'

They both laughed, wallowing in the shared ground they had found. Just as Danny reached across the table to take her hand, the waitress smacked the Garlic Bread Extreme right on top of his arm.

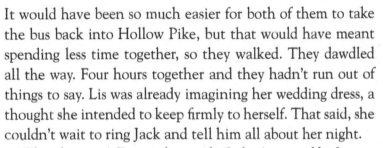

It would have been so much easier for both of them to take the bus back into Hollow Pike, but that would have meant spending less time together, so they walked. They dawdled all the way. Four hours together and they hadn't run out of things to say. Lis was already imagining her wedding dress, a thought she intended to keep firmly to herself. That said, she couldn't wait to ring Jack and tell him all about her night.

'The thing is,' Danny beamed, 'I don't even *like* horror films! I only said *Hacksaw* because I knew you wanted to see it!'

'What's wrong with horror films? They're fun!'

'I just think they're … nasty! I mean, who wants to see people being chopped up and stuff?' He casually grasped Lis's hand as they meandered up the hill towards Sarah's house.

'I do. It's a rush!' Lis replied.

'You like being scared?' he asked with disbelief.

'I'm getting used to it …' Had that been too weird? She scolded herself mentally for letting her mouth run away with itself.

'Well, you're safe and sound with me,' Danny said, pulling himself up tall.

Lis glanced at him. He had such a kind face; she couldn't

take her eyes off it, studying the rise and fall of his bone structure.

'This is my house,' she said as they reached the drive. Her stomach was full of butterflies; it was time for goodbye, and as much as she hated the thought of it, who knew what might come by way of a parting gesture?

Danny turned to her and took both of her hands in his. 'God, your hands are like ice cubes!'

'Sorry.' She smiled as sweetly as she could, tilting her face towards his.

'Lis, I've had such a cool night, even though everything went wrong! I promise as soon as *Hacksaw* comes out on DVD ...'

'Forget about it! I had a really good time too.' She moved her body a daring inch closer.

'I think you're awesome,' he muttered. 'If you want to go out again next week or something . . ?'

'Yeah, I'd like that a lot.' This was becoming hard work. She traced her toe around his foot, careful to make contact.

'Cool! Well I'll see you at school, obviously, so we can sort something out then.'

'Danny?'

'Yeah?'

'This is where you're meant to give me a goodnight kiss.'

'Oh, OK, I wondered when I was meant to do that bit!' He smiled, a wide, fantastic smile and then finally leaned forwards, his lips coming to meets hers.

Lis felt his warm, moist, beautiful mouth press against her own. She closed her eyes and it was as though all the feeling in her body had moved to her lips, sensing every intimate detail of the kiss. He moved his hands to her waist. Electricity ran up and down her spine at the tenderness of his touch. Even through her coat she could feel glorious heat coming from his hands, and couldn't help imagining how they would feel on her skin.

He drew her nearer, closing the distance between them as she slid her arms around his neck. The kiss intensified. She wanted it to go on and on and on.

'Oi!' came a loud Welsh voice. 'Don't you need a license for that sort of behaviour?'

Danny pulled back at once and Lis looked up to see Sarah standing on the front balcony, waving at them with a mischievous smile on her face. Luckily, Danny saw the funny side and laughed loudly, daring a shy wave back at her sister.

Sarah winked theatrically at Lis before heading back inside the house.

'Danny, I am so sorry about her.' Lis felt her cheeks turning pink. 'That's my sister.' *And she is so dead*, Lis added privately.

'It's OK. She seems nice. Plus, I *was* getting a little carried away . . .'

Lis felt her heart thump against her ribs, threatening to bounce clear out of her chest. *He'd felt it too!*

'So was I,' she murmured. 'I should probably head in – and kill her . . .'

Danny leaned in once more and gave her a much less risky kiss, his mouth pressing briefly against hers.

'Goodnight, Lis. I'm gonna be thinking about you all day tomorrow.'

'Yeah, right!'

He kissed her one last time, grinned like a lunatic and then turned and walked away, leaving her smiling and happy on the drive.

'Sarah Harvey, where are you?' Lis yelled, racing into the house and slamming the door behind her. 'That was so embarrassing! I could have died!'

Sarah feigned nonchalance, pretending to leaf through a magazine on the sofa in the lounge. 'So that was Danny?'

Lis paused in front of her, hands on hips, trying to muster anger but finding it lacking; the night had been too incredible to waste time being cross. Sarah looked up from the magazine, with a grin that Lis couldn't resist.

'Oh, Sarah, I had the best night!'

'I know, I saw!'

Lis threw herself onto the couch next to her sister. 'I meant before that bit! We went for a meal and just talked and talked about his family and his life and . . . just . . . everything! It was awesome. We're going out again next week.'

'Just one piece of advice, Lis, love. Garlic on a first date? Rookie mistake!'

'Do I stink?'

'You reek, hon! I hope he had some—' Sarah stopped abruptly.

'What?'

Sarah sat forwards, grabbing the TV remote from the arm of the sofa. Lis twisted to see the late evening news on the wide-screen. Filling the rectangle was Laura.

A middle-aged anchorman spoke to the left of her stunning image: the same school photo that had been so proudly displayed at her memorial.

'The parents of murdered schoolgirl, Laura Rigg, today made an emotional appeal for witnesses to come forward. Gita Nersessian reports from North Yorkshire.'

The image faded to one of those standard police set-ups you see on the news every day. A panel of tired-looking people sat in front of a screen displaying a regional police force logo. There were sporadic flashes and clicks from cameras, and journalists pointed microphones. At the centre of the panel sat Kitty's father with Laura's parents.

Sarah reached across the sofa and took Lis's hand. 'Do you want me to turn it off?' she asked gently.

'No,' Lis replied, taking the remote and turning up the volume.

'It has been over a week since the body of Hollow Pike teenager, Laura Rigg, was found at a local beauty spot, but police are yet to make an arrest. Today the parents of the deceased, Ian and Jennifer Rigg, made this heartfelt plea . . .'

There was a close up of a distraught woman in her early forties. She *was* Laura, only twenty-five years older: same hair, face, eyes. It was chilling.

'We have lost the most precious thing in our world,' she said, her voice shaking.

Next to her was a solid, handsome man, a George Clooney type. *Definitely* the same man Lis had seen on the street fighting with Laura. He wrapped an arm around his wife protectively.

Jennifer Rigg continued, 'We need to know what happened to our daughter. We won't rest until we know. Someone out there *must* know something, *must* be protecting someone. It's gone on long enough . . . Please come forward and contact the police. Please!'

Lis pressed the red button and the screen went black. Her buzz had been sucked into the television.

Without saying a word, she stood and took herself up to bed. Sarah looked on, speechless.

Once in her bedroom, Lis peeled off her coat and threw it over the chaise longue. She curled into a ball on her bed. Guilt. That familiar guilt was back again.

Tonight she'd experienced something so rare with Danny:

a perfect first kiss. There would be no more first kisses for Laura Rigg. She'd had her last kiss weeks ago and had never even realised. She'd thought she had a long life, bursting with kisses, ahead of her. Not any more.

Lis understood the whole 'death is a part of life' philosophy, but it meant nothing right now. She didn't know why she should feel so bad about life when Laura was dead, but she did. The nightly news had sent her a timely reminder, just as she was on the verge of being happy. From the depths of her handbag she heard a tiny twinkle. Sighing and leaning over the edge of the bed, she dragged the bag to her and dug out her phone.

One new message. From Danny: *I meant it – I can't stop thinking about you! Sweet dreams xxx*

He'd meant every word. She'd be safe and sound with him. Although she knew it was a little selfish, Lis couldn't help feeling a certain lightness inside. Her heartbeat quickened, and, closing her eyes, she smiled and replayed the kiss in her head.

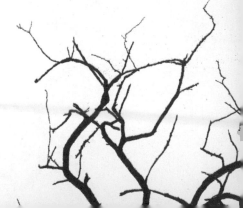

Part Three

*The devil is more eager and keen to tempt
the good than the wicked . . . therefore
the devil tries all the harder to seduce
all the more saintly girls*

THE MALLEUS MALEFICARUM, 1486

Offerings

The best way to tell if a boy is a virgin is to engage him in a conversation about sex, as Lis discovered the Monday after the half-term break.

'I think it went pretty well ...' she told Jack.

'Did you have sex with him?'

'Jack!' screamed Lis, as they walked towards their lockers. 'Do you mind?'

'OMG you did! What was it like?'

'Jack!'

'Well, is that a yes or a no?' he demanded, grinning salaciously.

'It's a no, you pervert!'

The hallway seemed especially downbeat that morning. First day back after the holidays, and it looked as if most of the pupils were already counting the weeks, days and hours until Christmas. The week off had gone far too quickly for Lis's liking; her body had reacted angrily when her alarm had gone off at 7 a.m. The only saving grace was that she would get to see Danny again.

Laura's funeral had come and gone during the holiday. It had barely made a blip on the news; some other, newer atrocity was more exciting for the TV channels. People were quietly forgetting about Laura Rigg.

'I was only asking!' Jack protested. 'Have you arranged a second date yet?'

Lis scrunched her face slightly. 'No. He's been texting all the time, but he hasn't actually asked me out again. I'm starting to worry.'

'Why would he be texting if he wasn't interested? Chillax.'

'I will as long as you never use the word "chillax" again!'

Jack smiled, stopping at his locker, onto which someone had kindly scratched the word 'faggot'. He pulled out a sealed envelope.

'What's that?' Lis asked.

'My weekly excuse for not doing PE. Mum's stopped fighting it. This week I have a bad back. Next week, who knows?'

'You'll have to do it at some point,' Lis laughed. How come she was the only one of her group who actually participated in PE?

'When Mr Coleman stops referring to me as "Dolly Denton", I'll start doing PE!' Jack told her.

Lis's stomach growled. 'Do you wanna head to the canteen?'

'Yeah, cool, I'm starving.'

'OK.' Lis sighed. 'I'll just get my kit ready for next session. *Some of us* have netball.' They moved down to her locker, ominously close to where Laura's was now sealed up with wasp-coloured police tape. Both fell silent. The tape made the red box look like a gift-wrapped Christmas present.

'That's grim,' Jack said, chewing on a nail. 'What do you think was in there?'

'I don't know.' Lis paused, fumbling for her padlock key in her bag. 'I guess the police cleared it out.' Only then did she see the padlock on her locker hanging open. She unhooked it and gave it a squeeze. The lock was broken, refusing to click shut.

'What's up?'

'My padlock's broken ...' Her voice trailed off, her hand reaching for the handle. Broken or *been* broken? Her heart was suddenly in her mouth. She started to open the locker door.

'Lis ... Maybe we should—'

A messy black shape swung out at her. Lis could only freeze as her mind tried to process the image. It was Jack who cried out first, jumping away as if he'd seen a shark's fin in the water.

Crudely stapled to the inside of the locker door was a dead crow, its wings grotesquely snapped open, crucified. Feathers tumbled from her locker and scarlet blood had soaked into her PE kit and textbooks. The bird's lifeless eyes gazed at her accusingly.

It took Lis a second, but then she screamed.

She fell back into Jack's arms, flooring him, as Ms Dandehunt emerged from her office.

'What on earth is all this noise?' she started, but seeing the terrified pair flailing about on the floor, she crouched to help them.

Mr Gray flew out of G2 and reached Lis at the same time. By now they were attracting attention from milling pupils.

'Lis?' Mr Gray grabbed her by both shoulders, trying to steady her. 'What's happened? Tell me!'

'Look,' she hissed. 'My locker!'

Ms Dandehunt looked up at the locker.

Mr Gray teased open the door, before whipping it shut again in disgust. 'What the—' he gasped. 'Lis, Jack, are you OK?'

Jack nodded, dumbstruck.

Lis struggled to her feet. 'Yeah. I'll be fine.' It was sick, what kind of person would do that? With the teachers there, she felt calmer, but dirty, very dirty. She had dry blood on her hands, sticky and brown. 'Can I go and wash my hands?'

Mr Gray looked to Ms Dandehunt, who nodded approval.

'Yeah, sure. I'll get someone to sort this out for you,' Mr Gray told her. 'Jack, will you make sure she's OK?'

'Of course,' he said quietly, cripplingly shy in front of the teachers.

'God, why would someone do that?' Mr Gray grimaced.

Ms Dandehunt took another peek inside the locker. She pursed her lips thoughtfully. 'Hmm,' was all she added.

As Jack led Lis away, she threw a glance back at the crow. She could think of only one reason why there would be such a morbid gift in her locker: it was a warning. From someone who knew she'd been seen somewhere she should never have been.

Even after a shower, the unclean feeling lingered. In her mind's eye, blood still coated her fingers. Lis wrapped her soaking hair inside a twisted towel and flopped down on her bed. Grabbing a Spanish textbook, she hoped to fill her head with the language, blocking recurring flashbacks of the mangled crow. Her paranoia was working overtime. All she could think was that it was a message from the phantom in their video, the hand on the tree – *I saw you, keep your mouth shut.*

Jack's locker had been fine, and she'd texted Kitty and Delilah. They hadn't got a warning. Just her. She'd been chosen specially.

Lis released the towel, letting her damp locks fall down

her back. Someone tapped on the door and she jumped, knocking a cup of tea off her dresser. She couldn't go on like this. 'Come in,' she said, mopping up the spill with a handful of tissues.

'You left your phone downstairs in your bag, honey. It keeps ringing,' Sarah announced, holding the phone out.

It *had* to be Danny. Lis crossed the room in a second. 'Thanks, Sarah.' She raised her mobile to her ear, her heart pounding. 'Hello?'

'Hi, darling. It's Delilah.'

Lis's face fell and she had to steady herself against the bed. She was pleased to hear from Delilah, but it was Danny she really wanted to call her.

'How are you feeling? Any better?' Delilah asked.

'Oh, hey. Getting there. Two showers,' Lis told her.

'Oh, you poor thing. Jack described it. It sounds simply horrific.'

'Yeah, it was. I just don't get why someone would do that.' She tucked her legs underneath her. 'Do you think it's a Laura thing?'

There was a pause on the other end of the line. 'I honestly don't know, darling. It could just be a very, very sick joke.'

'You don't really buy that, do you?'

'No,' Delilah admitted. 'There are only two things I don't believe in and coincidence is one of them.'

'What's the other?'

'The government.'

Lis managed a wry laugh at that.

'Darling, this might not be a random bird. It could be like an offering. A sacrifice.'

Lis scowled. What was it with the people in this town? 'What?'

'You know, Pagans, witchcraft, Satanism ... Some spells require an offering. A *blood* offering.'

'A blood offering to my locker?'

Delilah snorted down the phone. 'It was only a theory. The sacrifice is usually to the Horned God. After you mentioned witches, I started to think there might be something in it, that's all.'

'Yeah, well, witches are one of the things *I* don't believe in, at least I don't *think* I do,' Lis said, increasingly uncertain.

'Darling, you shouldn't be so closed minded; it's so last season,' Delilah purred.

Two pieces of a puzzle connected in Lis's mind. 'Dee? Did you take the book from Mrs Gillespie's shop – An Occult History of Hollow Pike?'

'No,' Delilah mumbled. 'Not guilty.'

Lis sat up straight on the very edge of her bed, suddenly tense again. 'Do you think Kitty could have it?'

'It's not really her thing, is it? You don't *still* think we had anything to do with Laura's murder, do you?'

Lis shook her head. 'No, no, of course not.'

'We'll get to the bottom of this, I promise,' said Dee. 'There's nothing to worry about. *If* there was someone else in the woods, they certainly don't want to be found out, do they? Why would they draw attention to themselves by leaving dead things in your locker? It doesn't add up. The police will catch Laura's killer. Until then, we lay low. Quiet as mice.'

Sighing, Lis flopped back onto the bed. 'OK. I can do that.'

'Good, now sleep tight. Sweet dreams, my love.' Delilah blew her an air kiss and hung up.

Lis massaged her aching temples. Rolling over, she buried her face in the pillow, muffling a scream that kicked inside her like a wild horse. When was she going to wake up from this nightmare?

At the other end of the line, Delilah hung up on her friend and gently put her mobile phone down – on top of an old, leather-bound volume entitled *An Occult History of Hollow Pike*.

The Babysitter

The tall, stained-glass windows scattered beams of multi-coloured light throughout the cavernous library. Lis wistfully watched tiny specks of dust pirouette through the rays. Now that it was November, more and more pupils were piling into the study rooms, escaping the exposed outside areas. It was becoming a struggle to maintain their hold over the toasty cushion corner, however much Daphne, the librarian, tried to reserve it for them.

Alone at a study bench, Lis flicked through her Spanish textbook, reading a feature on Mexico City. The Aztec ruins looked incredible – what was left of them. She imagined a time when she'd have the money to go exploring. How far away would that be? Ten years? Fifteen? An optimistic fragment of her mind allowed her to imagine that by then, the albatross that was Laura Rigg might have unwound itself from around her shoulders. Christ, she had a new-found understanding for Lady Macbeth – guilt sucks, and she hadn't even murdered anyone.

A pair of hands covered her eyes. 'Guess who?'

'Banquo?'

Danny sat down next to her, obviously baffled. 'What?'

'Never mind,' she told him, thrilled to see him. '*You* never text. I was waiting up all last night!'

'Sorry. Match against Blackheath Grammar. We lost.'

Lis giggled, did he think she was one of *those* girls? 'I'm kidding! Sorry about the match.'

'Nah, it's OK. And I did mean to text, honestly. I wanna know when you're free.'

Across the room, Daphne raised a finger to her lips before wagging it at them.

'Whenever,' Lis admitted. She was so over playing games. 'The last thing I need is me-time right now.'

His heavy brows dipped. 'What's up?'

Lis shrugged, not knowing how to put it into words. 'Uh, where to start? You heard about the dead bird in my locker? All a bit scary.'

'Yeah. I'm sorry. It was probably Connor O'Grady; he's proper mental. Why don't we do something tonight to take your mind off it? I'll keep an eye on you!' he said with a grin.

She pouted. 'I can't. I'm babysitting my nephew.'

Danny wrinkled his nose for a second. 'OK, what if I came over to help? Would your sister mind? We could watch a DVD or something.'

In Bangor, DVD had been code for only one thing. 'Oh, yeah?'

'Not like that!' So DVD meant the same thing here, then. 'I'll behave. I could download *Hacksaw 2* for us,' Danny suggested. 'Highly illegal, but you're worth it!'

Lis smiled – Danny was once again taking the edge off her problems. 'Sounds like a plan,' she told him. 'But *I'm* not promising to behave . . .'

What to wear for a DVD/babysitting date? Everything she'd tested looked try-hard. In the end, Lis stole Max's ancient *Guns N' Roses* tour T-shirt and stuck it over some leggings:

slouchy, cool and a little bit rock. She'd put Logan to bed already and now waited in her room, calming music playing in the background. Danny would be here in about an hour. *Deep breaths, Lis, deep breaths.*

Standing in front of the mirror, she messed her hair up, eager to look like she hadn't spent an hour getting ready. Downstairs, she heard a clatter of paws and raucous barking as Sasha tripped over her own legs to get to the door. Oh, God. He was early.

Lis crossed the hall and skipped down the stairs, swinging off the banister and into the kitchen. And then she frowned; Sasha was bouncing up and down at the *back* door. The porch had one door leading to the drive and another that connected to the back terrace. But there was no access to the back garden from the street. Then she realised she hadn't heard the doorbell, just Sasha. Odd.

'What's up, you crazy dog? You wanna go out?' She opened the door, putting it on the latch. A blast of cold November air flooded the house.

Sasha pelted onto the patio, barking like a thing demented. She shot up the stairs that led onto the back terrace, the one outside Lis's bedroom. Lis stepped onto the dark patio, the paving slabs icy through her socks.

'Sasha, do not run off,' she called. 'Do your business and get back inside!'

The rotating clothes line screeched as it turned in the breeze, a few old towels hanging on the line. Lis rubbed her arms against the bitter cold while Sasha continued to bark at the top of the garden stairs. With a glance back at the house to make sure she hadn't locked herself out, Lis jogged up the steps. The family dog was barking at shadows, a perfect little sentry. Thinking back to the shadows outside her bedroom all those weeks ago, Lis scanned the garden carefully. The only movement was Logan's plastic windmill twirling in the breeze.

'What has gotten into you?' Lis grabbed Sasha's collar. 'Come back in!'

Dragging the reluctant, shaggy creature behind her, Lis descended the stairs and pulled the dog back into the house. 'Stupid animal,' she said, ruffling her fur. She slammed the door shut and dropped the latch. As an afterthought she twisted the key to the mortice lock, just to be on the safe side, then pulled the keys out of both front and back doors and drifted back into the kitchen, tossing them into the fruit bowl where keys lived.

Checking the kitchen clock, she saw she had fifty minutes until Danny was due to arrive. What was she meant to do with herself until then? Pace? *Glee*, that was the answer. Episodes of *Glee* always chilled her out. Wiping her clammy hands on her T-shirt she entered the lounge and turned the TV on.

But Sasha's weird behaviour continued. She was now darting between the windows of the house, trying to look out into the night.

Lis wasn't about to let a hyper dog ruin her evening with Danny. 'That's enough,' she said affectionately. 'In your basket.'

She led the dog through to the conservatory, just off the lounge, where her basket was kept. 'Go to sleep, you nutcase.' Leaving Sasha, she re-entered the lounge. 'Right, what was I doing? Oh, DVD.'

She scurried up the stairs and burst into her room, locating the *Glee* box set on her bookshelf. She pulled it out and turned to leave. Only then did she notice that something was wrong. Even in the dim light of her bedroom lamp, she could see subtle changes. Her wardrobe door was ajar. The drawers in the chest by the door were pulled open – just an inch or so, but she always pushed them shut or they looked untidy. Even in a rush, she *always* pushed them shut. *Someone had been in her room.*

Her stomach turned over. Was there any way she could have done it? No. Had Sarah been in her room? No. Her hand flew to her mouth. The back door. She'd left it wide open while she fetched the dog. Oh, God.

She punched the off switch on the iPod dock. The house was silent, save for the noisy TV downstairs. Her eyes fell on the centimetre gap in her wardrobe door. No one could fit in there with all her clothes, could they? She looked around her room, grabbing a wrought iron candlestick from her desk.

She felt lightheaded and realised she'd stopped breathing. Eyes watering, she took a step towards the wardrobe. Her finger traced the line of the open door. Like ripping off a plaster, Lis flung the door open and stepped back, raising the candlestick, ready to strike. Nothing. Just a rail of coats and dresses. She pulled the clothes aside, but she already knew nobody could fit in there.

She heard a creak downstairs. A foot weighing heavy on a floorboard. *They were in the house.* Where was her phone? She had to call the police. Her mobile was nowhere to be seen. What had she done with it? She had to get out of the house! That's what she always screamed at those girls in horror films – *get out of the house!* She considered the French windows onto the terrace. No, that way only led into the copse.

She inched onto the landing. The coast was clear. The doors to the study and Logan's room were dark. Oh, Lord, Logan! Forgetting her own safety, she dashed into his nursery. Inside, a dainty night-light twirled, casting fairy tale silhouettes over the ceiling. In his cot, her nephew was fast asleep. Lis closed her eyes and let out a shaky breath. He was safe and sound.

There was a crash. It sounded further away, like a door banging. A glimmer of courage ignited in her gut. She had to know who had been in the house, get a look at them. Instinct told her this was the watcher – the one from outside her home. Maybe the one from behind the trees. She closed the door to Logan's room and tiptoed towards the stairs, still gripping the candle holder. Looking into the lounge she saw it just as she'd left it: TV blaring. Sasha in the conservatory. There was no motion and no shadows to hide in. From the lounge there was access to the balcony, but that was always locked, except on the hottest summer days. That left only the kitchen as an escape route.

She slipped down the stairs and through the saloon doors into the kitchen. It was lit up like Christmas, white light gleaming off the stainless steel surfaces. Crouching down, she looked under the kitchen table: nothing. What's more, both the front and back doors were deadlocked, the keys jumbled up in the messy fruit bowl where she'd thrown them. There was only one remaining option.

Behind her, the internal door leading down to Sarah's workshop stood ajar. A black two-inch gap leered at her. She rested the candlestick on the counter and pulled a kitchen knife from the block, the cool blade flashing in the light.

The cellar door groaned as she pulled it fully open. The stairs descended into a still, dark underworld. Lis pressed the light switch and far below strip lights flickered into action, filling the room with a jittery blueish glow. Knife in front of her, she crept down the first two steps. From this angle she still couldn't see into the basement. Anything could await her. This was Hollow Pike, after all.

Squatting down, she took the last steps like a tiger, ready to pounce. The smell of sawdust and varnish was overpowering; normally she loved the aroma, but not tonight. In the murky light, Lis made out four vintage wardrobes, all ready for Sarah to restore, all with their doors ajar. She backed away from them, leaning on the wall. This was a nightmare. Four empty boxes standing like coffins. An urge to laugh, or cry, or both shook her body.

This was a mistake. She should turn, run up those stairs and straight out the door. Her mind was screaming at her to get out, yet her feet carried her towards the first wardrobe. With the carving knife outstretched, she reached towards the edge of the door ...

There was a loud clatter to her right. Lis yelped, slicing through the air with the blade. She ducked behind the wardrobe. Another crash. Peeking out, Lis saw the workshop window wide open, the wind swinging it to and fro so that it slammed against the frame. That's how he'd got out, then. Lis tore over to the window and peered outside. She saw only Max's van on the tarmac, but somewhere in the distance, she heard footsteps sprinting across gravel.

An hour later, Lis clutched a cup of tea to her chest. She, Delilah and Jack sat in the lounge, each coiled like a too-tight spring.

'So what on earth did you tell Danny?' Delilah asked.

Lis shrugged. 'I said I had a migraine and needed to sleep. He sounded gutted, like I was ditching him.'

'You did the right thing. He'll understand,' Dee told her.

'You must have been terrified,' Jack said. 'I'd have been straight out the door, screaming "murderer, murderer!" at the top of my voice!'

'I had to know who it was. I couldn't stop myself,' Lis replied, seeing her actions now for what they had been – insane. The odd thing was, it hadn't been Danny she'd wanted afterwards. She'd needed her friends, the ones who'd been there *that* night.

'I wonder what they were looking for,' Delilah said, playing absent-mindedly with her hair.

'I have no idea.' Lis sipped her tea. 'I don't think anything's missing.'

Kitty smashed through the back door, swinging a torch in one hand and holding Sasha's lead in the other. 'Nothing. There's no one around, Lis. Whoever it was, they're long gone. I'm sorry.'

'Not your fault.'

'We'll stay the night though. Make sure you're safe,' Kitty promised.

Lis mulled over her words. 'The only way I'm going to feel safe is if we catch whoever this is.'

Delilah joined her girlfriend on the sofa. 'What do you mean?'

'The police aren't getting anywhere fast and tonight someone was *in my room*! Anything could have happened! We were there that night. We're the only ones who know what happened.'

'But we didn't see anything,' Kitty pointed out in a matter-of-fact tone.

Lis stood in the centre of the rug, making an impassioned speech to her friends, like a politician starting a rousing election campaign. 'There was someone in the copse and they *saw us*. Think about it. If *you'd* killed Laura and seen a load of kids filming you in the woods, what would your first instinct be?'

'To find them and kill them,' Jack said flatly. All colour had seeped from his face.

'My thoughts exactly,' Lis said grimly. 'But why isn't any of this shit happening to you?'

Delilah said very quietly, 'What if he's working his way through us, one at a time?'

'Oh, God,' Jack cried. 'You don't think that's true?'

Lis continued. 'Someone stuck that crow in my locker. Look what happened to Laura! I don't want to end up the same way. We have to find out who's doing this.'

Jack wrung his hands. 'Lis, that's crazy. What can we do?'

'Is it?' Kitty replied. 'We couldn't do a *worse* job than my dad. He's clueless.'

'Please, Jack,' Lis begged. 'I want my life back. It's never going to happen with all this madness going on.'

'Lis is right,' Delilah threw in her vote. 'If we want any semblance of normality we need to find Laura's killer. Before he, or she, strikes again. Until then, we're all in danger.'

All eyes fell on Jack who squirmed under the intense scrutiny. He was scared, and rightly so. Lis was scared too. Petrified. But Victim-Lis was in exile. It was time to fight fire with fire. 'Come on, Jack. I need you.'

'Sod it, I'm in,' he announced. 'I must be mad.'

Lis took a deep breath, not sure what she'd signed herself up for. It was terrifying, but she couldn't have another night like this one. What was she meant to do? Hide behind her friends for the rest of her life? She needed to be by herself without checking every shadow, looking under every bed. This was the only way. 'Excellent. So ... where do we start?'

Kitty sat up. 'I think we need to know everything the police know ... Dad's been bringing files home with him. Give it a little while longer and practically the whole case will be at my place, and then … Who's up for a sleepover at the Chief Inspector's house?'

That night, once Sarah and Max had returned and her friends had gone home, Lis nervously re-entered her room. Maybe refusing Kitty and Delilah's offer to stay over had been premature, but she hadn't relished the prospect of being a third wheel in her own bedroom.

Lis inspected the open drawers. Why would someone want to rummage through her room? What were they hoping to find? All she had in there was T-shirts. It all seemed so random – or like she was missing something blindingly obvious. She sighed. She hadn't mentioned the intruder to Max and Sarah, not wanting to worry them, but worry buzzed incessantly around her skull like a trapped fly.

Slipping out of her clothes and into her PJs, Lis pulled back the duvet. Tonight was definitely a 'sleep with the light on' night. Lis rolled into bed and, as she always did, slid her hands under the pillow to warm them. Only when her fingers brushed against something hairy, did she yelp and snatch them back. God, what now? First a crow … but this felt smaller, like an insect or something.

Hardly daring to breathe, Lis lifted her pillow. It was just a couple of twigs. Weird. Lifting them closer, she saw it was actually three sprigs of lavender bound together with a tatty black ribbon. The scent was strong. If it hadn't been for the ribbon, she'd have assumed this was something Sasha had dragged in from the garden, but paws can't bind flowers together.

Only hands can.

The Laura Files

Jack scratched his head, confused. 'So there were no witches?'

'We're not sure,' said Delilah. 'The girls were doing *something* in the woods, but they deny it was witchcraft.'

Kitty grinned. 'It might have been your usual seventeenth-century forest hijinks: Spin the Bottle, I Have Never!'

Jack slung his copy of *The Crucible* to one side. 'So what was all the fuss about then?'

'That's the whole point of the play. When little Betty gets sick, everyone wants someone to blame – so they blamed the so-called witches. It's about fear of the unknown,' Delilah said, chewing her pencil.

'It's blagging my head,' Jack sighed. 'Do we have to do this now? Can't we watch a film or something?'

They were all in Kitty's attic. The four of them lay like caterpillars in sleeping bags, nestled amidst empty pizza boxes.

'I should be writing my *Crucible* essay . . .' Lis worried from her prime position on the leather sofa. Two weeks had passed with no further incidents. Boring had never been so welcome, but she knew she should really attempt homework at some point.

Jack guffawed at that. 'No thanks. We have ice cream and we have DVDs. Why would we work? We deserve a little down time!'

'Fair enough.' Lis caved. 'I'll have another bowlful then.'
She lifted the tub from Delilah's hand.

'Sod it, shall we just watch *Mean Girls* again?' Jack
suggested.

'Yes! I vote for that,' Delilah cried, clapping her hands.

There were similar murmurs of approval from Kitty. Jack
slotted the disc into the machine and joined Lis on the sofa.

This feels so good, Lis thought. After endless hours of worry,
it was a blessed relief to be doing the same thing that every
other fifteen-year-old on the planet was doing. Of course, as
soon as the house was quiet, they would be doing something
else entirely: playing Nancy Drew. 'What time is it?' she
asked.

'Just gone eleven,' Dee replied.

'What time do you think your parents will be asleep?'

Kitty considered the question. 'Hmm. It won't be long.
But we need to make sure. If we get caught . . .'

Lis nodded. 'And you're sure the stuff will be here?'

'Dad's been bringing work home every night since Laura
died. There's a *ton* of stuff in his study now.'

'OK.'

'Let's go after the film's finished,' Jack suggested. 'The coast
should be clear by then.'

'Good luck concentrating.' Delilah rolled onto her front.

Jack pressed *Play*, and Lis tried not to think about the fate
that had befallen their very own *mean girl*.

By half-past one the house was silent and dark as the friends
emerged from the attic room. Kitty led the way by torchlight
as they tiptoed through the sleeping house. They must have
looked so comical, straight out of *Scooby Doo*, but it didn't

seem funny at all. Lis felt acutely sick, although Keith Monroe's snores reverberating through the walls brought her some peace of mind.

Clinging to one another in a human train they made it past the bedroom level and edged down the stairs. Kitty indicated they should miss out a creaky step just before the next landing.

Soon they were outside the study. Kitty depressed the handle and oh-so-gently inched the door open. It whined and Kitty cursed it under her breath, stopping as soon as there was a gap big enough for them to slide through.

Once inside, she shut the door behind them and flicked on a tall corner lamp. The office was a shrine to golf, with clubs, trophies and memorabilia cluttering the space.

'OK, we'll need to keep our voices down,' Kitty said softly.

'What are we looking for?' Jack whispered.

In the centre of the room stood a large mahogany desk, piled with Manila folders. 'These,' Kitty said, picking up one of the folders. 'The case files.'

Keith Monroe had apparently been working on the investigation well into the night; three mugs containing the dregs of black coffee surrounded the notes.

'Don't mess anything up,' Kitty warned. 'If we put things back in the wrong order, we're dead, and Dad could lose his job if anyone found out.'

Delilah lifted a folder off the pile and handed it to Lis. 'Knock yourself out, darling.'

Lis found an empty section of floor where she could study her folder. Did she really want to know what was inside? Yes! Taking a deep breath, she flipped the file open. Mistake. The first thing she saw was Laura's dead face. Close up. Blue-white skin, eyes wide open, staring into nothing. Mud and gravel studded her face like dirty jewels.

Lis did nothing, said nothing, frozen before the image. God knows how long she stared at the photo. It felt like hours. Laura was achingly beautiful, even in death. Gathering her strength, Lis turned to the next picture. This one was a wide shot, somehow less personal, but more informative. Laura's body had clearly been carefully positioned, not dumped. Her arms were crossed over her chest, her legs laid out straight together. She lay in the centre of a circle carved into the earth. Within the circle, someone had etched a five-pointed star, one point down by Laura's feet. A pentagram.

Lis's mouth fell open. 'God . . . guys . . . you should see this.'

The others were studying files of their own – Delilah at the desk and Kitty and Jack on the floor like Lis.

'Keep your voice down! What is it?' Kitty knelt up to see better.

Lis held up the picture.

'Oh my God!' Jack hissed. 'Who did that to her?'

'That is some messed-up shit,' agreed Kitty.

'She was an offering.' Delilah held up an even more graphic image from Laura's autopsy. 'Her heart was removed.'

Lis realised she was shaking. 'No!'

Delilah nodded. 'Witchcraft.'

'They left that out of the news report,' Jack said, eyes wide.

'Can you blame them?' Kitty whispered. 'What are they gonna say, "Try not to panic, but a schoolgirl was killed in a satanic sacrifice"?'

Lis shook her head angrily. 'This is crap! She was murdered. End of. If we go to the police and say "witches did it" they'll have us institutionalised!'

'Yeah,' Kitty said. 'At least now we know why they did it – some sort of offering.'

Lis's eyes fell back to the picture of Laura's face. It wasn't fair. The fact that someone who thought they were *magical* had done this somehow made it even worse. But was that it? Was it a witch, or was it someone who just wanted it to *look* like witchcraft? Uh, brainache.

'Hey, listen to this,' said Jack, leafing through crisp sheets of paper. 'They can't get a solid alibi for Laura's dad!'

'No way!' exclaimed Delilah.

'It's always the parents . . .' mused Kitty.

'What? You think her dad is a man-witch? Is that even a thing?' Lis asked.

'I dunno,' Jack went on. 'He says he was staying at some hotel in Birmingham the night she died, but the hotel hasn't been able to confirm it because he paid with cash. Or so he says. They're waiting for CCTV to clear him.'

Could it really be that simple? Laura's dad killed her? Perhaps it was the most likely explanation. The row on the street that day had looked pretty fierce, but it just didn't feel right. Lis remembered the strong, solid father at the police appeal. How could anyone sit in front of a TV camera knowing they'd taken a life?

'There's more,' Jack continued. 'Mrs Rigg won't back up his story. He says he rang her that night from Birmingham. She says he's lying!'

'If she thinks he killed her daughter, why would she lie for him?' Delilah said, shuffling through her own file.

'I've got Nasima's statement.' Kitty held it up for them to see. 'Apparently, Laura wrote in her diary religiously, like, every day. The police are convinced that if her dad was abusing her or something she'd have written about it. They've contacted Laura's parents, but they don't know where the diary is, and apparently Ms Dandehunt's reported that it isn't at school.'

'Hmm, so Laura might have written about the murderer?'

Delilah raised an eyebrow. 'Dear Diary, I think my dad might kill me tonight?'

Lis sprang to her feet, crossing to look at Kitty's document. 'It's possible ... The day I went to see Laura on the rugby pitch, she was writing in a flowery notebook. I didn't think anything of it, but maybe it's important. What if Laura knew someone had it in for her and wrote about it? We need to find that diary!'

'What? Are you mental?' Jack grimaced.

'I've never been more serious. Laura was scared of the copse and she was acting weird at school, right? Maybe she knew something. Maybe she wrote it in the diary.'

Kitty looked up. 'Lis,' she said, 'I know where Laura's diary is.'

At Laura's

'So this is it!' Kitty slammed a tattered photo album into the centre of the rug on the floor in her attic. The faded pages were the colour of tea where it had been stored in unforgiving sunlight. Leafing through the cardboard sheets, Kitty rested on a page displaying a single picture.

Lis, Delilah and Jack leaned over to get a better look. The image showed two young girls. The first had a cute black afro framing a cherubic face. It was unmistakeably Kitty. She was standing next to a plump little girl with thick brown curls.

'Oh, good God, look how fat Laura was!' Jack squealed.

'That's Laura? Crumbs!' Lis internally wrestled with a feeling of glee at seeing that Laura had had puppy fat. It was neither kind, nor relevant.

'Yeah, that must have been taken back in the day when she was on speaking terms with any form of solid food,' Delilah quipped.

Kitty giggled. 'Yes, but look at what she's got in her hands!'

Ignoring the subjects and looking at the setting, Lis recognised the hallmarks of a birthday party: bunting, discarded wrapping paper and cards. In Laura's chubby hand was a beautiful floral notebook, tied with a delicate pink ribbon.

'Her diary?' Lis asked.

'Yep!' Kitty pushed herself back onto the worn leather sofa

and crossed her impossibly long legs. 'I know, because I bought them for her!'

'There's more than one?' Jack frowned, scrutinising the photo.

'Yeah, it was a five-year box set; each diary was a different colour and had a different pattern. Believe it or not, when we were ten, Laura and I were pretty good friends.'

All of a sudden it made sense to Lis. The animosity between Kitty and Laura had always seemed so personal; now it turned out that it was. Lis remembered when she and her best friend Bronwyn had been carefree twelve-year-olds in Bangor. That was before Bronwyn had turned on her so disastrously. Friends can do twice as much damage as enemies.

'God, I remember that party,' Delilah said quietly. 'I was the only girl in our class that wasn't invited.'

'Yeah, that was when it all started going tits-up,' replied Kitty.

The smiles in the photo gave no indication of the years of bitching and torment that were to follow. Laura looked so soft, so innocent.

'You said you knew where she kept the diaries?' Jack broke in, shattering Lis's thoughts.

Kitty grinned. 'Well, I know where she kept them four years ago!'

'OK . . . spill!'

'In her en suite bathroom!'

'Gross! Dear diary, no bowel movements today . . .' Jack laughed.

'Eww! No. The panel on the side of her bathtub comes off. She was so proud of her genius hiding place that she showed me.'

Lis wrapped her chunky cardigan more tightly around herself. In the dead of night, the attic was freezing cold. 'Do you think they'd still be under her bath now?'

'I don't see why not. It *is* a good hiding place.'

The four looked at each other silently, all of them knowing what needed to be said, but nobody wanting to be the first to say it.

'Well?' Jack started.

'Well, we'll have to go and see if they're still there,' Lis finished.

Delilah glanced uncertainly from Lis to Kitty. 'Do we *really* want to do this? If we get caught we are in deep, deep trouble.'

Lis stood and paced across the attic. She was more determined than ever. 'Yes!' she announced. 'It would be lovely to just lie low and let all this wash over me. I would love nothing more than to just go to lessons and hang with you lot and snog Danny ... but it's not going to happen! Not while someone's playing with me – and I don't think they're just going to go away.'

'You're right,' nodded Kitty. 'First Laura, then the crow, then someone breaks into Lis's house. We don't know who could be next. The diaries are a long shot, but they're the best shot we have of finding a clue to who's behind all this.'

'Are we all in?' Lis looked around the room.

Delilah nodded earnestly and, although he didn't look thrilled, Jack also bobbed his head.

'Cool,' she breathed. 'Well, then I guess we need a plan.'

'A plan sounds good ...' Jack managed a tiny smile of encouragement.

'Well, somehow we need to get into Laura's en suite bathroom ...' Lis let the sentence trail away. She hadn't got further than that bit.

Kitty, from her central position on the sofa, took control. 'OK. This is what we'll do ...'

The Riggs' sycamore-lined street was so quiet, so still, it could be a painting. A painting entitled *The Middle-Class Dream*. Murder didn't belong on this cul-de-sac. School had finished for the day, and dusk was already drawing in, the sky turning a washed-out purple as the late autumn sun wilted.

'Make sure you keep her out of the way,' Jack told Lis.

'Stop talking!' Lis snapped. 'Right. Are you hiding or not?'

Jack pouted and ducked into the holly bush next to the front door, crouching out of sight. 'Ouch, this is sticking right up my—'

'Shh!' Lis stepped up to the door and rang the impressive bell; chimes rang from the hall within. Laura's house was only a short walk from Kitty's and it was just as imposing. A bright green lawn stretched for what looked like acres behind her.

'Maybe there's no one home,' whispered Jack.

'*Ssh!*' Lis repeated as footsteps approached the door.

The plan was simple, but that didn't bestow any confidence. Lis, new to the town and unknown to Laura's parents, would bring flowers to their home in a gesture of sympathy, try to get invited in and somehow engage whoever was there in conversation. Meanwhile, Jack, smaller and lighter on his feet than Kitty, would slip inside, check under Laura's bath and take the diaries if they were there. Kitty and Dee were back-up. Easy. What could possibly go wrong?

The door creaked open. Mrs Rigg stood on the threshold, an impenetrable expression on her face. She was immaculately dressed. Lis wondered if she was on her way out. Who wears heels around the house?

'Hi, Mrs Rigg?' Lis smiled. 'You don't know me . . . I'm Lucy from Laura's school. We were good friends and I just wanted to bring these flowers for you. I'm so sorry for your loss.'

Mrs Rigg frowned. She was stunning but, what was the word, *severe* maybe?

'Lucy? I didn't realise Laura had any friends called Lucy.'

'I'm new to the area,' Lis explained. 'Laura was in charge of showing me around Fulton. She was amazing.' The lies felt as though they should scald her tongue, but Lis was relieved at the ease with which they seemed to flow. Her heart pounded, but as long as she could continue a normal conversation, she'd be fine.

'I see. Well, it's nice to meet you, Lucy. I'm Jennifer, Laura's mother. Thank you for the flowers, they're lovely. I'm so sorry you didn't get an invite to the wake. We tried very hard to reach all Laura's friends.' Her manner shifted slightly. It was business-like: death etiquette. Jennifer reached for the bouquet in Lis's hands.

This was the only chance she had. Time to leap. 'I'm sorry, but would it be possible for me to use your bathroom while I'm here? I have to get the bus back to Fulton ...'

The mourning mother didn't look overjoyed, but she nodded politely and stepped aside. 'Of course, dear, come in.'

Mrs Rigg led her into the hallway. Lis turned and shut the door behind her, quickly setting the lock on the latch so Jack would be able to enter easily. Now all she had to do was play for time: how long would he need to find the diaries?

She found herself standing in a grand, tiled entrance hall with a handsome curved staircase leading to a landing upstairs. Luckily for Jack, all the doors off the landing looked as if they were ajar. She gasped as she took in a stunning chandelier hanging from the centre of the ceiling. 'Wow, Mrs Rigg, you have such a gorgeous home!'

'Thank you, and please call me Jennifer, all Laura's friends do. Did.'

But she wasn't really Laura's friend. Guilt made her queasy. *Keep your cool*, Lis told herself.

'The water closet is just this way, dear.' Jennifer's Yorkshire accent was noticeably clipped, as if she had trained herself to lose it.

Lis followed her down a short passageway that led to a vast family kitchen. Just before that was a little side door to a downstairs loo.

'There you are. I'll just be in the kitchen finding a vase for these,' Jennifer said, waving the flowers.

Lis shut herself into the frilly pink cloakroom and sat on the toilet seat, taking out her phone. She quickly called Jack – his cue to enter. Listening closely, she thought she heard the front door open and quickly flushed the toilet, making as much noise as she possibly could by running the taps at full flow and even humming as she dried her hands. Now she really had to buy Jack some time.

Leaving the little room, Lis made her way into the kitchen where she found Jennifer arranging the flowers in a tall black vase. Lis wondered how many vases of flowers this poor woman had arranged over the last few weeks.

'Don't they look great?' Jennifer said with a smile. 'Thank you again, Lucy.'

Lis rubbed her hands on her school uniform. 'I thought you'd probably have loads of flowers already, but I didn't know what else to bring.'

'It was very sweet of you,' Jennifer replied. 'The first round of flowers have all died now, so these are very welcome.'

Lis hovered at the island in the centre of the kitchen, trying to think of something else to say.

'Can I get you a glass of water or anything?' Mrs Rigg asked. She was obviously an expert hostess.

'Er, that would be lovely, thank you.' What was Jack doing?

Was he lost? He was meant to call her as soon as he was back outside.

Lis's gaze fell on a huge framed black-and-white photo on the wall. It was one of those glossy professional family portraits. Sarah had been trying to convince Max that they were classy, not tacky, for weeks.

In the photo Mr and Mrs Rigg stood at a jaunty angle, arms around Laura. They were such a handsome family. 'It's a stunning portrait, isn't it?' Mrs Rigg said, smiling slightly as she followed Lis's eye line. She handed her a glass of water before crossing the room to the picture. Lis followed.

'It was taken in the summer holidays. It's the last picture we have of her. Of course, she absolutely hated posing for it. She would have done anything to be with her friends instead of her boring old parents. We had to threaten to stop her allowance!' Her smile fell. 'Did she ever talk about us? Was she very unhappy?'

The question caught Lis completely off guard. She opened and closed her mouth like a goldfish. 'I ... I don't think so. She, er ... never said anything.'

'You know, Lucy, you look a lot like her ...' the older woman absent-mindedly fingered a delicate silver cross around her neck as she gazed at Lis.

'No, Laura was much prettier than me!' Lis exclaimed in surprise.

Mrs Rigg reached out and stroked her hair away from her face. 'Same hair. It's so thick and shiny ...'

She seemed to be looking past Lis and into another time, swimming in the memory of Laura. Lis flinched away from her touch.

Without warning, a solid thud sounded from the floor directly above them.

'What the bloody hell was that?' Jennifer Rigg immediately

dropped Lis's hair and started out of the kitchen.

Jack! Lis's mind raced as she instinctively followed Jennifer. Somehow, she had to stop her from going upstairs. What was Jack doing? Was he hurt? Would Mrs Rigg see him? *Think fast, Lis, think fast . . .* 'Was that your cat or something maybe?' she asked.

'We don't have a cat, so I doubt that,' Jennifer snapped as she marched across the regal entrance hall, her high heels tapping on the tiles. Lis continued to pursue her, searching for something else to say.

'Mrs Rigg, stop!' She grabbed the older woman's arm.

A fierce expression flashed across Jennifer's face, reminding Lis of Laura in fight mode. 'Let go of me, right now!' she said coldly.

'But, Mrs Rigg, if there's someone upstairs, it could be dangerous!' Lis knew she sounded like a crazy person, but the repercussions of Jack being found in Laura Rigg's house would be devastating. Inspector Monroe would hang them all out to dry.

'You're absolutely right, dear.' Jennifer strode into the adjoining drawing room – another pristine magazine spread with a roaring open fire. 'Which is why I shall take this!' With a single fluid move, she pulled an iron poker from the hearth. In a second she was back at the foot of the stairs, armed and ready. Lis watched helplessly, hoping inspiration would strike before Mrs Rigg did.

Jennifer edged up the stairs, brandishing the poker. As Lis tentatively followed, she heard further banging from the first floor. Would Mrs Rigg actually hit Jack with the poker? The disastrous state of their juvenile plan confronted her. What *had* they been thinking? They were in over their heads, sinking without trace, drowning in failure.

'Please, Mrs Rigg, be careful!' Lis scurried to her side.

Maybe she could stop her from hitting Jack if necessary.

'I'll be fine, dear. Stay well back.'

The pair reached the curved landing. The truth perched on the tip of Lis's tongue. Maybe if she just told her the full story, Mrs Rigg would turn a blind eye? Fat chance!

Thick silence filled the air as the duo strained to listen for the intruder. Nothing, the landing was silent.

'I think it came from Laura's room,' Jennifer hissed, '*Journalists!* I thought it was bad when they went through the bins, but this is something else! Scum!'

'Mrs Rigg, let's just get out! Or call the police!' Lis urged.

Mrs Rigg shot her a cold look that told her in no uncertain terms to shut up. Then she gave the door to Laura's room a gentle push. With a dry creak, it swung open.

Twilight seeped onto the landing as Jennifer stepped into the bedroom. Taking a deep breath, Lis followed.

It looked like a bomb site. This must have been exactly as Laura had left it before her last trip out: her meeting with murder. The duvet was in a heap on the bed, make-up and accessories were strewn across a grand dressing table and an entire handbag had been emptied out onto the floor. There were posters on the walls and photos on the mirror. It was a typical teenager's bedroom, only this one would eternally lack a teenager.

Jennifer looked around the room, turning in every direction, bewildered. Lis could see the internal door to what had to be the en suite bathroom. How could she keep Mrs Rigg out of that room?

'Strange. I could have sworn it came from in here ...' Mrs Rigg finally lowered the poker.

'Maybe it came from outside?' Lis suggested.

Mrs Rigg seemed about to nod, but then her gaze fell on the door to the en suite. Lis was all out of ideas. The older woman headed for the bathroom. They were busted.

But then the doorbell rang: an ostentatious bell chime. And again. Someone was pressing the button repeatedly so that the noisy chimes filled the house.

'Who on earth is making that racket?' Mrs Rigg snapped and rushed from the room.

Lis waited until she heard Mrs Rigg's footsteps on the stairs before flinging herself into the bathroom. It was small, just big enough for a bath, sink and toilet. She instantly noticed that one corner of the bath panel was loose.

'Has she gone?' Jack said from under the bathtub. He pushed the plastic panel aside and rolled out of his hiding place. It was a good job he was so slim or he'd never have fitted. In his arms were four pretty floral notebooks, each bound with a ribbon.

'You got them!'

'Yep, but I dropped the bath panel; it was dead heavy! I called Kitty straight away and she went to Plan B. Sorry!'

'Never mind,' Lis whispered, heading back to Laura's bedroom. 'We need to get out of here, right now!'

Lis ran onto the landing. She could see Mrs Rigg at the front door. On the threshold stood Delilah, ginger curls tucked into her old red Pizza Factory cap. 'This is the address I've got,' she was saying, her arms filled with pizza boxes.

'I assure you, young lady, I haven't ordered any pizzas!'

'Is this thirty-two Cedar Drive?'

'Yes!'

'Well, that's the address I've got ...' Delilah insisted.

Lis darted back into Laura's bedroom. 'Right, I'll go downstairs and try to get her into the kitchen. You have two minutes to get out, OK?' she told Jack.

Jack was way ahead of her, already hidden, waiting behind the bedroom door, the diaries in his rucksack. 'OK. And if

I can't get out that way, I'll go out the window – there's a tree I could climb down.'

'Jack, when this is over, you should join the SAS, seriously.'

He grinned like that was the biggest compliment he'd ever received. Lis left him alone and headed downstairs, wondering what lies to feed Mrs Rigg. Never mind the SAS, she wanted an Oscar. But they had the diaries. If Laura had left any clue to who her killer was, this would all be over soon.

Mission accomplished.

Dear Diary

The text message had simply read *Meet me in the rec?* Too intriguing an offer to refuse. Leaving Delilah to examine the diaries, Lis had set off to see Danny. Darkness was closing in as she pushed through the gate to Hollow Pike recreation ground and Danny was alone, swaying back and forth on a swing.

'Hey.' His face lit up on seeing her, and once more his smile left her breathless.

'So, this is what you do in the evening? Lurk in playgrounds waiting for passing girls?' Lis teased.

'Absolutely. Care to join me?'

'How could I resist?' She plonked herself on the swing next to his. 'What's up?'

He poked at the woodchip with his toe. 'My sister, the one at Oxford, is home for a few days. I so needed to get out of the house! You've saved me.'

'Any time.' She kicked off and swung out, remembering what it was like to defy gravity on these things – reaching that point when you fly so high you hover for a moment before lurching back down.

'It wasn't just that though. It's been a while and texting isn't the same. I thought it'd be cool to hang,' Danny continued.

'Literally!'

'Any more migraines?' he asked.

It took Lis a second to realise what he was talking about.

Her brain kicked in just in time. 'Oh, yeah. I mean, no, no more. I'm so sorry about that. It came out of nowhere.'

'So everything's OK now?'

'Yeah, everything's fine.' More lying. How much of her time was now taken up with these so-called white lies? They were still lies.

'Good. What've you been up to?'

Breaking into a dead girl's bathroom to steal her diaries. 'Nothing much.'

'It's always nothing with you.' Danny experimentally trundled back until his feet could only just touch the ground before letting himself fall into a swing.

'What do you mean?'

'You're very mysterious. It's pretty sexy!'

'Oh, yeah, right!'

He laughed. 'Are you, like, a spy?'

'Nope.'

'Or, or maybe a superhero, like Clark Kent – with a secret identity?'

'Nope, keep trying.'

'I know, I bet it's witness relocation! Are you secretly Amish?'

'What?'

'You know, like that film with the Amish boy?'

'You got me! My real name is Gerda. Promise not to tell?'

Danny stopped swinging and took the chain of her swing in his hand to slow her motion too. In a way he was right. Moving here *had* gifted her with an aura of mystery. In fact she'd been an open book in Bangor, but now she really did have secrets. *Real* secrets, not just high school gossip. She wished she could tell him, but telling him would be purely selfish, and she didn't want to drag him into her mess. Perhaps it would have been best if she'd followed head not heart and never agreed to the date with Danny. Of all the nice, normal girls at Fulton he'd picked her: pretty bad luck on his part.

'Is that why you asked me out? Cos I'm an enigma?' She wrapped the last word in a deep, spooky voice.

'Nah!'

'Good, cos you'd be very disappointed!'

'And what is that meant to mean?' he smiled. 'You're being enigmatic again!'

She said nothing, aware she wasn't really helping her cause. The silence was warm and treacly, heavy with expectation. The toe of his Adidas reached across and gave her own school shoes a playful kick. She threw him a coy glance and gave him a nudge back. Footsie: how infantile, but how electrifying!

Danny pulled on the chain of her swing, bringing her closer to him. With a glint of mischief in his eye, he kissed her lips and a wave of bliss ran through Lis's entire body. Suddenly she was miles from the chilly rec, somewhere bright and tranquil. For an ecstatic instant she forgot everything; there was nothing but the kiss.

In the distance, a phone rang, calling her back to the real world. Every time she spoke to Danny it seemed that thing interrupted them. 'I'm sorry!'

'No worries.' He smiled and licked his lips.

She retrieved the phone from the bottom of her bag. 'Hello?'

'Hi, darling, it's me,' said Delilah.

'Hey.' Lis twisted away from Danny in case he heard something he shouldn't.

'Can I see you? Could you come over?'

'Now?' Lis asked.

'Yeah, it's important. I wouldn't ask otherwise.'

Lis sighed, looking up at the boy who was now gazing away to the horizon, his handsome profile catching the starlight.

She wanted to stay with him forever. But Delilah, the fastest reader, had the diaries and their allure was strong. *This could all be over tonight*, Lis thought.

'OK. How do I get to your place?'

The Fulton Farm Estate was a far cry from the rest of Hollow Pike. The gateway to the housing estate had a burnt out minibus under a cheery sign welcoming residents home. The pebble-dashed houses were grey and tired, many entirely decrepit with sealed metal windows to prevent squatting. Some prouder members of the community had bravely tried to maintain pretty front gardens, but they were in stark contrast to the majority which had wild, overgrown jungles spilling onto the pavement. Lis couldn't help wondering why so many of the properties had bathtubs in their gardens, and why there were so many cars with no wheels parked in the driveways.

Lis was surprised that this could exist just a five-minute bus ride from Kitty's palace on the hill. Deprivation and menace hung from the broken street lights. Delilah's house was somewhere in the middle of the spectrum. There were no bathtubs or burned cars, but the garden was a borderline forest. Somehow, it worked; the most beautiful wild flowers grew up the sides of the house and trees with willowy leaves framed the home like a lace curtain.

Pushing through a rusty gate, Lis approached the front door and knocked. A loud television blared from within, and then a door swung open to reveal a tall man with a trim goatee and long grey hair secured in a plait. He was wearing overalls covered in oil paints.

'Hello,' he said, smiling to reveal a gold tooth. 'You must be this Lis we've heard all about. Come on in.' Lis warmed to him immediately. He looked like a friendly pirate.

Then Delilah pushed past him. 'Hey, Lis. Come up to my room,' she said, seizing Lis's hand and dragging her into the house.

The cramped lounge was stuffed with mismatched furniture and smelled a lot like cigarettes and marijuana. Lis vaguely made out the shape of Delilah's brother playing a console game, but was hauled past too quickly to be introduced.

They sprinted up stairs cluttered with mugs and telephone directories until they came to a landing. One bedroom was partitioned off with a curtain for some reason, but Delilah took her past that and into the next room. It was probably a small room, although Lis couldn't be certain as the space had been almost entirely filled with books. Every surface was piled with literature of all shapes and sizes. Delilah had even foregone a bed frame and wardrobe in order to create more storage for her novels. There was a single mattress pushed tightly into a corner and a rail to hang her clothes on. The room flickered in the glow of tea-light candles alight in jam jars on top of the book towers. The room was *so* Delilah.

'Wow, great room!'

'Thanks, darling. And thanks for coming so promptly.'

'That's OK.' Lis wondered where she was meant to sit. 'What's up?'

Delilah motioned for Lis to join her on the mattress. 'Lis, I'm freaking out.'

'Why?' Lis could tell she wasn't messing around. Delilah looked like she might vomit; she was even paler than normal.

'If I tell you something, do you promise not to tell anyone? It's really, seriously, *catastrophically* bad.'

'OK ...' Lis agreed, wondering what the secret was – there were some biggies flying around this town.

'Last summer, before you arrived, I got really drunk at this barbecue at Rachel Williams' house. Kitty wasn't there because, you know, she thinks they're all a bunch of wannabe tossers . . .'

Lis smiled despite herself. 'And?'

'And I ended up cheating on her.'

'Oh! Right. Who with?'

'That's the worst part. It was with Cameron Green,' Dee wailed.

'What?' Lis exploded like a firework. 'Don't tell me you . . .'

Tears rolled down Delilah's face. 'Oh, God, no! It was just a messy clinch really. On a pile of coats. I was so wasted. I regretted it straight away; it was so stupid.'

Lis was lost for words. What had Delilah been thinking?

'Please don't tell Kitty!'

'I won't, I won't,' Lis promised. 'But it's in the past now. Why worry?'

Delilah picked up one of the diaries – the baby blue volume. 'It's in Laura's diary. It's why she dumped Cameron. If Kitty sees this . . .'

Lis drew Delilah into a hug. 'What are we going to do with you, eh?'

'I didn't know who else I could tell,' Dee sobbed.

Lis took the notebook from her. 'Look, what if we tear out that entry? Could we do that without it changing anything else?'

Delilah wiped her eyes on the Pizza Factory fleece. 'I think so. But isn't it wrong? It's Laura's last word, you know?'

'I don't think it has anything to do with what happened, though, do you?'

'I don't know. Cameron didn't like being dumped.'

Lis opened the book and started flicking through the handwritten pages. Laura's girlish loopy writing sloped across the journal. 'Really? Well, look, Kitty's hardly likely to want to read these diaries word for word. We can just tell her the important stuff and fail to mention the bit about you and Cameron. What else was in the diaries? Any other clues?'

'Not really.' Delilah pulled herself together, looking happier. 'The first three books were pointless – mainly lists of people she did and didn't like.'

'I used to keep a death list,' Lis admitted. 'Not now though, I'd like to make that *very* clear!'

Dee managed a feeble smile. 'There were a couple of interesting things in this one. Listen to this ... "Dear Diary", blah, blah, blah, "I can't believe what Cameron did with that pikey skank bitch". Nice, thanks, Laura. "I'm done with Fulton boys – except Danny, he's different".'

'She didn't sleep with Danny, did she?' Lis didn't think she'd be able to handle it if Laura had.

'I don't think so. If she did, it's not in this volume.'

'Where's the next one?'

'I don't know. This is the last one and it finishes in July,' Delilah said. 'But things seemed to change in this one.'

'How?'

'Well, Laura thought her dad might be having an affair, for one thing, and she also wasn't very well. She was seeing a doctor for a sleep disorder.'

What little stale air there was in the poky bedroom seemed to be sucked out through the walls and Lis struggled for breath. 'Wh-what was wrong?' But she knew the answer before Delilah even opened her mouth.

'She was having nightmares. Listen. "Dear Diary, I'm so tired, but I'm scared to close my eyes. Why can't I just dream about Taylor Lautner like everyone else? No. I get to crawl about in the copse. It's so stupid. Now, in the day time, it doesn't even seem scary, but I can't think of any words to describe what it's like once I'm asleep. I'm soooooo tired. Mum says the doctor will help, but every night is the same and I don't see how the doctor can change my dreams".'

Delilah stopped. 'Lis? Are you OK?'

The room was now spinning all around Lis. 'No, I am seriously not OK.'

'Darling, you're freaking me out a bit. Have you taken something?'

'No. Dee ... I have the same nightmare.'

'Eh? I don't know if that's—'

'Possible? Well, looks like it is,' Lis snapped.

Delilah put the diary down, but she was unwilling to meet Lis's gaze.

'What is it?' Lis asked.

'Well, if you're having the same dreams ...'

'Delilah, just spit it out, for God's sake!'

'Well, listen to the final entry. "Dear Diary. WTF? How random is this? Got home and there's a dead bird on my bed. How grim is that? It must have flown in through my bedroom window, or something, and died! It's minging. Mum is clearing it away now, but she's being really weird about it".'

Delilah stopped and looked at Lis pointedly. 'Another bird. What do you think that means?'

Lis stood up and paced across the room, her head spinning. 'Laura got a bird and she died. Dee, I got a bird too ...'

Delilah shook her head. 'No, I didn't mean that!'

'Is it a sign? Am I next?'

Her friend had no answer to that one. Needing to steady herself, Lis leaned on one of the towers of books that rested against the wall. She started to feel her heartbeat slowing down. Then she saw the book her hand was resting on: *An Occult History of Hollow Pike*.

Tick Tock

Delilah realised at the same time Lis did. She sprang off the bed, red-faced and caught red-handed. She dove for the book, but Lis whipped it off the top of the pile and out of her reach.

'Delilah, why do you have this book?' she demanded.

Delilah groaned. 'Oh, Lis, I know what it looks like ...'

'Really? What does it look like? I think it looks like you blatantly lied to my face!' Lis snapped.

'Well, what was I meant to do?' said Delilah, back on the verge of tears. She tried to take the book, but Lis held onto it. 'After Laura died, the papers said it was a ritual thing and I panicked! I mean, what would you have done?'

'Erm, told the truth? Delilah, what am I meant to think? You have the book and you were in the forest. Did you ... ?'

Delilah collapsed onto the mattress. She pulled her knees to her chest, rocking back and forth. 'No, of course I didn't. Don't be insane!'

'OK ... gonna need some sort of explanation in the next five seconds ...'

'You don't know what it's like, Lis. I always screw up. Everything I touch turns to crap. It always has. Just ask my mum; she couldn't get out of here quick enough. You'll leave me. *Kitty*'ll leave me when she finds out what I did with Cameron. Everyone leaves me sooner or later.'

Lis saw the lost little girl on the mattress and felt for her.

She seemed almost frail, like a baby bird that had tumbled out of the nest. She crouched down next to Delilah, not letting go of the book. 'No one's going to leave you, OK? But you'd better tell me what you're doing with this book, right now. Dee, I'm not kidding.'

Delilah peeked over her knees. 'What can I say? I'm a witch.'

'Oh. My. God.'

'A *modern* witch. No brooms, no pointy hats and no ritual sacrifice! Is it that hard to understand? My mum was Wiccan, so are my dad and step-mum. Earth magic – it's songs and chants and charms. It isn't *Buffy*. I can't do lightning bolts or fly! And it's *peaceful*. What happened to Laura is nothing to do with Wicca. That was something else – something much, much darker.'

Lis scanned the bookshelves: *Teen Witch*, *A Modern Guide to Wiccan Practice*, *Candles for Beginners*. It all seemed pretty innocent. Nonetheless, she needed to be sure. 'Delilah, how can I believe a single word you say? You lied!'

Exhausted, Delilah rolled her eyes. 'Lis, sweetie, it's only a silly little book at the end of the day. I took it to *read*. I haven't been using it as an instruction manual for ritual murder!'

A wry smile edged across Lis's face. 'But it doesn't look good, Dee. Think about how Laura died. It was a ritual thing. We saw the photos.'

'And it was way beyond me. I don't even know what kind of magic that is.'

'What does Kitty think?'

'Kitty doesn't even know I stole the book,' Delilah confessed.

Lis sensed that she was getting the truth now. 'Fine. Does the book shed any light on what's happening?'

Delilah reached for it and this time Lis handed it over. 'It's actually fascinating.' Delilah opened the book to a page she'd marked. 'I didn't realise the extent of the legends.'

'About Hollow Pike?'

'Absolutely. Did you know Roman soldiers wouldn't attack the village because they thought it was protected by the gods?'

Lis shook her head.

'Infertile women used to come here to see witch doctors. Druids used to make a pilgrimage here for summer solstice – pretty major stuff!'

'What changed?'

'The witch trials in the seventeenth century,' Delilah said, and her eyes looked dark in the candlelight. 'All the Hollow Pike witches were hanged, burned or drowned.' Delilah turned to another bookmarked page showing an old etching of a young woman bound to a stake as tongues of fire licked at her feet. All around, the villagers of Hollow Pike looked on, watching her burn.

Lis puffed out her cheeks. 'Well, it looks like they missed one because someone in this town is still all about weird ritual sacrifices!'

'It looks that way,' Delilah agreed sombrely.

Companionable silence fell over the room. The thought of tiny little Delilah taking on Laura was ridiculous, Lis knew that, but when would she finally feel like an insider? She was getting tired of all the skeletons tumbling out of closets (or lockers). 'Tomorrow we're taking that book back to Mrs Gillespie, OK? She's pretty pissed off.'

Delilah opened her mouth to argue, but on seeing Lis's Kitty-like expression, she gave in. 'OK,' she sighed.

The next morning, Lis and Delilah skipped first period in order to return the stolen tome to its rightful owner. There was something taboo about being in town during school hours, and Lis felt closer to Delilah now that they were both playing truant. The fact that they'd shared secrets had also created a strange sense of sisterhood.

Lis saw Hollow Pike in a totally different light now that the witchcraft fiction was rapidly becoming fact. Every dark corner and slim alleyway was now filled with imaginary witches and murderers. The market was all hustle and bustle. It seemed bright and friendly but, through Lis's knowing eyes, it was suddenly sinister. She saw a stall holder reach under a curtain to hand a customer a plain brown package – was it just fruit or something magical and mysterious?

One stall was selling pet supplies and some smaller animals, such as hamsters and gerbils. As Lis passed, just for a split second, she thought she saw the salesman hand a woman a thin green snake, the serpent briefly coiling around the lady's wrist before she dropped it into her handbag. What sort of town was she living in? Or was her imagination simply working overtime?

They turned off the main street and headed down the winding cobbled alley that led to the Friends of the Church shop. Lis felt nervous, but she was glad to be out of the claustrophobic market.

'What are we actually going to say?' Delilah asked when they reached the door.

'I think we should be honest. I don't think she's *that* bad, underneath it all,' Lis replied.

'Careful, you're sounding a bit *Sesame Street*, Lis.'

Lis laughed and the pair burst through the door on the count of three.

They immediately froze. They were so busted; at the

counter was Mrs Gillespie, looking as hideous as ever, with Ms Dandehunt, their headmistress. The oddest part was that the look on the head's face suggested *she'd* been caught in the act. Whatever conversation the two women had been having stopped dead, the pair as rigid as the ancient mannequins in the window.

'Hello, children!' Ms Dandehunt said brightly, snapping out of her statue state. 'How are you on this lovely morning?'

Lis was unsure how to respond so she remained silent. Unfortunately so did Dee. Lis attempted a smile, but the atmosphere in the store was so tense she could hardly move her facial muscles.

'Mrs Gillespie and I were just finalising some plans for the Winter Fayre,' Ms Dandehunt went on. 'Mrs Gillespie always donates some things to the bric-a-brac stall.'

'That's right. Bric-a-brac,' Mrs Gillespie put in, touching her ruby red lips with a gloved hand.

'Oh, OK,' Lis replied.

Ms Dandehunt zipped up her bright green cagoule and pulled an orange pom-pom hat over her bowl cut. 'Righty-ho! I'd best be off, although it's always lovely to see you girls.'

Their headmistress wobbled out of the shop. Without a doubt, it had been one of the strangest encounters of Lis's life. Ms Dandehunt hadn't been able to get out of the shop fast enough, and she hadn't even mentioned their obvious truancy! Lis longed to know what the two women had been discussing. She seriously doubted it was bric-a-brac. Lis found it hard to imagine the women even being friends. They were both bonkers, of course, but Ms Dandehunt was as cuddly as Mrs Gillespie was creepy.

As Lis wondered about it, Delilah approached the counter.

'I didn't know you knew Ms Dandehunt,' she said to Mrs Gillespie.

'Small town like Hollow Pike, everyone knows everyone,' the crone said, picking up a pricing gun. 'Now, I assume you're here to return something you picked up *by accident?*'

'Me *gustaría tres pasteles, por favor,*' Jack's accent butchered the Spanish tongue once again.

'You want three pastels?' Lis asked.

'Three cakes.'

'Oh, OK.'

Lis and Delilah had rejoined school before second period and were now safely in their Spanish class. They'd told Mr Gray that they'd needed to visit the Family Planning Clinic and he'd ushered them in without another word. Male teachers were always so easy in that way, mention sex or periods and they turned to stone – a modern Medusa effect.

Kitty looked over her shoulder and whispered, 'So what did Laura's diary say?'

'Nothing juicy,' Delilah hissed back. 'She thought her dad was having an affair with someone at work. She saw them having a steamy lunch.'

'That'd explain the Birmingham hotel bit,' Jack pointed out.

'*And* why Mrs Rigg won't back him up,' Kitty added. 'But I can't see why he'd cut out Laura's heart for that. Bit extreme!'

Delilah then told them of the dead bird that Laura had discovered on her bed. Lis's blood ran cold once more. Too many similarities: the dreams, the birds, even the same crush! And Laura's mum had commented on how she and Laura looked alike.

Chancing a glance over her shoulder, Lis saw Danny

watching her. Flushing red, he turned away, pretending to be interested in the Spanish exercise. Then he looked back, his gaze lingering longer than it should, and it was Lis's turn to blush.

'Maybe we should keep looking for the fifth diary,' Delilah finished. 'It seems likely she carried on after the last entry.'

'No,' said Jack. 'It could be *anywhere*. I'm not creeping around her bathroom again!'

Lis brushed her dark curls over her shoulder. 'No. I have a feeling that it's in school. Laura was writing it here when I confronted her. That was the day she ... we ...'

'But the police cleared her locker,' Jack pointed out.

The friends looked at one another, completely stumped. Across the aisle, a sniggering Cameron Green leaned over to Kitty. 'Oi, Monroe. When you get bored of girls you can *comer mi pollo!*'

'Thanks, Cam, I'd love to eat your chicken,' Kitty said smoothly, 'but I think you mean *polla*, tosser.'

Even Harry and Nasima laughed as Cameron turned back to his mates shame-faced. Danny mouthed 'sorry' at Lis.

Lis stole a glance at Delilah, who'd gone deathly white. Lis knew why. Poor thing – what a mistake to have snogged such a gorilla!

The bell for morning break rang out and everyone started to gather up their books.

'Don't stampede!' pleaded Mr Gray as the students lunged for the door. 'Lis, can I see you for just one sec, please?'

Lis nodded, swinging her bag onto her shoulder.

'We'll see you on the quad,' Jack said, filing out with the girls.

'Cool.' Lis drifted to the desk at the front of the classroom and hovered at Mr Gray's desk until the crowd had disappeared into the hallway. 'Is there a problem?'

Mr Gray frowned, a mixture of concern and annoyance. 'I don't know. Is there anything you want to tell me, Lis? Is there something going on?'

There were about a million things going on, but none that she'd tell him. Sure, he was a great teacher, but she'd never been a touchy-feely, talk-to-teachers type. At her last school, they'd made things about ten times worse. 'No, everything's fine, thanks,' she said cautiously.

'In that case, could you explain your homework please?'

Her homework? The piece on modern Mexico City? 'I don't understand. I handed it in yesterday.'

'I know you did!' Mr Gray opened her red homework exercise book and flicked to the last page, where her report was written. Only now, over the top of her neat italic handwriting were three angry words, scrawled in what could only be blood: NOT LONG NOW.

The Solution

The words were ugly red gashes, carved into the flesh of the page. Lis's eyes teared up as she stumbled back from the desk.

'Well?' asked Mr Gray.

'I didn't do it!' Lis cried. She could hardly believe what she was seeing. It was horrible, and yet she was unable to look away. The words were clearly a threat. NOT LONG NOW – her time was coming.

'I'm not saying you did. Lis, is someone giving you a hard time? You know, you can tell me.'

'Someone must have . . . Someone's . . .'

'Someone's what?' His earnest expression was unbearable. 'Lis?'

She couldn't tell him the truth and she couldn't think of any decent lies. She just wanted to be out of the classroom. 'It's nothing. Nothing,' Lis croaked.

'It doesn't look like nothing. "Not long now". What does that mean, anyway?'

'Look, it was a stupid joke between Kitty and me. I'm sorry,' she lied clumsily, her tongue in knots. She dearly needed fresh air to take the bitter taste of bile out of her mouth. 'Can I go?'

Mr Gray looked far from convinced. 'This isn't funny, Lis. I was worried about you.'

'I'm sorry,' she repeated, staring at the carpet.

'You'll redo this piece of homework tonight. Is that understood?'

'Sure.' She practically ripped the exercise book out of his hands and then swept out of the classroom, not stopping to say goodbye.

It was all so clear now. Lis sat on the front steps of the library, her knees drawn up to her chin. The light was somehow brighter here, and even the morning air seemed sweeter. It was quiet. She'd needed to get away from the hustle and bustle of the school to collect her thoughts. It was time to face reality. This wasn't a game and, if it was, she certainly wasn't winning. Lis had had enough; the malicious red words were the final straw. Her mind was made up. She had to leave Hollow Pike.

After minutes or hours passed (she wasn't sure which), she heard footsteps crunching along the approach to the library.

'There she is!' Jack announced. 'Lis, what's up? We've been looking all over for you.'

'Hey, what did Mr Gray want?' Kitty asked, concerned.

Feeling justifiably dramatic, Lis handed over her exercise book, open at the offending page. They all looked at the bloody lettering and fell silent.

'Jesus, Lis.' Kitty slowly looked up from the grim message. 'Who did this?'

'Who do you think?' She was almost trembling. Part fear, part anger, it was all spilling out now, boiling over.

'It *must* have been the killer. Witches, not-witches, sodding pixies – I don't care any more. I'm going home! Back to Wales . . . back to my mum.'

A moment of silence followed. She hadn't planned to blurt

out her plan so suddenly, but it was the only way. If she couldn't go to the police, which she knew she couldn't, then she had to leave town. This had all started since she'd decided to come to Hollow Pike. Maybe it would finish when she left. Maybe in a parallel world where Hollow Pike contained her friends and Danny and *no murderers*, everything would have been different, but this wasn't the time to play *let's pretend*.

'You can't just leave, though!' Jack's voice was barely audible.

An exasperated, defeated laugh escaped from Lis's body. 'Jack! Me coming here was some sort of catalyst for a shit explosion! From the second I got here, my life has become a living nightmare. Laura was only the beginning. I'm so tired of being scared.'

Delilah leaned forward, looking businesslike. 'Lis, we're all having a hard time dealing with this. You're not alone. We were *all* there that night.'

'But none of you are getting death threats,' Lis protested.

Jack's voice was starting to crack. 'I know, but what about us? You met *us* here. That's not a bad thing.'

'Of course it isn't!' She fought an urge to sob. 'But I think if I just go home, I'll at least be safe. Things can go back to how they were before.'

'What? Miserable and bullied?' Kitty was relentless, testing Lis's resolve.

'I don't see how it can be worse than this mess.'

'What about Laura?' Delilah asked.

'What about her? Why is she still ruling our lives? She's dead! I've changed my mind. The police can work out who killed her; I'm not loving playing Nancy Drew! You can carry on if you want, but I'm out. I don't care any more. This isn't worth dying for.'

'But we're so close, Lis. What if the last diary *is* somewhere in the school? We just have to come up with a plan to search the place,' Delilah said.

Kitty stood up. 'This is crap. You're scared. Simple as. Where are you going to run away to next time, Lis?' With that, she stomped away.

'Don't worry about her. She's upset. That's her typical response, but we really don't want you to go,' Delilah said, patient as ever.

Jack nodded in eager agreement.

'I'm sorry.' Lis felt her eyes filling with tears. She didn't want to cry. 'I'm going to talk to my mum tonight. She's coming to Sarah's for Christmas and I'll go back with her then. I won't say anything about what we did. I'll keep it a secret.'

'But we'll miss you.' Jack half smiled, half frowned. 'It's been *better* since you got here.'

The friends embraced in a group hug. Lis knew she *would* miss them, more than any friends she'd ever had before, but she was determined not to back down.

'What about Danny?' Jack asked, wiping his damp nose on a sleeve.

The name hit her like a punch to the face. But Lis had wasted enough of that poor boy's life. It was time to let him off the hook.

Her mind gremlins wrestled amongst themselves as Lis made her way to the rugby pitch. She knew she couldn't leave Hollow Pike *and* keep Danny, and just the thought of him was making her want to change her mind. She had to talk to him before she crumbled.

She *had* to leave; reason dictated it was the only thing that would keep her alive, but something inside her, something *beyond* reason, wanted Danny. That single thought threatened to overpower every other idea in her head. Besides, it didn't seem fair. She'd practically given up hope of ever falling for someone the way other girls seemed to every week, and when she finally did, she had no choice but to throw it all away. *Be strong, Lis*, she told herself. *Just do it.*

Pulling the red trench coat tightly around her body, she tentatively stepped onto the edge of the rugby pitch, her ballet pumps sinking into the mud. Practice was taking place on the far side of the pitch. Was Danny even there? Then she saw him.

A new, particularly ferocious mind gremlin pounced. This one reacting to the sight of Danny in his rugby kit: muscular, mud-splattered and with those impossible eyes that she found entirely irresistible.

As she watched the rugby game play out, Lis realised she'd come to the end of her plan. She had only thought it through up to the point of seeing Danny after his practice. She had no idea what she was actually going to say to him.

A whistle blew sharply. Mr Coleman, PE teacher and ex-army man, stood, hands on hips, in the centre of the swamp. 'Lads! What have I said about cheerleaders?' he hollered.

It took Lis a second to get it. He was referring to her.

'Marriott's, sir!' yelled back one massive youth.

Danny looked to the sky from his distant corner. Wonderful, she'd embarrassed him in front of his team.

'Marriott! Get rid of her! Now!'

His face scarlet, Danny jogged over to Lis. As he came nearer, she couldn't help noticing the curve of his chest under his rugby jersey. She quickly drew her gaze up. When boys stared like that at *her* chest, she hated it.

He reached her side and Lis briefly smelled his sweat on

the air. It was intoxicating. Her cold lips parted, but to her utter horror, no words came out. Nothing.

'Hi, Lis. What's up? Were we meant to meet or something?' He gently steered her towards the path, out of the view of his laughing team-mates.

'I needed to see you . . .' Lis began.

Danny smiled, checked that there was no one looking and gave her a sneaky kiss. 'Cool, but you'd better be quick or Mr Coleman might remove a piece of my anatomy that I'm very attached to!'

Her lips turned to stone. 'I . . . I . . . We need to talk,' she managed to stutter.

'Now?'

'Yeah. God, I'm sorry. I shouldn't have come. I'm such an idiot.'

'Lis, you're worrying me. What's going on?'

'Danny, I don't know how to say this . . .'

His face fell into a carbon copy of the expression he'd worn the day he heard about Laura's death. 'Are you breaking up with me?'

Was it too late to change her mind? The look on his face was painful. Lis felt like she was kicking a puppy. *Don't be a coward.* 'No. Yes. I have to,' she replied.

'What?' His voice went up about ten octaves.

Lis clutched his hand, but he snatched it back.

'It's not you, it's—' Lis began.

'Don't you dare finish that sentence!' Danny snapped, but he sounded as if he might cry.

Please don't, Lis thought, *I couldn't stand it.*

'Lis, I thought we were a "thing"?'

'No, Danny, we *are* a "thing"!'

'So what's up?'

'I'm going home. Back to Wales, and my mum.' Danny's

brilliant eyes bored into hers, but he said nothing. 'Danny?'

'Sorry, but I can't do this,' he said at last. 'It's messing with my head!' He threw his hands up, turned and headed back up the path, leaving Lis desolate and alone.

'Danny, please don't go!' she called after him.

'What's the point in staying?'

'We need to talk about this!'

He looked back, his face grim. 'If you've already decided to go then there's nothing to say, is there?'

'Danny, I can't stay in Hollow Pike!' This time she could not hold the tears back. 'I wish I could explain but I can't. You were my last reason to stay.'

'Is that meant to make me feel better?' he asked. 'Grow up!'

'No! I meant—'

'You know what?' Danny interrupted angrily. 'Maybe you *should* piss off back to Wales. Things were easier before you got here.' He stalked back to the rugby pitch like a wounded wolf rejoining the pack.

Lis cried in public and didn't care who saw her.

Making Up/Out

Struggling to be the rock-solid big-sister, Sarah gave her a tearful glance. 'But why, Lis? You've seemed so much happier here. When I saw you *last* Christmas you were so thin you looked ill!'

Lis traced the grain of the wood in the kitchen table with her fingers, unable to look at Sarah directly. 'I know, but it's complicated.'

'Then for God's sake, *tell* me!' Sarah begged.

Lis dearly wished she could tell Sarah the whole story, but she was scared that whoever was coming after her would also come after the people she loved if they knew too much. Even the thought of someone prowling around the house while Logan slept made her flesh crawl.

'There's nothing to tell,' Lis lied. 'I just want to go home. I miss Mum.' Only partly true, but certainly easier than the *whole* truth.

'Is this about Laura? Or Danny? Whatever it is, you can tell me,' Sarah pressed.

Lis shook her head sadly. It was all of those things and then some.

'Something's going on, Lis. I'm not daft.'

Lis paused. Sarah had given her such glorious freedom since she'd arrived in Hollow Pike. Maybe her honeymoon period was over; it now seemed that her sister was going to wait for her to crack under interrogation.

Just as the tension became unbearable, Max ambled into the kitchen. 'Are there any Frosties left?' he asked, peering into the high cupboard.

'Bottom cupboard,' Sarah stated, not taking her eyes off Lis.

'All a bit serious in here,' Max muttered, grabbing the cereal box. 'What's up?'

Lis seized her chance. 'Nothing. But I'm going to move back to Bangor. I miss Mum.'

Her brother-in-law paused, genuine disappointment on his face. He put the Frosties down on the table and joined them. Sarah continued to view Lis sceptically.

'Lis, that's a bummer,' Max told her. 'We love having you here. You don't think you're imposing, do you?'

'No, it's not that. I just want to go home,' Lis said again.

He made a comical sad face. 'Does that mean we'll have to start paying for babysitters?'

As always, Max softened Sarah. 'Max!' she snapped, but the steely expression had left her eyes and Lis sensed her easing off. 'Think about it some more, Lis. The house won't be the same without you.'

If her time in Hollow Pike had been just this: her, Sarah and Max sitting around the kitchen table, with Baby Logan asleep in his cot, then Lis would never have to leave. But it wasn't; someone was coming for her.

The doorbell rang and Sasha tore through the house barking her standard visitor alert.

'Who's that?' Max asked. He seemed to think Lis and her sister were oracles of the gateway or something.

Sarah hauled Sasha out of the way by her collar and opened the porch entrance.

From outside, Lis heard a familiar voice. 'Hi, I'm Danny. Is Lis home?'

Lis froze in her seat. Danny was at her house.

'Ah, yes,' Sarah said, smiling. 'Come on in.'

As with any guest, Sasha jumped up to lick Danny, who didn't seem in the least bothered by the red beast rearing up at him as he entered the kitchen.

Lis, unsure of him after their earlier exchange, stood quietly by her chair at the table. All eyes looked to her, but she didn't know any of the steps to this dance.

'Hi, Lis,' Danny said, and smiled awkwardly. 'Can we talk?'

'Yeah. Sure. Er ... come up to my room.' Head down, she led him through the lounge and onto the next level.

'Wow, cool house!' Danny remarked, making polite small-talk.

'I know, right? Max built it all from scratch,' Lis told him.

'Cool.'

Lis paused for a moment before opening her bedroom door. Had she left any knickers, bras or tampons anywhere in plain sight? She couldn't be certain, but she was ninety-nine per cent sure she was safe to let Danny into her inner sanctum. She held her breath and swung the door open. 'Come in.'

Only a bedside lamp illuminated the room, throwing elongated shadows and shapes onto the floor. Deliberately, Lis sat at her desk, safe in her own personal space. Danny perched awkwardly on the chaise longue.

'Well,' Danny began, 'I wanted to come and say sorry face to face. I was a total dick earlier.'

Lis felt a flame miraculously reignite within her belly. 'You don't need to apologise. I shouldn't have turned up at rugby practice like that.'

'No, I do. I shouldn't have said I wanted you to leave town. I don't want you to go.'

She did and didn't need to hear that. 'I wish I could stay,' she admitted. 'Maybe if things were different … but they're not.'

'But why? Why can't you stay? Have I done something?' Danny asked, looking mournful.

Lis laughed, but the sorrow of it surprised even her. 'No. God, no! It's everything *but* you.'

Danny smiled ruefully, kicking at the edge of the rug with his toe. 'I knew something like this'd happen. It was bound to go wrong sooner or later. I've never been out with a girl I like as much as you. It was too good to be true!'

'But it *is* true. I swear.' Lis had never wanted anyone more. How could someone so beautiful have so little self-esteem? 'I don't want to sound too mental … but I'm, like, crazy about you, Danny! These haven't been the best few weeks of my life, but you've made everything so much better.'

Danny smiled, letting her words sink in. 'Oh. I didn't know if you liked me or not.'

'Are you kidding?' Lis snorted. 'The question on everyone's lips is what do *you* see in *me*? The whole school thinks I'm a total freak. I *am* a total freak.'

Danny got to his feet, took Lis by the hand and pulled her up to join him. They stood just inches apart.

'Well, I must be into freaks then,' Danny said. 'I have a freak fetish!' He grinned, brushing her hair back from her face. 'Can we just forget what happened earlier?' he went on. 'You're not like any other girl at school, Lis. You're a one-off. I love it.'

'Yeah. OK.' She retreated under her hair again, her face burning.

'I do! You're awesome. I mean, look at you, you're gorgeous!'

She made a little huffing noise at that madness.

'Come on, you are ... Well, I think you are. And you're clever, *really* clever and funny – even funnier than my mates. And you don't let people change your mind. And I love how you look out for your friends. I could go on ... It's quite a long list of stuff I like!'

Lis looked into his eyes, knowing how dangerous that could be.

'I don't want you to leave, Lis. I only said that because I was upset. I want you to be my girlfriend. Like properly.' This time he didn't need an invitation to kiss her. He took her face in his warm hands and leaned towards her.

As if they belonged together, their lips locked effortlessly. Danny's kiss was skilful and gentle. Heat radiated from his fingertips across her cheeks, fuelling a fire inside her that felt *so* good. Lis wanted him to warm her all over, cleansing her of everything bad that had happened in Hollow Pike.

With his free hand, Danny reached around to the small of her back and pulled Lis towards his body, closing the inches between them. No other thoughts clouded her mind, she was too aware of Danny's touch, every magnetic point of contact between them. She traced the lines of his shoulders, then ran her hands down over his chest until she found the smooth skin just above his belt.

He grinned, grasping her wrist. 'That's bad!'

'Want me to stop?'

'No.'

They kissed again, with more urgency. This was the most alive Lis had ever felt. Tangled in each other's arms, they fell onto the bed.

This is how it happens, Lis realised, *no planning, no games, just the moment.*

She lay back as Danny kissed her neck. She was almost

completely lost in him, but something caught her attention: *why was the outside security light on?*

Her eyes snapped open as Lis was shocked back into reality. She stared at the French windows. Beyond the fine muslin curtains, a hooded human shape glided across the terrace. The movement was precise, effortless and fluid as a shark fin cutting through waves – and just as deadly.

Danny sensed Lis freeze. Confusion spread across his face as her body went rigid. Unable to find the words, Lis jabbed a finger towards the figure, who darted away from view.

Danny was up and over to the window in a heartbeat. 'What the—' He peered out of the window, then turned back to Lis, his eyes alive with fire. 'There's someone out there!' He started to open the doors, but Lis seized his arm.

'Stop!' she gasped.

'Let go, they're getting away!' Danny cried.

Images and words tangled together in Lis's head as her brain caught up with what was unfolding in her room. 'You can't go out there, Danny!'

'Why not? I'll kick the sh—'

'Because you'll get yourself killed!' Lis spat through gritted teeth. She didn't know who was out there, but she was pretty sure they'd killed before and that she was next on their agenda.

Danny continued to tug towards the doors and it took all her weight to stop him. 'What are you on about?' he demanded. 'It'll just be some stupid kids, and now they're getting away.'

This was not the time to play hero. 'I wish it was, but it's not. Danny, sit down!'

He stopped dragging her across the carpet and she let him go. Hands on hips, he waited for an explanation.

'Sit down,' Lis repeated. Danny cast her a dark glance

and sat on the bed, waiting for an explanation she couldn't provide.

Lis sat next to him, shoulders hunched. 'You know how I'm a bit weird sometimes?'

'I had noticed, yes!'

She tucked her hair behind her ears, trying to remain as matter-of-fact as possible. 'Well, it's all to do with Laura's death.'

Danny immediately tensed and inched away from her. 'Go on . . .'

'Danny, we were there,' Lis breathed, the words trembling on her lips.

'What?' Arctic cool fell over the room.

'It's not like that. We didn't do anything!' Lis exclaimed. She hated the distance growing between them on the bed. She just wanted to feel his body against hers again.

'So what *is* it like?' Danny asked.

'We were in the woods that night,' Lis went on. She decided to omit some vital details, unable to let Danny think of her as a monster. 'We saw Laura, but there was someone else there and I think they saw us.'

All the colour drained from Danny's face as he processed that information. 'You think . . .'

'I think they're after me now. Whoever it is.' She knew she shouldn't be saying any of this. If Kitty ever found out, she really would kill her.

Danny looked away, frowning as if he were trying to answer the hardest Maths question ever set. 'Who's "we"?'

'I can't say,' she replied firmly, although she suspected it was more than obvious. 'Do you get why I have to leave now?'

He said nothing for what felt like a month. 'I guess. But why don't you go to the police?'

'Because we were there . . . And everyone knows Laura and

I hated each other. It looks really bad! I can't tell them, Danny. I just can't.'

Again, he had no comeback to that.

Lis went on, 'But Laura had these diaries: five flowery diaries. We think she might have written about whoever killed her.'

'Really?' Danny looked intrigued. 'Where are the diaries now?'

'That's the problem. We know where some of them are, but the latest one's missing. We think it might be at school somewhere. If we can find that, and work out who's after me, things might be different, but …' She didn't want to give him false hope.

'You should have let me go after whoever was out there. I could have stopped this!' Danny told her.

Lis slid across the mattress to where he was slumped. She took both his hands in hers. 'No. Because if anything happened to you, I wouldn't want to be in this *world*, let alone this town, got that?'

He blushed and nodded. Lis picked a bit of fluff out of his hair and took a moment to memorise his incredible face. Soon, she'd never see it again and she didn't ever want to forget. 'I'm leaving Hollow Pike. It's the only way I'll be safe.'

He didn't say anything further, but laid her down, pulling her into a tight embrace. He held her from behind and Lis felt his warm breath on her hair. She closed her eyes to commit every last second to memory.

From the tangled bushes at the end of the garden, a figure watched the house intently. Pale fingers pulled leaves aside, seeking a better view of the building. Only one light was on.

Through the thin curtains over the French windows, the figure could see a young couple holding each other tenderly. *Enjoy it while it lasts.* Did they know what was coming? Did they know how little time they had left?

The figure took one last look before melting into the infinite darkness of Pike Copse.

Head

Lis had almost fallen asleep in Danny's arms – a rare moment of perfection. It was refreshing to know such moments were still possible *and* could happen to her. She'd been starting to think they only occurred on TV. She would never say the 'L Word', but she was kind of thinking it.

Lis remained resolute, however. She *had* to leave Hollow Pike. There was no doubt about it now. There'd been someone on her terrace. She'd felt safe with Danny, but he wasn't going to be around forever. He couldn't be her one-man security team.

She walked to school alone, feeling the solitude acutely. *Witches are not real. Witches are not real*, she told herself repeatedly, like it was her own personal mantra. Looking through the trees, shrouded in morning mist, the idea of witches seemed almost plausible. The scenes from *The Crucible* wouldn't be out of place in these woods – the girls dancing around tongues of fire, dark spirits emerging through the smoke. Lis could almost hear the low chants.

Lis promptly filled her head with thoughts of Christmas in an attempt to distract herself. There was a glistening frost on the ground and misty lanterns of her breath hung in the air. If she could get through the last few weeks of term she'd be free of this town. God only knew what she'd face back in Bangor, but Bronwyn and her bitches had to be better than the murky figure who watched her, violated her room and sent her sinister threats.

The morning roads seemed quieter than normal. Why wasn't there anyone around? Every time a leaf rustled, Lis's head whipped to face it and she didn't dare put her iPod on in case it masked footsteps behind her. She couldn't shake it – the feeling of eyes staring at her. It was as if the trees themselves were watching, waiting.

Feeling tightly wound, Lis finally arrived at Fulton High. Entering the main gates she noticed Nasima and Fi buzzing around Harry, their new queen bee. There must have been a coronation over half term or something, because Harry had taken Laura's place. Her hair was bigger, her skin more tanned. Without Laura around to knock her down, she even appeared to have grown taller, although Lis figured that was purely psychological.

'Y'all right, London?' Harry sneered. 'Nice shoes, where'd you get them? The market?'

Lis couldn't be bothered with this today. 'No, Harry, I stole them off a tramp, right after I shagged him. Satisfied?'

Harry had no comeback for that one and Lis felt suddenly smug. Kitty would have been proud of that. Don't act bothered, but don't ignore them either – stand your ground. Maybe she was going back to Wales stronger after all.

Jack, Kitty and Delilah were already in G2. Lis slipped into her seat next to Jack, waiting for registration.

'Hey, how come you weren't on the bus?' he asked.

'Missed it again.'

Kitty obviously wasn't going to apologise for her stroppiness yesterday, but she did act as if nothing had happened, which was fine with Lis.

'Morning. What did you get up to last night?' Kitty said.

'Nothing,' Lis fibbed. She wasn't going to tell them about

her conversation with Danny just yet – especially the fact that she'd given away their darkest secret. 'What did you get up to?'

'Just hung out at Jack's,' Kitty said absent-mindedly.

'All of you?' Lis didn't want to seem like she was interrogating them, but she needed to know.

'Yeah,' Jack answered. 'I sent you a text but you never replied.'

That was true, she did have an invitation from him. Their story checked out.

Mr Gray, who probably liked Lis a lot less after yesterday's performance, bumbled into class sporting a large tea stain on his pinstriped shirt. He put a mug down on his desk and looked around the class, his eyes falling on her. 'Ah, Lis. Could Ms Dandehunt see you in her office please?' Her face must have fallen all the way to the floor, because he added quickly, 'Oh, I don't think you're in any trouble.'

'Oh, OK.' Still, she frowned at Jack, feeling anxious.

Delilah wagged a finger at her admonishingly. 'Good luck, darling,' she said and winked.

She'd never in her whole life been summoned to a head's office. Wasn't that fate usually reserved for terrorists and stuff? Even when things were really bad at GCC, Lis had always dealt with her class teachers. Slipping out of G2, Lis made her way down G corridor. Halfway down the hallway, she stopped at Ms Dandehunt's room and found the door standing open for her.

'Ah, Lis,' called the head teacher. 'Do come in and take a seat. You won't mind if I finish my Ready Brek, will you?'

'No,' Lis replied, entering the office and ignoring the bizarre spectacle of a grown woman eating mush from a plastic bowl. It was a simple, square room with one wall of shelves filled with an enviable collection of snow globes.

Enviable if you're a mad woman who collects tacky ornaments, that is, thought Lis.

Hanging from the walls were various photos of Ms Dandehunt with pupils of Fulton. Some of them looked *old*, like *Antiques Roadshow* old! How long had Ms Dandehunt worked in Hollow Pike?

Lis seated herself at the grand central desk as the head popped the last of the goo into her mouth.

'Yummy!' she declared, letting the spoon clatter into the bowl.

'Mr Gray said you wanted to see me?'

'Yes. You're not in any trouble,' she echoed Mr Gray's sentiment, 'but I have had a phone call from you sister.'

Ah, that explained it then. 'OK, what did she say?'

Ms Dandehunt rested her chubby chin in her hands. 'She said you were dead set on leaving Fulton High School. Is that right?'

'Yes. I'm going back to live with my mum.'

'I see. I imagine you've missed her terribly.'

'Yeah. It's been hard.'

'And it hasn't been easy for you here at Fulton, either, has it?' Ms Dandehunt regarded Lis with owl eyes, full of knowledge. Lis remembered that Mr Gray had told her weeks ago that the teachers were always listening – what did Ms Dandehunt know?

'Sorry, I don't know what you mean,' Lis said carefully.

Ms Dandehunt smiled knowingly. 'Well, first of all there was trouble with Laura Rigg, God rest her soul. I heard about her little internet rumour.'

'Oh, that was nothing.'

'Nonsense! It was a very cruel thing to do to a newcomer,' Ms Dandehunt insisted. 'And then you fall in with Miss Monroe, Miss Bloom and that quiet young man they hang around with. Charming, clever pupils, but . . . not the easiest of friends, I'd hazard.'

'They're fine. Really.' This was excruciating, worse than Mr Gray's little chats.

'Good. I hope so, because I'd hate to think that your decision had anything to do with problems at Fulton. That's not the kind of establishment I want at all,' Ms Dandehunt said seriously.

First-period Maths was suddenly more tempting than it had even been before. 'My friends are awesome, really.'

Ms Dandehunt walked over to her shelves and gave one of her snow globes a shake, making the glitter swirl and sparkle around the kitten inside. 'We never spoke about the bird in your locker, did we?'

'The raven?'

'Crow.'

'What?'

'Crow, dear. It was a crow. They're different. Ravens are a *type* of crow, but not all crows are ravens. Do you see?'

Lis nodded, although wasn't entirely sure she understood.

'Strange business that, wasn't it? You know, many hundreds of years ago, the crow had much greater significance than it does today. It was a very powerful symbol; an omen, too.'

Lis's palms felt sweaty all of a sudden. 'OK . . .'

'You know, many witches had birds as familiars. Do you know what a familiar is, Lis?'

Lis felt panic setting in. She couldn't look Ms Dandehunt in the eye, so she focused on the cluttered desk before her instead. There were more snow globes, a photo of Ms Dandehunt with a furry black cat, and about a hundred files overflowing with paperwork.

'No, I—' Lis broke off, her jaw locking in horror, because underneath some of the paperwork, only visible because she'd accidentally moved a file with her hand, was a hardback notebook covered in apricot flowers and tied with a yellow ribbon.

Laura's final diary.

Lock-in

'You what, dear?' Ms Dandehunt looked for her to finish the sentence.

Lis dragged her eyes away from the diary. It had to be Laura's. She'd seen Laura with it that morning on the rugby pitch, and it was the *same one*. Why did Ms Dandehunt have it? Why wouldn't she have handed it over to the police? Why? Why? *Why haven't I answered her question?* Lis thought frantically.

'I was just going to say that Fulton High has been great,' Lis gabbled, 'but I didn't realise how much I was going to miss Wales. I'm Welsh through and through at heart, I guess.' She knew she sounded like a crazy person, but she felt like she had to get out of the office in the next ten seconds or the scream building in her chest would burst from her lips. Because the only reason Ms Dandehunt would be hiding that diary was if she had a secret to protect.

And that was when Lis saw it. On the second shelf from the top of the wall, almost hidden in the museum of snow globes, was an inconspicuous sprig of lavender bound with a black ribbon.

Lis almost fell off her chair. The old woman was a witch! As insane as it sounded, it suddenly made sense. After all the weeks of whispers, rumours and ghost stories, Lis found herself living in a world that contained witches: a new, impossible reality.

'Lis, are you all right, dear?' Ms Dandehunt asked, fixing her in a hawk-like glare from behind her thick glasses.

'Yeah. I, er, just saw the clock and thought I'd better get to class,' Lis replied. 'I don't want to miss Maths.'

'Good girl. What a dedicated student you are. If only they were all like you.'

Wasting no further time, Lis sprang out of the chair and made for the door, almost tripping over her own legs in her hurry. 'Thanks, Ms Dandehunt. Bye.'

'Take care, Lis,' the headteacher called after her. It could have almost been a warning.

As soon as she left the office, Lis spotted Kitty's purple hair bobbing towards the exit at the end of G corridor and, ploughing through the stream of pupils, she raced to catch up with her. Knocking a group of Year Eight boys out of the way, Lis was relieved to see Jack and Dee alongside the taller girl.

Falling into step with them, Lis hauled Kitty to one side before she could enter her Maths lesson.

'Christ, Lis, what are you trying to do? Pull my arm off?'

'You can't go to first period – any of you. We need to talk NOW.'

The library was almost empty, save for Daphne running a feather duster over the bookshelves. The four friends crammed themselves into their usual toasty corner by the pipes.

'And you're sure it was the same diary?' Jack asked, tucking into a ham sandwich.

'Dead sure. Same book,' Lis told him.

Delilah looked at Kitty, doing that telepathic thing that couples do. 'Oh my God. That means ...'

'... that she had something to do with Laura's death!' Kitty finished. 'Otherwise, why wouldn't she have handed it over to the police? She knew they were looking for it; the police file said she'd been contacted about it!'

Lis spoke in a low whisper. 'I'm going to say something completely mental now, but just listen for a minute. I think she's a witch.'

Jack nearly choked on his lunch.

Delilah raised a delicate eyebrow. 'Oh, *now* you believe in witches?' she said.

'I know, I know!' Lis checked to make sure no one in the old library was listening. 'She has a black cat *and* the same flowers that I found under my pillow. It's her.'

'The super-grim way Laura was killed *was* more like a sacrifice than an attack,' Kitty admitted thoughtfully.

'And we live in Hollow Pike,' added Delilah. 'Maybe the witch trials didn't get all the witches. Maybe they just drove them underground.'

Jack finished his sandwich. 'Can you hear yourselves? Laura was killed by a psycho with a big knife. End of.'

'But, Jack, look at the way Laura was killed ...' Delilah spoke with urgency now that the picture was taking shape.

'OK, she was killed by a psycho with a knife who *thinks* she's a witch,' Jack amended. 'And what's more psycho than that? Literally nothing!' Then he looked thoughtful. 'Ms Dandehunt is kind of crazy. I guess it could have been her ...'

Lis had to admit, Jack had a point. She didn't believe in magical flying witches, but she certainly believed in people losing the plot. At the end of the day, isn't that why people do terrible things – because of the dark beliefs they harbour? A chill ran up her spine. 'We have to get that book from Ms Dandehunt's office. If it's evidence, we can give it to the police, and ... ding-dong the witch is dead.'

'How can we get it?' Delilah asked.

'I don't care,' Lis said emphatically, 'we just have to. And then we can live happily ever after. Me and Danny, you and you, and Jack and ... whoever the hell he fancies.'

'Gee, thanks, Lis.' Jack laughed.

'You're welcome. So, we need a plan ...'

All eyes turned to Kitty, their fearless leader.

'What am I? 0800-Dial-A-Plan?' Kitty groaned. The others nodded and Kitty rolled her eyes. 'OK. But we are going to be in so much trouble if we get caught!'

The clock had to be faulty. It was moving at half the speed of a regular clock; every minute seemed to span an hour. Agitated, Lis drummed her pencil on her exercise book, willing the time away. The sooner the bell rang at three, the sooner they could get this deranged scheme over and done with.

Kitty threw her a dark look from the other side of the Food Technology classroom, signalling her to relax, but Lis couldn't. She'd been unable to sit still all day and she had purposefully avoided Danny; he didn't need to see her looking like a wreck.

She stared at the blank page before her. The recipe for a diabetic dessert was just going to have to wait; she couldn't focus at all. This was it. This really was her last attempt to solve the mystery. If it didn't work, all she wanted was to spend her final weeks in Hollow Pike with Danny and then head home to Wales.

Finally, Miss Cook (yes, the Food Tech teacher was called Miss Cook) announced that any unfinished (or indeed, un*started*) work must be completed at home, and then told them to pack away their things.

At last! Let's get this show on the road! Lis thought. She tossed her things carelessly into her bag and rushed to Kitty's side.

'For Christ's sake, will you please chill out?' the taller girl snapped.

Lis pouted. 'Would you please become human?'

Kitty softened and rubbed her arm. 'Lis, it's going to be fine, seriously. Let's go.'

Wishing she could have even a fraction of Kitty's bravado, Lis followed her friend out of the cooking room and down the stairs to the courtyard, where Jack was already waiting for them. His expression was much closer to hers than Kitty's, and Lis found comfort in this fact.

'OK, now I'm really nervous,' he whispered to them.

'Thank you!' Lis exclaimed. 'Me too.'

Kitty ignored them both. 'Hurry up, Delilah's waiting for us.'

Swimming against the tide of pupils moving down the driveway and out of the gates, the three of them ducked into the library. Sliding straight past Daphne at the counter, they pushed through the interior door that led to the Sixth Form computer suite. During school hours, this was the exclusive domain of Years Twelve and Thirteen but, after school, this smaller ICT room was a dedicated homework area for children who didn't have computers at home. As most did, it was never busy, especially since October when a Year Nine boy had got into huge trouble for downloading porn.

Delilah was already there, tinkering away on the internet. 'You guys, quick, come look at this!' she called.

They walked around the little island of computers to see her monitor. She was looking at some sort of etching from the Middle Ages. It depicted a grotesque old man surrounded by cats, leaning over a bubbling cauldron.

'What's that meant to be?' asked Jack, frowning at the image.

'It's called *The Mage with Familiars*,' Delilah explained.

'That doesn't really help!' Jack said.

'I've been thinking about Laura,' Delilah went on.

'Makes a refreshing change,' joked Kitty.

Delilah ignored her. 'Her heart was removed, right? Well in the sixteenth century, goat or sheep hearts were often left as offerings to the Horned God. Witches believed he'd do their bidding if he accepted a worthy sacrifice.'

Jack grimaced at the engraving. 'So, Ms Dandehunt wanted Laura's heart as a sacrifice!' he exclaimed. Then he added jokingly, 'Ms Dandehunt's a cat person. I've never trusted cat people.'

'That's what I was searching for.'

'Crazy cat people?'

'No!' Delilah huffed. 'Familiars. I was trying to work out why Laura and Lis got the crows. I think it has something to do with those birds being witches' familiars.'

'That's what Ms Dandehunt said,' Lis added thoughtfully.

The school courtyards were now empty and the December sky was turning mauve already. Lis was twitchy, and Dee's sinister theories weren't helping. In a short time, they were about to risk everything to retrieve the diaries.

'When can we leave this room?' Lis asked.

'Rugby practice until five, Spanish club until six and then it's game on,' Kitty stated.

'Good.' Lis bowed her head. 'Now, who wants to help me write a diabetic recipe while we wait?'

There was something inherently wrong about the dark, silent school. It was a contradiction. No shouting, no bells, no life. As six o'clock approached, Lis found herself oddly calm, resigned to what they had to do.

Daphne had long since left the library, instructing 'you nice Year Elevens' to drop the latch when they'd finished their homework.

The four of them noisily made their way past the CCTV cameras trained on the library counter and the exit. They needed to be filmed leaving. Lis had to admit, Kitty's plan was airtight. She was wasted on schooling; the secret service needed her.

As soon as they stepped beyond the camera's gaze and into the dagger-sharp winter air, the group stopped.

'Right,' said Kitty with authority, 'does everyone know their positions?'

'Aye, aye, captain!' Jack saluted.

'This should be relatively simple,' Kitty went on. 'In and out in ten minutes. If the diary's not there, game over.'

Lis nodded, refusing to think about the ten billion things that could go wrong.

Kitty continued. 'Stick to your posts and if you see anyone coming, send a group text. Phones on vibrate?'

They all checked their phones.

Lis turned to Kitty. 'Are you sure this'll work?'

She nodded. 'The CCTV is like a normal video machine. Just press *Stop*.'

Kitty had invented an errand earlier to take her to the

main office. She was, of course, casing the joint, and she'd learned everything she needed to know about the school's limited security.

The CCTV was an old style video recorder system; no one would question a 'malfunction'. The trickier part was the burglar alarms, but 'Spanish for Adults' in G2 classroom didn't finish until eight, so they couldn't turn the intruder alarms on until then. The plan was to get the diary while the Spanish class was in progress, so they'd have to deal with the cameras but not the alarms.

'Remember,' said Delilah, 'don't go anywhere near G2, or we've had it.'

'Cool.' Lis's stomach fizzed like it was full of acid. 'Let's do it.'

They gathered at the top of the end staircase and peered cautiously down the corridor. The dark passageway stretched before them, the only light spilling from G2 at the farthest end of the hallway. On this stretch they were vulnerable; if someone came out of Spanish for Adults, they'd be busted.

'Coast's clear,' Lis breathed from her vantage point.

'What about the Spanish class?' hissed Delilah.

'Looks like they're all in,' Lis replied.

'OK. Stick to the wall and stay low,' Kitty instructed.

Jack had left them already for his role as early-warning look-out. His spot was outside the main entrance to the B corridor – the only access to the G corridor other than the main staircase, which Dee would cover. Lis edged down the corridor, hardly daring to breathe and keeping her eyes fixed on the end classroom. Her rubber soles made only the lightest tapping sound, but she cursed them nonetheless. Three strange girls creeping down a school hall must have looked hilarious, but in the moment it was serious as a funeral. Her heartbeat reverberated through her skull, but Lis ignored it, hastening on till she reached the central junction to the T Block, where the lockers and staffroom were located.

Turning the corner, she pressed herself in alongside the metal lockers. Kitty and Delilah joined her. From this hideout they couldn't be seen by anyone in G2.

'Christ!' The whites of Delilah's eyes shone. 'I don't know if I can handle this.'

Kitty gave her a slow, steady kiss on the lips. 'We're nearly there. Hardest bit's over – this is your spot. If anyone comes out of G2, let us know.'

Delilah tucked herself between the rows of lockers, vanishing into the shadows. 'Please be careful. Love you.'

'Right back at ya!' Kitty smiled and Lis drew strength from their affection. 'Lis, the office is just at the bottom of those stairs.'

'OK,' Lis whispered. She took a last look at the shadows moving within G2 and then started down the stairs to the main entrance hall. The grand old clock ticked louder than she would have thought possible as she reached the last of the stone stairs. Once in the hall, on her right was the exit to the school driveway, and to her left were the boys' toilets – two escape routes if she needed them. Sticking to the walls, avoiding patches of light on the floor, she tiptoed across the hall and onto the short staircase that led to what was essentially the basement of the school. On this level there was only the deputy head's office, the bursar's room and the main school office in which the surveillance equipment was located.

Although not as vital as Kitty's role, Lis knew she couldn't mess up. They shouldn't be in school at all, and if cameras caught Kitty going into Ms Dandehunt's office then there would be major hell to pay. It was Lis's job to make sure the tape from the CCTV didn't have any footage of them after the point where they were seen leaving the library.

It shouldn't be too hard, Lis told herself. *It's a video machine, for crying out loud. Stop, rewind, tape over. Easy! In theory.*

Just as Kitty had predicted, the door to the office stood ajar. Lis pushed the door softly, cursing the shrill creak it gave. Through the gloom she could make out three untidy desks and numerous filing cabinets. On top of one was a simple VCR and TV unit. A light on the VCR indicated that it was recording, but the TV wasn't on.

Lis darted over and pushed the *On* button on the CCTV monitor. The standby light glowed red, but the TV failed to come on. OK, so she needed a remote control. Great. Where was it? She swivelled to the desk behind her and started rummaging through the crap piled all over it: dirty mugs, paperwork, calendars, mouse mats, the phone, a stapler, but no remote! She was starting to lose patience when her hands found the slim plastic device underneath a crumpled copy of *Take a Break*. Lis switched on the monitor.

The TV buzzed to life, displaying twelve grainy boxes showing the different camera feeds from around the school. Each was labelled CAM1, CAM2 and so on. Jack was visible on CAM4, waiting by a rubbish bin outside the B corridor entrance, hopping from foot to foot to fight off the cold. Delilah and Kitty were still hiding by the lockers on CAM6.

Lis studied the remote and found the stop button for the video recorder. She pointed the remote at the machine and pressed the button. A red LED went out immediately. Job done. The cameras still showed *her* what was going on around the school, but now none of it was being committed to tape. Lis let out the longest breath of her life.

Taking her phone from her pocket, she expertly tapped in a text to Kitty: *Cameras off. Go go go!!!*. A couple of seconds later, Lis saw Kitty look at her phone, say a few words to Dee and prowl out of range of CAM6. In another few moments, her shadowy form crept onto CAM5, which filmed the entire length of the G corridor. This was risky because Ms Dandehunt's office was only two doors down from G2. Lis watched the slender figure edging down the corridor, unable to look away. This was must-see TV. She swallowed, her throat and tongue dry as a desert.

Wait. Something moved in the final row of cameras. Just for a split second, a dark shape had moved across CAM9, drawing Lis's attention. She left her perch on the desk to get a closer look. CAM9 showed the atrium outside the humanities rooms in the T Block. There shouldn't be anyone in there, so who could it be? They'd already seen the cleaners go home ages ago.

There it was again. Underneath the camera, a figure shifted in the darkness. The image was so poor it was as if a spectre moved through the hallway, but there was no mistaking it. *There was someone else in the school.*

Lis instinctively reached for her phone as the shape moved out of range of CAM9. She cursed under her breath. Where would it go next? Should she call Kitty? Call off the search? She slapped the side of her head, trying to knock some logic into her brain. T Block – where did that lead? Middle corridor, staffroom, G corridor. Scanning the cameras, Lis located the staffroom on CAM7. Sure enough, the mysterious figure emerged in the darkest corner of the screen. Squinting at the image, Lis could now see that the stranger was caped, with a hood over their head. This was not good.

Suddenly she realised that CAM7 was right next to CAM6. Delilah! Her friend was peeking out from the lockers, obviously waiting for Kitty – who, Lis could see from another camera, had now reached the entrance to the head's office. Dee's back was to the staffroom, and she clearly had no idea that someone was coming up behind her.

Lis watched in horror as the shadow glided towards her, a tiger stalking its prey. 'Delilah!' Lis bellowed, her shrill voice shattering the silence. Too late. As her scream echoed through the school, the hooded predator clamped a hand over Delilah's petite face, sealing her in a tight hold. In a single, fluid movement, the attacker swept her friend out of sight.

She had to help Delilah. Sprinting to the office door, Lis failed to see what was happening on CAM 11: another figure was walking along the bottom corridor right towards the CCTV office.

'Lis?'

She screamed, dropping her phone and watching it bounce under the desk. Danny Marriott stood in the doorway, blocking her path.

'Danny? What are you doing here?' She had to get to Dee, but this didn't make sense. He'd appeared out of the shadows, like something in a horror film.

'I was just about to ask you the same thing! Why are you in school so late?'

She started to blurt out their cover story, 'Delilah thinks her house keys are in lost property. Actually, never mind that … Why are *you* still here?'

He seemed to stiffen, backing away from her. Shadows occluded his handsome features. 'I asked you first.'

'Danny, I haven't got time for games, just tell me why you're here. Delilah's in trouble! And what are you holding behind your back?'

'Nothing!' he said far too quickly, stepping further backwards.

Little alarms started ringing in her head, but she advanced on him anyway. He was by the door and she needed to get out of here and help Delilah. 'Seriously. What's in your hands?'

'Lis . . .' he started, but before he could finish, she pounced. She darted towards him and he instinctively raised his hands in a move to put whatever he was holding out of her reach. Lis had played netball enough times to counter his defence and with a single swipe she knocked the object clear out of his grasp.

A notebook fell to the floor: hardback, decorated with little apricot-coloured flowers and tied with a yellow ribbon. Lis recognised it at once: Laura's diary.

Lis's brain went into overdrive. They'd assumed Ms Dandehunt was the killer because she'd had the diary and hadn't given it to the police. If it contained clues to Laura's murderer then obviously the killer wouldn't want the police to get hold of it. But now Danny had the book. Danny or Dandehunt? Dandehunt or Danny? *The killer has the book.*

'Lis . . . It's not what you think,' Danny said.

'What do I think?' she demanded, her heart pounding against her ribs.

Danny opened his arms and took a step towards her. She reflexively ducked back out of reach. 'Oh, God, I know it looks bad,' Danny muttered.

'Why do you have that diary?' Lis asked, trying to keep panic out of her voice. She'd been so blind . . . Laura had told her she and Danny were involved, but Lis had ignored it, willing to believe anything Danny told her. Had he killed Laura himself, or had it been his masked accomplice who'd now grabbed Delilah?

'I . . . I found it,' Danny stammered.

'Yeah, right!' The fight or flight impulse kicked in and flight won hands down – not least because, right now, Delilah needed her. Lis threw herself past Danny towards the open door, but he caught her in a second. Double her weight, Danny pinned her against the door frame, grinding her spine against the wood. She cried out in pain.

'Wait!' he urged. 'Lis, I need to explain!'

'Get off me!' Lis screamed, but he retained his hold on her. Desperate now, she delivered a hard kick to his shin. He howled and let go of her instantly. Lis took off up the stairs.

Even with a sore leg, she knew a rugby player wasn't going to be stopped that easily and she could hear him right behind her, limping as fast as she ran. She bounded up the first flight of stairs and was then faced with the choice of main exit, boys' toilets or the stairs up to G2. Danny would just as easily catch her on the drive as the stairs, she realised. Her only option was strength in numbers. She headed for the Spanish class in G2.

She made it halfway across the entrance hall before he caught up with her. He reached out, seizing a handful of her blazer. Lis shrieked and wriggled out of the jacket, letting him pull it clean off her body. Slowed, but still burning adrenalin, she ran on to the longer flight of stairs.

'Lis! Stop!' Danny called, throwing the blazer to the floor. He sprinted forwards, grabbing at her legs from a lower step. 'Will you give me a chance?'

She raced on up the stairs, focused on reaching the top. Danny's footsteps were close though, and getting closer every second.

'Goddammit Lis, you are bloody hard work!' Danny cursed and reached for her again.

This time Lis felt his hand close around her ankle.

Instinctively, she kicked backwards and Danny lost his grip. She heard a messy scrabbling sound behind her and looked to see Danny fall backwards down the stairs. He hit the floor with a dull thud. The force of it twisted his head around at a painful angle and his startled eyes closed. He lay there, limp and still like a rag doll. From his nose or mouth, Lis couldn't tell which, crimson blood spilled over his chin.

Lis stared at him, unable to breathe. This was the part where she knew she had to run. He was bound to get up and come after her. Murderers always do in films. Yet she found herself unable to move. It was as if the struggle had drained her whole body. She watched, waiting for any slight movement from the foot of the stairs.

'What the bloody hell is going on here?' an authoritative voice boomed from the very top of the staircase.

Lis turned to see Mr Gray jogging down towards her.

'Lis?' he said with concern. 'Lis? What happened?'

He put his arm around her and slowly she felt her brain defrosting: she was safe, it was fine, she wasn't alone. Lis fell into his arms like a marionette with its strings cut.

'Mr Gray, Danny's the killer!' Lis sobbed. 'He killed Laura. He was after me. And Delilah – someone's got Delilah!' The words tumbled over themselves.

'What?' Mr Gray pulled back. 'Are you kidding?'

'No! It's all true!'

He looked into her eyes, searching for truth, and then glanced down at Danny. 'Jesus, Lis! Is he OK?'

Mr Gray pushed her behind him and headed down the stairs to his unconscious pupil.

'Stop,' Lis begged. 'He's dangerous!'

'Just wait there!' Gray commanded. Her teacher cautiously leaned over Danny. Lis could see the blood, but was he breathing? Had she killed her boyfriend?

'He's alive,' Mr Gray announced. Danny stirred and the teacher recoiled in shock.

Lis wasn't going to wait for round two. She raced down the stairs, slowing only to step carefully around Danny's body.

'Where are you going?' Mr Gray asked.

Lis continued to run across the entrance hall back towards the main office. 'To call the police!' she shouted back to him. 'Then this whole thing will be over. We've got proof now.'

She trotted down the last few steps and into the office, now more familiar with her surroundings. Hauling a phone across the first desk she came to, she lifted the receiver and began to dial nine, nine, nine. She'd never done this before; she hoped it would be pretty self-explanatory. This was it. After this phone call it was out of her hands forever. She could find her friends, make sure Dee was OK and live happily ever after.

A warm hand pulled the phone out of her grip and calmly placed it back in its cradle. She turned and found her face inches from Mr Gray's.

'I was just calling the police!' she exclaimed, utterly confused.

'Oh, Lis,' Mr Gray said in a new, patronising tone. 'You can't call the police.'

'Why not?'

'Because Danny didn't kill Laura.'

And then he took a step back and swung his fist at her face so fast she didn't even have time to blink. The fist made contact and, after a split second of the most crushing pain she'd ever felt, Lis stopped being aware of anything at all.

Witches

This dream topped them all. This time, Lis had broken into school after hours, watched a hooded figure kidnap her mate, and then essentially kicked her boyfriend down the stairs! What could it all mean?

No, wait ...

Her eyes fluttered open to see long, white rectangles moving past her face. Where was she? Searing pain emanated from her nose and she tasted coppery blood in her mouth.

Oh, God, it wasn't a dream. Danny ... Mr Gray ... It had all happened. It was *still happening.*

Lis realised her legs were in the air. The oblongs she'd observed were strip lights. She was being dragged. Snapping into action, she wriggled like an eel, letting out a pitiful cry for help.

'Lis, hush,' said Mr Gray, who was doing the dragging. He pinned her feet together to stop her from kicking out. 'We're almost there now. Don't make a fuss.'

Using her arms, she tried in vain to claw her way in the opposite direction, digging her nails into the tiled floor, but she couldn't get a grip. Gray had the drop on her and all the momentum.

'Lis, will you calm down? You'll only hurt yourself!'

She swore, and again tried to kick herself free from his hold. She felt herself starting to cry with fear and frustration.

'Please don't cry. Men are physically incapable of dealing with crying girls. It's a fact of life.'

Lis swore again, more loudly. Why was he being so weirdly pleasant? Why not just finish the job?

Suddenly, the texture against the small of her back changed as a mighty pull from Gray dragged her through a doorway and onto carpet. The niceties ceased as he grabbed a handful of her hair and yanked her onto her feet.

They were in G2 and it was full of people. Lis's head spun wildly from the horizontal to vertical shift and the overpowering peppery smell that filled the room. She took a second to adjust.

Her gaze first fell on Kitty and Delilah who were both taped to chairs in the centre of the classroom. All the other chairs and tables had been stacked neatly around the perimeter of the room. Lis gasped: relief at seeing her friends alive, mixed with an equal measure of terror. Kitty and Dee had been crudely bound with brown packing tape, their arms, legs and mouths restrained. It was something you'd expect to see in a terrorist's home movie, not in real life.

Lis twisted round in Mr Gray's hold, searching for Jack. He wasn't there. But several other people were. She immediately recognised Jennifer Rigg, Laura's mum, standing elegantly in the corner, immaculate as she had been in her own home. Sitting next to her and holding a pile of ancient-looking books was little old Daphne from the library.

This was too weird. Why weren't they helping her? Why were they just sitting there?

'Help me!' Lis yelled, staggering as Gray pushed her towards a chair. 'Please!'

At least Mrs Rigg had the good grace to look away. Daphne seemed to find her plea funny.

'Welcome to Spanish for Adults,' Mr Gray sneered. He

shoved her down into a chair and Jennifer Rigg strutted to his side, carrying the tape. Within seconds Lis's hands were secured behind her back.

'Leave her mouth,' Gray instructed. 'Now, let's talk.'

'I don't understand,' Lis begged. 'Please, just let us go. We haven't done anything wrong!'

Gray looked at her, genuine sympathy in his eyes. 'You know what, Lis?' he breathed, leaning in so close he was almost nuzzling her neck. 'I'm gutted it's you, I mean it. I prayed and prayed for it to be someone else, but it's not, is it? It's you.'

'I don't know what you mean!' Lis screamed. She saw tears well up and spill from Delilah's eyes. Even hard-as-nails Kitty was wide-eyed with fear.

'Really?' Gray smiled. 'That's not true, is it? *Witch!*'

He was calling her a witch? Shouldn't it be the other way round? She glanced around the room, absorbing everything. Candles burned on the window ledges and on the teacher's desk where they surrounded a bronze bowl of burning incense, which filled the air with the pungent peppery smell Lis had already noticed. It was as if they'd all been transported back in time, hundreds of years, to the dark days – the *darkest* days – of Hollow Pike. Lis remembered the old etchings of burning torches and burning bodies, and the tortured faces of the witches tied to the stake as eager crowds looked on in glee.

And then she got it. *The Crucible*. The jigsaw was finished and it wasn't a pretty picture.

'What are you?' she asked in a low voice.

'Well, that's exactly what I was going to ask you!' He smiled. 'We are The Righteous Protectors. I doubt you'll have heard of us; we're not really down with the kids. We don't have a Facebook page.'

Oh, she'd heard of them. Suddenly she wished she'd taken the time to read Dandehunt's book herself.

'I've heard about you,' she said.

The adults in the room bristled. The colour drained from Jennifer Rigg's face. 'I knew it. They've known about us the whole time.'

'Be quiet,' Gray ordered. 'And just what did you hear?'

Lis paused. Play dumb or tell the truth? She figured it was much too late to play innocent. These were the professionals after all. 'You're some sort of church group ... From years ago. You protect Hollow Pike? You chase away the ghosts and goblins.'

The adults laughed, except Gray, whose expression was suddenly overcast, a storm brewing.

'Do you think this is a joke?' he growled. 'Our ancestors founded the Righteous Protectors almost four hundred years ago to purge this town of people like you! The townsfolk, your so-called "healers" and "wise women" were sinners. They danced with the devil and look what they got: children started to disappear, plague arrived. The witches hexed this town. We purified Hollow Pike.'

He reached under the neck of his shirt and pulled out a delicate silver cross, identical to the one Lis had seen Jennifer wearing at her home. 'Our families have continued God's work for hundreds of years,' he went on.

'You're related?'

'Not all of us. Names change over the years, but *we're* all Sternes. Meet my cousin and my grandmother. The Sternes were right there at the beginning, the proudest witch-finders – we even helped translate the *Malleus Maleficarum*. You're not the first witches we've dealt with.'

'We're not witches!' Lis exclaimed truthfully.

Again, the little congregation laughed heartily. 'Then

what would you call yourself, deary?' Daphne spoke up from her chair.

'Nothing! I'm just a girl.'

'Lis!' Gray chastised. 'You have such low self-esteem! You're so much more than just a girl!' He knelt before her, examining her keenly. 'Haven't you ever had a dream, Lis – a dream where you see things that haven't happened yet? Haven't you ever had a feeling of déjà vu that you couldn't quite place? Haven't you ever noticed the way birds seem to follow you?'

A tear stung Lis's eye and rolled down her cheek. He knew her better than she knew herself. She gave her ties an experimental tug but she was tightly bound. 'I don't know what you mean.'

Mr Gray wiped her tears away, and she flinched at his touch. 'That's interesting. In the past, witches couldn't cry under torture – it was one way of spotting a *malefica*. You must be very powerful indeed. We've been watching and listening closely, Lis. Does the name Rushworth mean anything to you?'

Saying nothing, she nodded. Her gran – her mother's mother – had been Vida Rushworth, that much was true.

'Everything changed when *you* arrived,' Jennifer spat. 'Laura's dreams began ...'

'Please,' Lis begged. 'I don't know what you mean!'

Gray sighed, becoming impatient. 'OK, I suppose there's time for a brief history lesson. Sitting comfortably? So, our ancestors, the Righteous Protectors, first rode into this hellhole nearly four hundred years ago. It had quite the reputation, as I'm sure you're aware. They stormed the forests and dragged the witch women from their homes. In accordance with the holy law, the witches were tried, convicted and executed.'

'You mean they were tortured until they confessed?' Lis demanded angrily.

Gray's nostrils flared, but he didn't rise to her taunt. 'Unfortunately,' he continued, 'some of their bastard children survived. Some of the locals felt sorry for them, can you believe that? They looked upon the witches as "healers" and that sort of thing. The pitiful creatures got wind of us coming and agreed to hide the witches' spawn.'

Suddenly, Lis saw where this was heading. It was impossible, though. She would have known. Someone would have told her – her mum or gran ...

'The Rushworth family was one of those suspected of taking in these devil children and raising them as their own. We could never prove it though ... until now. Laura was a Rushworth witch. And so are you.'

'What?' Lis demanded softly.

Jennifer spoke very quietly, candlelight flickering across her glacial features. 'She was adopted. I ... I couldn't have my own children ...'

Daphne moved across to Jennifer's side. 'It wasn't your fault, Jenny. You couldn't have known you were taking in a witch.'

Gray gripped Lis's shoulders, his voice suddenly deep and deadly serious. 'How could we have been so stupid? The oldest Protector family in Hollow Pike and we almost allowed our bloodline to be tainted.' Suddenly, the weird light tone returned. 'That's right, Lis, your grandmother was Laura's great-aunt. Only neither of them knew it because Laura's *real* mother never told anyone she was pregnant!' With a flourish, Gray produced Laura's journal from his inside pocket and showed it to the room.

He must have picked it up in the office after he punched me, Lis thought. She saw Mrs Rigg flinch.

'Jenny, do you want to do this bit, or shall I?' Gray asked.

'Simon, please don't,' she replied in her clipped, fake accent.

Gray smiled. 'We don't know how you did it, but you somehow managed to get hold of Laura's other diaries, didn't you? But you've been looking for this one, I understand. And rightly so! It's a page turner! The one where Laura finally learns who she really is – a witch.'

Lis pursed her lips. She tried to make eye contact with Kitty, wondering if Kitty's restraints were any more breakable than hers, but Kitty was nearest to Daphne, and on Daphne's lap lay a nasty-looking ornate knife. It was some sort of ceremonial dagger with a leather hilt and a long, wavy blade. Lis was too far away to see it, but she knew the blade had a delicate pattern inscribed into the metal. She knew it because she had seen the knife before – in her dreams.

'So I'm guessing Laura was your coven leader, right?' Mr Gray asked Lis. 'She wouldn't have had it any other way.'

Lis was about to deny this when she noticed Kitty shaking her head. Did Kitty have a plan? Lis wasn't sure, but as long as Mr Gray was talking, he wasn't using the dagger. *Play along with him.* And where was Jack? And Danny? *Oh, God, poor Danny!* If one of them had called the police, all she had to do was keep Gray talking. At the same time, she continued to rub her wrists together, trying to loosen the tape that held her.

'Whatever,' Lis said with as much conviction as she could muster.

'Four witches make a coven. A new coven in Hollow Pike. We can't have that. Now Kitty and Delilah we've suspected for a long time – Kitty, you're a witch through your grandfather of course, and we all know about your mother, don't we, Delilah?' Behind their gags, Kitty looked puzzled, obviously oblivious to her supposed witch bloodline, while Delilah's eyes flashed with rage. Mr Gray continued. 'You made four when you came here, Lis, and that's when Laura started having the dreams, started asking her father questions. He told her she was adopted and then it was only a matter of time before the four of you started practising dark magic. We had to end it.'

Lis's heart broke on the spot. Oh, poor Laura, suffering the nightmares all by herself. She'd been going through the same things as Lis but with no one to talk to. No wonder her last few months had been so tumultuous! Lis knew exactly what that felt like, but at least she'd had the others in the end. If only Laura had opened up that day on the field, things could have been so different. But the Righteous Protectors had killed her, just like they were going to kill Lis and her friends now.

A hot tear trickled down her cheek. She understood everything now. They were linked. All of them. On her first day at Fulton she'd been drawn to Laura as much as to the others. Perhaps some sort of magnetism in their bloodline had pulled them together. But Lis had been too late to reach Laura. Much too late.

Her gaze fell on Mrs Rigg and something new blossomed in Lis: anger. 'You killed your own daughter!' she exclaimed, aghast.

'She wasn't my daughter, not any more,' Mrs Rigg replied icily. 'She belonged to Satan. You all do. When she told me about the dreams, the birds, I knew she was in league with the devil. There was nothing I could do. She had to die.'

'Right, you keep telling yourself that!' Lis snapped. She couldn't keep that one in.

The older woman marched across the room, rage burning across her face. 'You little bitch!' She pulled back her arm ready to strike, but Gray intervened, catching her hand.

'Don't get too close,' he told her. 'It could be a trick. Remember what you're dealing with.'

'You said the pepper would protect us from spells,' Jennifer said, pointing at the pot on the desk.

'You can never be too careful with witches . . .'

They're scared of me! Lis realised. Could she use that? She tried to give them a compelling look, but it probably just came across as sullen. The tape around her wrists was loosening, though. As subtly as she could, she tried to wriggle her fingers out from the bindings. *Play for time*, she told herself.

'So you killed Laura?' Lis remarked. 'Nice. She hadn't done anything wrong.'

'We knew there'd be four of you so we started the search straight away,' Gray told her. 'We traced the family trees. You three, all from old Hollow Pike families, thick as thieves. Didn't take much to figure it out, to be honest. We've been watching you ever since.'

'It was you outside my room last night!' Lis suddenly realised. 'You pervert!'

Gray winked. 'You put on quite a show with Mr Marriott, by the way. It was so easy – I heard you tell him you were looking for the diary at school, we just had to wait here until you were dumb enough to break in. I wish it had been someone else though, not you guys. You guys are great! Every school needs its freaks!'

'Well, then, let us go! We haven't done any witchcraft. We're not *evil*.'

He stood tall, serious and business-like. The fire of hatred burned in him. 'I'm sorry, Lis. Do you know how important being a Righteous Protector is? It's everything. A blessed role. A *God-given duty*. The Righteous Protectors are what stand between good and evil. We're everywhere, Lis, quietly keeping the world safe from your kind.'

'Your power is evil,' chipped in Daphne. 'It's in your blood.'

'That's not true!' Lis cried. 'Do I look evil to you?'

'Sorry, Lis. That's not how it works. It doesn't matter how you *look*. Evil can take many forms.' Gray turned to the others. 'Right, how do we do this? Which one first?'

'Wait!' Lis pleaded. 'Kitty and Delilah have nothing to do with any of this. They're nothing ... It's just me! Let them go.'

Daphne shook her head. 'Always four!' she screeched and grinned. 'You, Laura, Kitty and Delilah!'

And then, out of nowhere a silver object flashed through the candlelight – a pair of scissors curling around Mr Gray's neck like the deadliest of snakes.

A skinny hand clutched the blade to the teacher's throat.

'And Jack,' said Jack.

Living the Dream

Jack's hand trembled, one blade of the scissors digging into the stubble on Gray's neck. Lis could see that Jack's eyes were wide open and wild with fear. 'Right. This is what's gonna happen,' he said. 'If anyone moves I will cut Mr Gray's throat, and I mean it, I will.'

'Who's he?' asked Jennifer, staring at Jack.

Lis had never been so pleased to see anyone in her entire life. This was her moment. She finally managed to tug her hands free and bent down to pull the tape off her legs. As she did so, Jennifer snatched the dagger from Daphne and swung in for the kill, but she stopped when Gray yelped in pain.

'Put down the knife! Now!' Jack barked, drawing a drop of blood.

'Jack. Just relax. We all know you aren't going to hurt your teacher. You're one of the good boys ...' Gray cooed, trying to charm him.

'Yeah, well, it's always the quiet ones ...' Jack muttered. 'Now, let them go. All of them. Do it!' he snapped at Daphne and Jennifer.

Lis finally freed herself and kicked the chair out of the way. Jennifer had placed the dagger on the floor as instructed, but it was still nearer to her than to Lis. If Lis grabbed for it, Jennifer could easily get to it first.

'What are you waiting for? Move!' Jack lacked conviction,

panic broke his voice into a high-pitched squeak. Nonetheless, Daphne slowly started to untie Delilah.

What happened next was a blur. Moving like lightning, Mr Gray, a good five inches taller than Jack, swung to the side and wrapped his arms around him. In a heartbeat, he had floored Jack, despite Jack's efforts to jab him with the scissors. Distracted, Lis failed to see Jennifer reach for the dagger on the carpet until the woman was already bearing down on her with the blade. Thinking fast, Lis grabbed a plastic chair and swung it at her face. The metal legs clanged against her skull and Jennifer fell back into Daphne's arms with a pained screech.

'Lis, run! Get help!' Jack yelled from where he was pinned underneath Gray.

She hesitated for a moment, watching Jack's rescue crumble and wondering what she should do.

'Lis, go!' yelled Jack. 'Get the police!'

Lis didn't wait any longer. She turned and ran.

The clatter of classroom furniture ringing in her ears, Lis sprinted to the fire exit. As she hit the metal bar, the fire doors mercifully swung open and she tumbled out into the freezing winter night. Which way to go? This was the back of the school, with no access to the front driveway. *Think, brain, think!* On this side she had netball courts, the rugby pitch and the copse. Of course ... the copse. It all became horribly clear. Mrs Gillespie had told her that her dreams were a warning ... a warning about *this*, and she knew exactly what awaited her in the black trees.

Lis turned back to the fire escape, but heard heavy footsteps from inside the school, getting closer. Dream or no dream, there was no other way out – literally. Maybe she could even *use* her dream – a map of the tangled paths through the copse formed in her mind. She was certain she could reach the other side of the wood, the safety of home. This time, she would ensure the nightmare had a happy ending. Besides, what choice did she have? It was do or die. Hopefully do.

'Go get Danny Marriott. He's by the main entrance,' Lis heard Gray shouting to Daphne and Jennifer inside the building behind her. 'We can't have any witnesses. Kill him! I'll get Lis!'

Move! Now! Lis told herself. She squeezed down the side of the netball court, heading towards the rugby pitch. If she could get into the copse then she could employ the darkness, the trees, the little secret dens. Gray would be just as lost as her. And if she could reach the other side ... Hollow Pike, the police, safety.

Looking back she saw Mr Gray emerge from the fire doors. She'd been spotted.

Back in G2, Jennifer knelt on Jack's chest, crushing him to the floor.

'Got you now, you little bastard!' Jennifer snarled. Jack responded by spitting straight into her face.

Jennifer slapped him. Daphne came to her side and the women dragged Jack across the carpet as he kicked and shouted.

'Against the table!' Jennifer commanded, pulling out the tape and wrapping it around and around Jack and the table legs as if trying to mummify him. 'You have to kill Danny!' she added. 'If he wakes up, we're all in deep trouble.' She handed Daphne the ornate dagger.

'OK, deary. I'll be back in a minute, don't you worry.'

'Just you wait till Lis calls Kitty's dad,' Jack growled. 'He'll make you wish you'd never been born.'

Jennifer laughed. 'Idiot! Your little mate's never going to reach the police. She's exactly where we wanted her! You didn't think we were going to kill you in the classroom, did you? She's dead meat.'

As soon as she reached the dilapidated boundary wall that separated the playing fields from the copse, Lis yanked her skirt up and clambered over the crumbling stone. She scrambled over the top and fell down the other side, now oblivious to minor aches and pains. Her crushed nose was entirely numb, what were a few more cuts and scrapes?

Landing awkwardly in the undergrowth she picked herself up, deliberately heading away from the light of Fulton High and into the deepest darkness; it was now an ally in her escape.

'You're not going to make it, Lis!' Gray called. She saw him appear at the top of the boundary wall. 'Give up now! It'll be easier that way.'

Not bloody likely. Lis fled, her muscles aching. Her legs weren't used to this punishment, she was no runner. Blackness enveloped her and she could no longer see where her feet landed. Brambles ripped at her tights, and her feet sank in sticky mud. But she had to keep going: deeper and darker, deeper and darker.

Mr Gray's footsteps behind her grew closer, driving her forwards. How close was he? *Keep running. Don't stop.* Her lungs seemed to be shrinking, retracting into useless, painful weights within her chest. She couldn't go on like this, she was making too much noise and her pursuer had a longer stride. As thin branches scratched against her face, she grasped the rough bark of the nearest tree trunk. Pressing her body close, she clung on, lowering herself to kneel among the twisting roots.

She listened hard. Where was he?

Suddenly, a brilliant flash of lightning rocked the copse, shaking birds from their sleeping perches. It was followed a blink later by deep, furious thunder.

What is it they say? Lis thought. *The sooner the thunder follows the lightning, the nearer the storm.* Another white bolt of energy forked across the sky with another thunderclap so loud Lis could feel it shake the air.

A storm was on its way.

A pair of sheep's-wool-lined winter boots shuffled down G Corridor. The dagger held out in front of her, Daphne reached the top of the long stone staircase that led to the entrance hall. The school was silent, save for the steady ticking of the clock. Spread-eagled at the foot of the steps lay an unconscious youth. He looked heavy – and although they weren't supposed to kill anyone inside the school, how on earth was she meant to get him outside? Too bad, she'd have to kill him there. You can't plan for everything, can you?

Holding the bannister, because the stairs were steep and she had a bad hip, Daphne started to descend towards the boy Simon had called Danny. Poor thing. None of this had anything to do with him. Oh, well – one boy wasn't worth the risk of exposing the Righteous Protectors, not after so many centuries of secrecy.

Halfway down the stairs, she stopped and drew a deep breath in through her nose. Lavender. Without any shadow of a doubt the school smelled of lavender. 'Lavender?' she muttered to herself, feeling anxious now. 'Who's there?'

She didn't see the rounders bat swinging at the back of her head until it was far too late. Daphne slumped to the cold stone steps.

The rain fell heavily; sheets of water streamed down through the branches. Lis's uniform was plastered to her skin as she dared to peek out from behind her tree trunk. Somewhere close a twig snapped underfoot. The storm was a hindrance and a help; the brilliant lightning could easily illuminate her position, but at least the roaring thunder disguised her ragged panting.

High above her, in the skeletal branches of the trees, birds circled like bats. It was as if they shared her panic. She couldn't stay here all night. Gray would find her eventually. Becoming the darkness, Lis slunk away from her hiding place. If she ran uphill to the highest point of the copse she'd be halfway to Hollow Pike.

The rain created a swamp under her stupid canvas pumps, yet she ran with renewed vigour, the birds noisily chanting their support. Her sprint was childlike, too frantic and desperate to be athletic. Fire burned through her thighs as she struggled to keep going over the uneven earth, the footpath utterly lost. Gnarled branches reached down from the trees like talons and clawed at her hair, which hung in tangled ropes around her face. Freezing water ran into her eyes, blurring her vision. Time and time again Lis smacked into trees, her only comfort the knowledge that Gray was at an equal disadvantage.

She paused, trying to regain her bearings. Was she going up or down? Had she changed direction? She was surrounded by trees that seemed identical in the dark. There were no landmarks, no sign posts. She was lost.

'Lis!' she heard Gray cry, bloodlust in his voice. 'I see you!' She ran.

'You know, the devil bore children with the witches through incubi and succubi,' Jennifer said, as she strutted up and down the classroom, looking oddly beautiful in the dancing candlelight.

'You're a nutjob!' Jack snapped.

'The Beast walks the forest.' She stroked Delilah's hair. 'But you know that, Delilah, don't you? You've felt it too.'

Delilah could only scowl at her.

'Why do you think your mother left town in such a hurry? We discovered her little secret ... She just ran away and left you, didn't she?' Jennifer whispered.

A muffled expletive tore from Delilah's mouth and she rocked her chair back and forth, dying to get her hands on Mrs Rigg.

'You're one to talk about parenting,' Jack spat. 'Great job you did with Laura!'

Jennifer wrapped her fingers in Jack's hair and twisted his head back. Jack yelped. 'Don't think I won't kill you here, you little fairy,' she snarled. Then she froze and sniffed the air. 'Lavender,' she stated.

'What?' Jack struggled against his bindings.

'For protection ...' Jennifer went on, though she seemed to be talking to herself now.

The scent of lavender grew more potent, filling G2. The air almost seemed to thicken, filling with a sweet-smelling, hazy fog. Jack's eyes began to water, but at least Jennifer released her grip on his hair. 'What the hell?'

Disconnected voices drifted into the room like wraiths in a mist. They came from nowhere and everywhere, as if the walls themselves were speaking. The voices were soft, gentle, dreamlike. The words became louder and clearer. *Safe in your light. Safe from harm. Safe from fear. Safe in your light. Safe from harm. Safe from fear. So mote it be.'*

The chant was repeated, round and round like a carousel, the room starting to spin with it. Jack felt nauseous and light-headed; the lavender fumes were overpowering. His vision swam in and out of focus.

'Stop it!' barked Jennifer, picking up Jack's scissors from where he'd dropped them in the struggle. 'What's going on?'

The voices grew deeper and stronger, less childlike and more sinister, this time seeming to come from below, from the bowels of the earth. *Safe in your light. Safe from harm. Safe from fear. Safe in your light. Safe from harm. Safe from fear. So mote it be.*

Jennifer blinked hard and peered through the lavender smoke. Was it her imagination? Had writing suddenly appeared on the walls, or had it always been there? Old Latin incantations seemed to seep out of the plaster, blood red letters transforming into pentagrams which then swirled and reformed, taking a new shape. The images merged together to form a shadow that rose up the walls, sweeping onto the ceiling. The shadow was roughly the size of a man, but the head was more like that of a goat or bull, with two curved horns on either side of the face. Thick arms ended in hawk-like talons.

The silhouette loomed over Jennifer Rigg, bearing down on her as it grew larger and larger. The woman backed into the farthest corner of the room, cowering away from the monstrous shadow. 'Please, no. This can't be happening,' she croaked. 'Our father, who art in Heaven, hallowed be thy . . . Save me . . . NO!'

As she screamed, the windows shook in their frames.

Keep going! Lis powered forwards, swiping at hanging branches that got in her way. She no longer cared in which direction she ran as long as it was away from the footsteps behind her.

And then suddenly the ground wasn't there any more. Lis's legs gave way, and she fell, landing painfully on her left hip and tumbling awkwardly down a slope. As she ploughed through thorns and brambles she wondered if she'd fall forever. She closed her eyes and waited for the end to come. Eventually, she slid to a halt in slick wet mud.

A freezing, creeping sensation rose up about her legs. She was in water: the brook. Fresh, hopeless tears streamed down her face. Clawing at reeds she tried to pull herself clear of the stream, but found herself sliding back in the slippery mud. No! This couldn't be happening. But it was, and she'd been here before.

The water, the pebbles, the rain, the birds . . . *the dream.* Everything about this situation was the same and also different. Her dreams had merely *felt* real. This *was* real: surround sound, high definition. It all made sense now, of course. Lis and Laura, linked by blood, by Hollow Pike, by Pike Copse, *by murder.* And not just Laura's murder, but the murders of all those women who had died at the hands of the Righteous Protectors. *Were they drowned in this very water?*

Lis was well rehearsed at this part. This was where she had to crawl. Maybe this time it would end differently . . . She hoped so. She started to move forwards. Rain pelted her, streaming down her body and into the brook and she wondered if she could let the stream's little current take her, but she wasn't sure in which direction it would carry her: into Hollow Pike or right back to Fulton?

She couldn't take the risk. Delving deep within, she struggled with muscles she'd never used. Snarling, she pulled herself through the swollen stream, biting her lip against the cold. She crawled for everything she had: Sarah, Max, Logan and her mother. Kitty, Jack, Delilah. And Danny ... all the things she needed to say to Danny. There was no ice water on the planet that would stop her, no bleeding nose, no twisted ankle or throbbing hip.

Lights. In the distance she saw lights: houses, people and safety. She was going to make it! Relief broke like dawn in her heart.

There it was. The strong, silent hand in her hair.

She should have known better.

Through the billowing, lavender-infused smoke, stepped two figures, arms outstretched. The first carried a stone mortar, from which the thick smoke billowed. The second figure coughed and spluttered, wafting her way through the fog.

Ms Dandehunt pulled back her hood and fully entered the room. 'It seems we got here just in time, Celeste.'

Mrs Gillespie extinguished the smoking bowl and rested it on Mr Gray's desk. 'So mote it be,' she finished her incantation.

'Kitty, Delilah and, er ... Jack. We'll have you out of here in a jiffy.' Ms Dandehunt strode over to Jennifer and hauled the sobbing woman out of the corner. Mrs Rigg was pale and stiff with terror.

Jack looked over at Kitty and Dee, both blinking hard against what was left of the dizzying smog. Mrs Gillespie soon had Delilah free, and started work on untying Kitty. Jack's head was still throbbing and he could hardly see straight. Whatever was in that bowl was strong stuff. His vision gradually came back into focus, and he regained his senses.

'Daniel was coming around,' Ms Dandehunt said as she tied Jennifer Rigg to a chair with her own tape. 'He'll have called the police by now.'

'Where's the librarian?' Kitty asked, as Mrs Gillespie pulled the tape from her mouth. Delilah was busy unwrapping Jack from the table legs.

'She's resting,' Celeste Gillespie said flatly.

'Now, I think we'd better get our stories straight, don't you?' Ms Dandehunt nodded at each of them.

'But Ms Dandehunt,' Jack begged. 'Lis! She's in trouble!'

'I'm sorry, Lis. This is the only way.'

His empty apology was the only new chapter to this experience. Lis pulled away, gasping, filling her lungs with much needed air. He was so strong! Her wet body had managed to slip through his fingers a couple of times, but he always regained the upper hand.

Even though she knew how this ended, with a vacuum of nothingness, she wasn't going to go without a fight. She dug her fingers deep into the flesh of his forearms and spat in his face, deriving satisfaction from the brief flash of red-hot anger he exhibited before he regained control.

'Relax, Lis. It'll be better for you if you just let go.'

'Go to hell!' she screamed, but he just pushed her down into the black brook. The sky vanished. She pushed and kicked and squirmed but his grip held fast. Rearing up, her face managed to break the surface, but Gray took a hand off her neck and forced her face back under.

Water rushed up her nostrils. She remembered this bit vividly from her nightmare. Soon everything would become peaceful; the battles in the forest and in her head would momentarily cease fire, allowing her a moment's silence before the end.

If death is like this, it's nothing to be afraid of, she thought as the calm set in. She knew she should be fighting, but the sense of peace was oddly gorgeous, akin to going under anaesthetic. Lis didn't want to die. She thought of all those things she wanted to do, all those places she wanted to go. They were nothing now. Only dreams.

It could be worse. She'd come this far. Maybe the others could overpower the older women? Without Gray, they might have a chance of escaping. *That is a good last thought. Hang on to that*, Lis told herself. She felt Gray's stranglehold relax slightly as the life ebbed out of her body. *Is this how he killed Laura?* Death wrapped its soft petals around her and started closing up.

Suddenly, Lis felt Gray let go. Why? She wasn't dead yet. Did he think she'd gone already? His hands left her throat and she felt him stagger away from her. With a last surge of energy she forced her tired body to sit upright. Her face broke the surface of the stream, and as muddy water poured out of her mouth, sweet, sweet air flooded in. She choked and coughed, spluttering as she cleared her eyes.

What was going on? Lis peered around. Gray had fallen backwards and now sat in the fast-moving brook, looking stunned. A huge, sleek crow squawked as it flew at the teacher's face, pecking at his skin. Lis had been saved by a bird. If she weren't so cold, she'd have laughed out loud. Velvet, blue-black feathers flapped in Gray's bewildered face.

He struggled to his feet and stumbled out of the stream, staggering left and right. As he did so, another crow joined the first, needle-sharp talons clawing at Gray's eyes and face. Then another. The teacher slapped at himself, trying to hit out at the birds. Lis seized her chance to scramble out of the brook and onto the bank. Then, with a whispered 'thank you' to the crows, she started running towards the comforting orange windows of Hollow Pike that glimmered just over the hill.

With a last swipe at the birds, Gray came after her again, but she felt stronger now – as if Death himself had given her a second chance. Gray grabbed her shoulders, but Lis whirled around and scratched at his already bleeding face.

'Get off me!' she snarled.

Gray tried to wrap his hands around her throat, but she yanked his head back by his hair so he couldn't get a firm grasp on her wet body. Sliding through the waterlogged mud, the pair slithered away from the stream. They trampled through the undergrowth, throwing body blows at each other. There was no way Lis was giving up now. With a final war cry from her gut, she threw all her weight at him. They both fell forwards into a black abyss.

She could be flying. Her hands grasped uselessly at thin air, the shock of the fall taking all the scream out of her. It was slow, effortless, silent and weightless. Freezing air rushed up around her and she tumbled away from Gray, closing her eyes. When the flying ended, this was going to hurt. A lot. As she fell, Lis braced herself for impact.

She squealed when she hit the ground, but needlessly. Whatever was underneath her was wet, but soft. Her face smacked into it, reminding her of Mr Gray's punch, but she was fine. She heard a loud, moist snap beside her – and then near silence. Only the cawing of the crows could be heard faintly over the polite whisper of the rushing stream.

Lis finally dared to open her eyes. The rubbish dump. Of course. The fly-tipping heap had broken their fall. Lis was face down on a stained yellow mattress, but Mr Gray was motionless. She didn't understand – why wasn't he coming after her? Then she saw why: Gray had landed at an impossible angle on a mound of derelict furniture and a metal chair leg now protruded through a ghastly red hole in his neck. His blood trickled down the long, thin metal pole as the rain ran off his perpetually shocked face.

If this were a horror movie, Lis knew she should shoot the bad guy in the heart or chop his head off, or something; the killer's never really dead, he always comes back for one last scare. But from where Lis was, crouching on her dirty mattress, he looked pretty bloody dead. Yep, he was dead. And at this point in time, she couldn't find it in her heart to feel anything but relief.

From the other side of Pike Copse she heard the beautiful singing of police sirens and started to cry.

Ms Dandehunt led the three scared youths down G Corridor, ready to face the police. 'Now, are we all clear on what we're going to say?'

'Ms Dandehunt, stop! We have to go after Lis. He'll kill her!' Kitty seized Ms Dandehunt's arm.

Mrs Gillespie smiled, her face ghoulish in the candlelight. 'You don't need to worry about Lis,' she said. 'A little bird tells me she'll be just fine ...'

Drip

Lis had dozed all through the night, cushioned by the drugs the doctors had pumped into her. It had been a shallow, unsatisfying sleep, fraught with panicky moments where she'd woken and not remembered where she was. Now it was morning, although it was almost as black as night outside her window. Clouds remained like steel giants in the sky, a stark reminder of last night's storm. She was propped up in bed, Sarah's blonde head resting on the corner of her mattress.

A plump, jolly nurse entered the room and as she did so, Lis glimpsed the fluorescent jacket of the police guard posted outside her door.

'Good morning, my sweetheart,' the nurse said in a thick Jamaican accent. 'You feeling any better? Hypothermia is no laughing matter now, is it?'

Lis pulled herself up, waking Sarah in the process. 'Yeah, I'm OK,' she replied.

The nurse smiled. Lis hadn't seen a mirror, but if the padding across her nose looked how it felt, she didn't want to.

'Sorry, Lis, I must have dropped off,' Sarah apologised.

'That's OK, don't be daft.' Lis's throat felt sore. It must be from all the screaming. She dimly recalled collapsing into the arms of the policewoman who'd found her, although it was all a flashy blur of torches and searchlights and rain. For a brief but terrible moment, Lis had thought they might not find her in the labyrinth of trees and she'd be left there to die.

The nurse pressed a plastic cup of water into her fingers and watched her swallow some more pills. As she did, the door opened again and Kitty's father entered, his imposing bulk filling the doorway. The last time she'd seen him, he'd been with Kitty in the back of an ambulance, clinging to his daughter, hugging her to his chest and kissing her forehead.

The nurse angrily stepped up to him. 'You leave her alone to get some rest!'

'I just need five minutes.'

With a frosty glare at Monroe, the nurse left the room.

Sarah gave him an equally warm reception. 'Do we have to do this now?'

'I'm afraid so.' He was so different this time, so much softer. 'How are you feeling, Lis? Last night must have been awful. Quite a storm, eh?'

Lis just about managed to nod.

'Well, you can rest now. It's all over. Mr Gray is dead.' Was he going to tell her something she didn't know? 'You were the only person to see what happened ... I'm sorry, I have to ask ...'

Closing her eyes, Lis saw the same image that had played on a loop all through the night. 'The weather was so bad. He was chasing me and we fell off the edge. It was impossible to see where we were going.'

'That's what we assumed. Don't worry, Lis, you're not in any trouble. The dagger recovered at the school is a positive match to the injuries on Laura's body. We can't be certain it was Gray who used the knife on her, but it had his prints on it. It seems a safe bet.'

'Good. Did you hear that, Lis?' Sarah asked.

'Jennifer Rigg and Daphne Gray are accessories to murder, of course; they aren't even denying it. Once they're out of hospital they'll be detained until trial.'

'They're here?' Lis gasped.

'No, love. Different hospital in Leeds, and they're under armed guard, don't you worry. We haven't even begun to question them yet. Lord knows what possessed them ... but we'll get to the bottom of it.'

But Lis knew they wouldn't; somehow Hollow Pike always kept its secrets. She looked over at Sarah who smiled warmly. Her poor sister, what was she meant to make of this mess? 'What about my friends?' Lis asked.

'Danny, Jack, Delilah and Kath– Kitty are all doing fine. They only had minor injuries. They've already given statements.'

'Can I see them?'

'No!' Sarah put in. 'Not yet. Wait until you're better. You need to rest.'

Lis saw tears well up in her sister's eyes. Did she blame Lis's friends? Did she think they'd dragged her into this mess?

Monroe shifted his enormous frame around her metal bed and pulled up an armchair. 'Lis, there are just a few more questions. What happened in that classroom? I've never seen anything like it.'

There was a clatter at the window. All three turned to see a huge black shape beat its wings at the glass. The bird's feathers glistened the colour of sapphires as it perched on the window ledge.

Hollow Pike awaited her answer. The crow was its messenger.

Lis turned back to Monroe and lied through her teeth. 'I don't know. When Jack distracted the others, I just ran.'

Monroe's eyes bored into her. She noticed that the white

parts around his irises had a slightly orange tint.

'I'm sorry, I just don't know,' she repeated.

'And you have no idea why you and the others were targeted?'

Oh, she had a very good idea. But though the reason was ridiculous, she knew to say nothing. 'No. They just seemed fixated on us for some reason.'

Monroe flopped back in the armchair, apparently exhausted. 'OK, last question. We still haven't recovered Laura Rigg's diary. Danny Marriott says he dropped it on the floor of the main school office, but our team has been unable to recover it. Any ideas?'

'No, I'm sorry,' Lis whispered.

'Me too. We might have found some answers there.' He seemed sad, a knowing sadness. How long had he served in this town? What kind of things had he seen? How many 'unexplained' cases? How could the police ever tackle the darkness she'd witnessed?

He stood and shook Sarah's hand before patting Lis on the shoulder. 'Get some sleep, Lis.' The police inspector regarded her thoughtfully one final time, before gliding out of the room, his long winter coat flowing behind him.

Outside the window, the crow took flight.

A couple of weeks passed in a mix of the hospital's regime and Sarah's. Lis was allowed books, magazines, her Nintendo, Max, Logan. She was *not* allowed her mobile phone, her friends, newspapers, to watch TV. In Sarah's eyes, she wasn't 'strong enough'. Perhaps Sarah was right. The nightmares stopped, but were replaced by an unnatural black absence when she slept – a peaceful nothingness, worryingly close to her final seconds under the water of the stream. It was too quiet.

Dealing with her mother had been tricky to say the least. Deborah had travelled up from Bangor the day after Gray died, bringing a tide of questions that Lis couldn't answer. Her mum blamed Sarah for not looking after her properly, they'd bickered non-stop, and Lis had felt even worse. Things had calmed down by the time Deborah had gone back to Wales for work, but no doubt the arguments would flare up again when she returned for Christmas.

On the plus side, they were letting Lis go from hospital tomorrow. She'd be home in plenty of time for Christmas. Though once they let her out she'd have to face the journalists, of course. Sarah said the news people had been camped outside the house.

Lis often thought about Mr Rigg, alone in that enormous house in Upper Hollow. How many TV cameras were pointing at him? That poor man. He'd lost his daughter and his wife. She quickly turned the page of the magazine she was reading. Every time she thought about Laura, even for a second, a new wave of guilt swept over her. Could they have helped her? Could they have *saved* her? Maybe if Laura had had friends like Kitty, Jack and Delilah – people she could really talk to ... But she had kept everyone at a distance. In the end, although it was Kitty, Jack and Delilah who were considered 'freaks', Laura had probably been more alone than they ever were.

There was a gentle knock at the door.

'Come in,' Lis called.

Behind a towering bouquet of flowers, Ms Dandehunt entered the room. 'Hello, dearheart, these are from the school.'

'Oh, thanks!' Lis smiled. You couldn't not smile when Ms Dandehunt was around. 'You didn't have to.'

Her headteacher sat down in the armchair. 'Of course we did. I think it's the very least we could do, given ... what happened.'

Lis stared at her hands, unsure what to say.

Reaching into her handbag, Ms Dandehunt produced a DVD and placed it on Lis's lap: *The Crucible*. 'I thought you might enjoy the film.'

Lis laughed. 'Just what I always wanted!'

'I won't keep you long, Lis, dear. I just wanted to make sure you were all right. I know your view of Fulton High School must be astoundingly poor at the moment, but I like to think that a brave, strong girl like you will be ready to join us again after Christmas. It'd be such a shame to lose you.'

'I wouldn't say I was brave or strong.'

Ms Dandehunt's kind, round face beamed at her and she took Lis's hands into her own. Her skin was warm and soft, reminding Lis of her old Gran Rushworth.

'Oh, I would,' Ms Dandehunt insisted gently. 'We make 'em strong and brave here in Hollow Pike. You and your friends ... What you did ... Quite, quite spectacularly bonkers! You ought to have your heads examined, all of you – but it was extraordinarily brave and very, very strong.'

Lis choked up with tears. She looked out of the window, sensing some of her birds not too far away in the nearest trees. It was comforting. 'Yeah, but I'm not from Hollow Pike, am I?'

Ms Dandehunt stood to leave. 'Oh, you're definitely a Hollow Pike girl. It's in your blood, my dear.' She gave Lis a tender smile and trundled towards the door.

'Ms Dandehunt?' Lis sat up. 'Did you have a relative called Reginald?'

'Yes, dear. He was my grandfather.' She lingered in the doorway. 'A thoroughly insightful chap.'

'Who . . . *What* are you?'

Ms Dandehunt smiled an old, world-weary smile, and returned to Lis's bedside. 'The most important thing you need to know about me is that, first and foremost, I'm a teacher. Like any *good* teacher, my priority is to protect the children in my care. Remember this: as long as you remain in Hollow Pike, Lis, there'll be someone on your side.'

Once more she reached into her bag and pulled out a sprig of lavender, sealed with a black ribbon. 'Lavender. For protection. Black is the colour of protection, you see.'

'It was you.' Lis understood now. 'You put the lavender under my pillow!'

Ms Dandehunt chuckled. 'All this started when you arrived, Lis. I don't believe in coincidence, so I knew you were either Laura's killer or in danger yourself. When the bird appeared in your locker, I knew we had to protect you. In the seventeenth century, the Righteous Protectors took to nailing a familiar to the homes of suspected witches. A gruesome practice, intended to warn people away.'

'I thought it was you,' Lis whispered. 'You had Laura's diary.'

'Yes, although perhaps don't mention that one to Chief Inspector Monroe. I knew what Laura's death meant. I knew more than the police could ever comprehend – so I took her diary from her locker.'

'What did it say?'

Ms Dandehunt turned to the window, just as a ray of weak sunshine battled through the overcast sky. 'Poor Laura, so lost and lonely. Desperate to know who her real family was, what her dreams meant. She threatened to run away.'

With Danny, Lis thought. *Just like she'd said that day on the rugby pitch.* 'But Laura wasn't a witch! None of us are!'

Smiling sadly, Ms Dandehunt said, 'Hasn't that always been the way though, Lis?' she tapped *The Crucible.* 'Paranoia, fear, malicious rumours. Some people don't seem to be able to see *who* people are, only *what* they are.'

'Why did they hate witches so much?'

Ms Dandehunt chuckled. 'If humans didn't hate each other so much, what would the papers have to write about?'

Lis felt her cheeks reddening, but she had to ask. She had to know. 'So you're ...'

'Witches?' Ms Dandehunt finished for her. 'If you like, yes.'

'But white witches?'

'You watch too much TV, Miss London,' she said, stroking Lis's hair.

Lis shook her head. 'But I don't believe in—'

Ms Dandehunt put a finger to her lips, silencing her. 'And perhaps that's for the best. Is it easier to think of Simon Gray simply as a madman rather than a witch-finder? Will it help you sleep at night?'

Lis couldn't answer, overwhelmed by the enormity of it all. Ms Dandehunt gave her a soft kiss on the forehead. 'Sweet dreams, Lis.'

Christmas

Frosty morning light flooded her bedroom, and Lis dived out of bed and headed straight to the mirror to inspect progress on her nose. It was her new morning routine. The swelling had gone down considerably, but although everyone denied it, Lis could tell it wasn't its normal shape and size. At least the raccoon-like black eyes had faded. Still, there would be no family photos *this* Christmas.

Laughter drifted up from downstairs. It was Christmas morning. Sighing, Lis threw her dressing gown on and slouched out of her room.

Max had the fire going like *The Towering Inferno* while Sarah was trying in vain to interest an eleven-month-old infant in presents. And her mother presided over the scene, cup of tea in hand. Lis looked on like the Ghost of Christmas past.

'There she is!' exclaimed her mum. 'Merry Christmas, sweetheart.'

'Merry Christmas!' Lis replied, adopting the faux-cheery tone she needed to escape scrutiny. Ow, that still kind of hurt the healing bone in her nose. She moved over to the rug and received a welcome kiss from her mum before planting a similar one on Logan's fluffy head.

'Morning, Sleeping Beauty!' Max grinned.

'Hardly.' She pointed to the centre of her face.

'I think there are some presents under the tree for you ...' Max told her.

Sarah leaned back and checked. 'Sorry, babe. None for you, actually! Bad times!'

Lis snorted. 'Very funny. Check again.'

With a grand flourish Sarah pulled a neat pile of parcels out and slid them towards her. *I wonder if I'll get a diary this year*, Lis suddenly wondered. She squashed that thought before it could take over. These were normal things. Normal things were good. Normal things helped to paint over the cracks.

Lis had always found Christmas Day to be quite boring. Once you've opened all your presents and got dressed up, there isn't a lot left to do other than eat.

'Mother, will you do the drinks and just let me worry about the bloody food?' Sarah's wilting patience echoed from the kitchen. Logan was pulling a piece of wrapping paper across the floor and Lis channel-hopped while Max entertained the next-door neighbours.

'Do you want a glass of champagne, Lis, love?' he asked, refilling glasses.

'No, thanks.' Her attention rested on the news channel. A striking blonde anchor woman sat in front of a picture of Mr Gray.

'A spokesperson for North Yorkshire Police yesterday refused to comment on growing speculation that local schoolgirl, Laura Rigg, had been a victim of a ritual-style killing. Since her death—'

Max stepped in front of the screen, putting down the champagne and turning the TV off.

'Max!' Lis objected.

'You shouldn't be watching that,' he said gently.

'I can't hide from the TV.' She gave him a cold stare. Why wouldn't anyone let her talk about it? She hadn't left the house since she'd been discharged from hospital. She'd escaped only to become a prisoner in her own home. She knew Sarah meant well, but wrapping her up in cotton wool was making her feel worse.

'You can today. It's Christmas, love, and we have guests,' Max insisted.

She nodded silently. There was so much she wanted, *needed*, to say, but no one wanted to listen. Maybe it was just too scary.

'Lis!' Sarah hollered. 'Door!'

Which nosy neighbour was it now? Even for Christmas, an unusually high volume of guests had 'dropped by' since the night of the Great Storm. Lis was almost at the stage where she was ready to sign autographs. She shuffled past her bickering mother and sister to the door.

Outside stood Danny Marriott, his cheeks cartoon-red from the cold. 'Merry Christmas!' he announced, a grey beanie hat hiding the stitches Lis knew he'd had in his head.

Merry Christmas, indeed. Danny had been one of only two things on Lis's Christmas list, the other being news from her friends.

'You're meant to say "Merry Christmas" back and invite me in,' Danny told her. 'It's fricking freezing, Lis!'

She opened the door wider and bowed her head, completely overcome with embarrassment. 'Come on in.'

He stepped past her and entered the sweltering kitchen. 'Something smells good! Hi, Sarah.'

'Hi, Danny. Merry Christmas!' Sarah replied, briefly looking up from a large pan of gravy.

'Oh, this is Danny, is it, Lis?' Her mum wiped her hands on a towel and came to greet Danny. 'I'm Lis's mum, Deborah. You never said he was so lovely looking!' she told Lis.

Jesus Christ. 'Thank you, Mother!' In fact, after everything that had happened, Lis was so weirdly thankful for her mum and family that she only *half* died inside. But she grabbed Danny by the hand before her mum could locate any childhood pictures, and pulled him straight through the party in the lounge and into the conservatory on the other side. Seasonal goodwill drifted through the double doors, but they were alone.

'Sorry about her! She's always like that,' Lis said.

'She seemed . . . nice.'

They stood awkwardly in the glass box, which was a tinsel jungle of Christmas decorations at present. Many times Lis had thought about how to apologise to Danny. She'd written so many scripts in her head, but she hadn't considered stage fright in her plans.

'Danny, I'm sorry!' she blurted out.

'Sorry? What for?' He frowned.

She reached up and pulled his hat off, revealing the wound from the fall.

'Oh. That wasn't your fault.' He guided her onto the futon. 'Well, yes, it was your fault, but what were you meant to think? I had Laura's diary, plus the school was full of magic mushroom smoke, or whatever!'

'That's the thing that really bugged me while I was stuck in the hospital,' Lis told him. 'Why *did* you have Laura's diary?'

He unconsciously rubbed his scabby stitches. 'I saw it on Dandehunt's desk. She called me in to ask if I knew why you were leaving, and I thought that if I stole it for you, you might be, like, impressed. I sneaked in after rugby.'

As romantic gestures go, stealing a dead girl's diary from your headteacher was certainly original. A faint suggestion of a smile appeared on Lis's face.

'And you know what?' Danny continued. 'That psycho bastard's dead. The rest of them are going to jail. It's over.'

'What do you think happened?' Lis asked him. This was her chance to gauge what people had been saying in her absence.

'It's been all over the news. Mr Gray was like a Bible freak or something! They're saying he was in a cult. Some people at school have been saying it's something to do with the Hollow Pike witch trials, but ...'

'You don't believe in ...'

'In witches?' Danny laughed. 'Are you kidding?'

Lis merely shrugged. She honestly didn't know what to think any more.

Danny continued. 'Anyway, I didn't come here to talk about that crap. I haven't been allowed to see you for weeks!'

Brilliant. Someone else who didn't want to talk about it. 'So why did you come?'

'Er ... hello? It's Christmas! I brought you your present!' Danny told her with a grin.

Internally Lis slapped herself. Gifts, of course! Exchanging gifts is what human beings do on Christmas Day. Living in Sarah's protective bubble, with no access to shops, Lis had figured that not being dead would have to be her present to her family. But what about Danny?

'You got me something? Danny, I didn't get you anything!'

'Good!' he said and grinned. 'That will make my present look even better and earn me points! I didn't expect one, seriously.'

He reached into his coat pocket and produced a long, slender package, neatly wrapped in gold paper. Taking it from him, she ripped the paper off and pulled out what could only be a jewellery box. 'It's not a silver cross, is it?'

'What? No, why?' Danny asked, confused.

'Never mind!' She snapped the box open and pulled out a web-fine silver chain with a little silver swallow suspended from it. Its eye was a tiny, glistening blue stone. It was perfect.

'I thought that after all your encounters with birds, you could use a nice, friendly one.'

If only he had the first clue how apt his gift was. Tears, the good kind, threatened to spill down Lis's face.

'Danny,' she began, 'I adore it! You have no idea!' She gave him the only gift she could at that moment: a slow, tender kiss on his lips, which he happily accepted.

'That'll do me,' he said, and grinned.

'And, now that I'm safe, I don't have to go back to Wales,' Lis told him.

'You're staying?' He jumped off the futon. 'That's the best present ever!'

He pulled her up and kissed her again, holding her face in both hands. Lis felt a happy glow. This was the best Christmas since she'd been given the *Sylvanian Families* tree house when she was eight.

St Wilfred's Church was a typical village church in rural England. Its elegant spire glistened in the early morning frost on Boxing Day. Behind the church was a graveyard, full to capacity for well over a hundred years, the headstones eroded and cracked, some leaning perilously close to collapse.

A couple with a poodle rested some flowers on a grave, before walking away hand in hand. It was a crisp, fresh December morning.

But at the very edge of the graveyard, beyond the crumbling perimeter wall and behind the hanging willow trees, there lay an overgrown wasteland. It was covered in shrubs and litter and junk, but at that moment, four friends reunited stood around a burning dustbin.

'This is where they buried the witches,' Delilah explained. 'The church ground is holy, so a woman suspected of being a witch was buried outside the graveyard. No headstones, no memorial, no nothing.'

'Those poor women. It's so unfair,' Lis said, looking mournfully at the five floral notebooks in her hands. She couldn't bring herself to drop them into the flames. This was the only record of the *real* Laura Rigg. 'Can we really do this?'

'We have to!' Kitty replied. 'Laura's secret dies with her. No one has to know she was . . .'

'An *actual witch?*' Jack finished. Thank God he'd had the presence of mind to shove Laura's diary into his trousers seconds before the police arrived. This was for the best.

'If people read these,' Kitty went on, 'there's a chance they'd track us down too. Like it or not, it's in our blood.'

They'd all looked up their family trees, of course. Gray had been right. All of them, even Jack, had Hollow Pike roots going back hundreds of years. Maybe, *just maybe*, they were all descended from those women in the woods.

'Do you think there are more of them? More Righteous Protectors?' Delilah asked. The worry that they could still be hunted down and burned at the stake had crossed Lis's mind too.

'I don't know. Dad says Jennifer and Daphne are refusing to speak. It's like they've taken a vow of silence or something. They just sit in their cells, staring at the walls. They're protecting the Protectors.'

Lis imagined the women, still and silent, waiting. But

waiting for what? It was hard knowing that Righteous Protectors might still be out there with their murderous beliefs.

'You know what I think?' said Delilah. 'I think the police know more than they let on. How could you live in Hollow Pike and not realise there's something peculiar going on? Everyone has heard the stories; everyone knows what happened to all those women, but they just ignore it.'

'Because it's too scary to admit something so dark happened on your doorstep. How would you ever sleep at night? It's easier if it's just a bad dream.' Lis closed her eyes tightly, blocking out the image of Gray's dead face that flashed through her mind.

Kitty gently reached over the flickering fire, taking the diaries from Lis's hands. She looked at each of her friends in turn. They all silently nodded agreement. And Kitty let them drop. Initially, the books squashed the flames, but first the corners blackened and then vibrant, yellow tongues of fire licked the pages. Ashes swirled into the December air, taking Laura's final words away with them.

'It's over.' Kitty walked away from the fire.

'But we have to go back to school.' Jack shuddered. 'I don't know if I can go back there after what happened.'

'Jack, we have to. The exams.' Kitty took his hand. 'If we're ever going to get the hell out of Hollow Pike, we need good grades.'

Jack nodded sombrely.

'So we just go back to normal?' Lis queried. For a second she almost thought that could be possible.

'I wouldn't say that. We're not exactly normal, are we?' Jack lamented.

'And we never were in the first place!' Delilah laughed, searching in the undergrowth for something.

'And I say, thank God!' Kitty added brightly, folding her arms across her army jacket.

Delilah fashioned a rough cross out of two long sticks, binding them with a long black ribbon, pulled from her hair. Then she wedged it into the earth: the witches of Hollow Pike finally had a memorial.

Their work done, the friends helped each other over the wall and back into the official graveyard.

'That only leaves one question,' Lis murmured, staring into the distance. 'Which is worse? Being a witch, or being Laura Rigg's less pretty cousin?'

Jack and Kitty laughed and Lis couldn't keep a straight face for a moment longer. Their giggles rang around the churchyard like bells.

Delilah's green eyes twinkled. 'Can you smell that?'

'What?' Lis, Kitty and Jack chorused.

'Snow. Snow's on its way.'

Like a winter fairy, Delilah skipped around the deserted graveyard gazing up at the gentle clouds in the milky sky.

'How do you know?' Jack looked up too.

'I just do.'

As she said it, the first feathery snowflakes fell, carelessly drifting down from the clouds.

'OMG!' Jack said gleefully.

The first flakes were soon joined by a polar flurry, drifts first clotting on the grass and then the pathways. The graveyard soon turned radiantly white: a clean, fresh page stretching before them, ready for new stories.

'White Christmas!' Delilah turned back to them.

Kitty shook her head, grinning in disbelief. 'Dee, sometimes you scare me a little!'

Lis caught the intricate flakes of snow in her hands. They were real. *She* was real. It was impossible to think of herself as the same girl who'd come from Wales. She was something new. Maybe a witch – or maybe she'd turned into a butterfly. It was too early to tell. A smile full of hope burst across her face. At that moment, she knew only one thing for certain: she had *friends*.

'Right, then. Who's up for a snowball fight?' Lis yelled. Her feet crunching in the snow, she darted through the headstones, as carefree and unique as the snowflakes spiralling around her.

Acknowledgements

This is all a bit Oscar winner's speech, but here goes. *Hollow Pike* was made possible with the help of the following people, and I owe them a lot because this book means everything to me.

I'll start by thanking my agent, Jo, for recognising the good in *Hollow Pike* when it was in a much sketchier state than you find it today. You've supported me every step of the way *and* took me to The Ivy. Amazing. Next, to the wonderful team at Indigo/Orion, you've made *Hollow Pike* flesh! I'm grateful to Amber and Jenny, my editors, for intuitively knowing exactly what I wanted to say; Nina for her PR witchcraft; Alex and the rights team; and Fiona for her sophistication and wisdom.

I'd also like to thank my own growing coven of internet followers on Twitter and Facebook. This book feels supported even before its release, and that is just lovely. I pray you like the finished product.

Finally, and most importantly, to my family and friends for your unwavering support. We're *so* not a mushy family, so I'll simply say thank you for *everything*. Particular thanks to Sam Hudson for the countless times she has read *Hollow Pike*, and to the talented Stuart Warwick for the music. Sarah, Lou Lou, Kat, Fi, Joe, Niall, Gavin – I love y'all for being believers!

And to K, P and B. You were there – you know what it was like. I treasure that time and always will.

Join the Hollow Pike online community today:

www.facebook.com/junodawsonbooks
www.twitter.com/junodawson
www.junodawson.com